THE FALCON PRINCE

THE FALCON PRINCE

KAREN KELLEY

BRAVA

KENSINGTON PUBLISHING CORP.

www.kensingtonbooks.com

BRAVA BOOKS are published by

Kensington Publishing Corp.
119 West 40th Street
New York, NY 10018

All Kensington titles, imprints, and distributed lines are available at special quantity discounts for bulk purchases for sales promotion, premiums, fund-raising, educational, or institutional use.

Special book excerpts or customized printings can also be created to fit specific needs. For details, write or phone the office of the Kensington Special Sales Manager. Attn.: Special Sales Department. Kensington Publishing Corp., 119 West 40th Street, New York, NY 10018. Phone: 1-800-221-2647.

Brava and the B logo are Reg. U.S. Pat. & TM Off.

ISBN-13: 978-0-7582-3838-2
ISBN-10: 0-7582-3838-X

First Kensington Trade Paperback Printing: August 2010

10 9 8 7 6 5 4 3 2 1

Printed in the United States of America

For Manda Brooke Wheeler.
Someday you can dedicate a book to me.

Chapter 1

Rianna Lancaster's feet pounded the winding trail, adrenaline rushing through her veins, wind on her face, her heavy breathing the only sound in the quiet of the piney woods. That, and the cry of a hawk circling somewhere overhead. This was what being alive was all about. Just her and nature. Inner peace. Pure freedom . . .

Yeah, right. If you'd listen to me, we could be flying. Talk about wind on your face. I can almost feel it now. So close, yet so far away.

Ria missed a step but quickly recovered.

Almost freedom.

It was just her, and the voice inside her head, running along the trail. Ria's parents had told her that everyone had a voice inside their head. She had a feeling it wasn't quite like the voice inside *her* head.

Maybe insanity ran in her family. It was possible. She'd been adopted when she was three and knew nothing about her biological parents.

The voice did cause her some concern, though. She frowned. And it caused a few of the townspeople concern, too. That was her problem. Well, one of her problems. The major one. Living in the small Texas town of Miller Bend, which had a population of a whopping three thousand, made it pretty much a gimme that everyone knew everyone else's business. It seemed they thought she was a little, well, daft. Unfortunately, sometimes she had a tendency to agree with them.

I said we could be soaring through the sky. Were you listening to me?

"No, I wasn't," she panted, not wanting to break her stride. "Go away."

Not gonna happen.

No, Ria hadn't really thought the voice would leave her alone. It never had before.

The delusional voice inside her head had a name—Shintara. Because it had a name, did that make Ria crazier than the usual, say, run-of-the-mill, crazy person?

Probably.

She worked around animals too much. Another problem. Not that she didn't love her Pet Purr-Fect Grooming shop. She was proud that she was doing a booming business, but maybe she did need to get away for a while. If her new assistant worked out, she would seriously think about taking off for a week or two.

Okay, she needed to clear her head. Nothing in life mattered when she was out running. This was her time. She didn't have to worry that people thought she was a little mentally off-balance. She didn't have to . . .

A hawk swooped down, landing on the trail in front of her.

She came to a grinding halt, feet still running in place, and then stopping altogether.

What the hell? Hawks didn't just land in front of people. And it should have taken off as soon as it spotted her.

Ria stared at the bird as she tried to catch her breath, bending over and resting her sweaty palms on her knees.

The hawk was magnificent, with a creamy white breast and speckled, dark-brown wings that blended into black tips. The bird was so close she could see its sharp talons. Talons that were made for catching and holding prey. Something about this wasn't good. Probably because the hawk still hadn't moved. It stared at her as though it were silently trying to communicate. This was weird. No, it was more than weird.

Almost as weird as the thick fog rolling in. She straightened, her gaze flitting from tree to tree until she could no longer make them out. An icy chill raced down her back as if someone had run an ice cube over her spine.

Fog wasn't that unusual. Right? It was early morning, and the trail behind her house was in a low spot. Except this fog wasn't like any fog she'd ever seen. Kind of *Friday the 13th* creepy.

Alrighty, maybe this was her cue to leave.

Someone groaned, but the fog was so thick now she couldn't see a thing. Ria hesitated. What if the hawk had been trying to tell her that his owner was hurt? That . . . that . . .

It had finally happened. She had completely lost her freakin' mind.

But the fog began to dissipate enough that she could make out a man's face. A very tall man. At least six-two. With short dark hair. Strong chin. Green eyes that studied her. Tanned skin. Muscular chest . . .

Her assessment came to a screeching halt.

Muscular *bare* chest.

Yum! Shintara's voice came through to Ria's thoughts.

"Shut up," she told the voice.

Well, he is hot.

The man stepped forward. "I'm Prince Kristor, from New Symtaria. I'm here to take you back to my planet," he said in a deep, commanding voice.

The fog vanished.

The man was totally naked.

Ria screamed.

Birds took flight.

Small animals scurried into hiding.

Fear cemented her feet to the ground, and no matter how much her brain screamed—*Run, you idiot!*—they weren't budging.

Her sweaty hands fumbled with the small can of mace hooked onto her waist purse, her heart slamming against her ribcage.

She got it loose, raising it as he stepped closer. "Like hell you will! Take this!" She thrust out her arm and sprayed. He grabbed his face and yelled, his voice a thundering boom that bounced off the trees. She didn't waste any time turning and running as if the devil were on her heels and, as far as she knew, he just might be.

"Oh, God, oh, God, oh, God. Please don't let me die!" she prayed as she stumbled down the path toward her house, accidentally dropping the small can of protection. There was no way she was going to stop and pick it up.

Why hadn't she gone to church last Sunday? This was her punishment. She was going to die. She could almost feel a knife plunging into her back. Not that the guy had had a knife. He hadn't had anything. He'd been bare-assed naked.

But he could choke her to death. He'd had big hands.

That wasn't all that was rather large, Shintara said.

"Shut up," she wheezed.

Home. She had to make it back. There she would be safe. She tried to take a deep breath, but it was as if she'd lost her ability to inhale.

Who was the naked man? A mugger?

No, a serial killer!

She needed to call the sheriff. Phone! Crap. She had her cell with her. Why hadn't she already thought about calling the cops? She fumbled with the zipper of her waist purse, not stopping in case the guy was behind her.

Ria finally tugged it out, did a juggle that any circus performer would've been proud of, steadied the phone, then punched in 9-1-1 as she ran up the steps of her house. She shoved the door open, gasping for her next breath right before she slammed the door behind her.

"Nine-one-one, what's your emergency?"

"A man. He was naked. In the woods. Hurry." God, she still couldn't take a deep breath. She leaned against the door, gasping for air and trembling all the way down to her toes.

"Calm down, ma'am. I need an address."

"This is Ria. Rianna Lancaster. I'm inside my house, but I was running . . ."

The dispatcher distinctly cleared her throat. "Oh, it's you, Ria."

Ria moved the phone away from her ear and glared at it before bringing it back. "And what's that supposed to mean?" Why did Tilly have to be the dispatcher on duty? She was a real pain in the butt, besides being the biggest gossip in town.

Deep sigh. "I'll send Heath over."

"Fine! And tell him to hurry."

"They always do, dear."

The line went dead.

Ria straightened and reared back her arm, but stopped just short of throwing her phone against the wall. Destroying her cell wasn't an option—she needed it. Besides, it wasn't her phone's fault the dispatcher was a moron—of epic proportions. In the end, she only snapped it closed. But really hard. Life was so not fair.

She began to pace the living room. Tilly hadn't believed her. No one ever believed her. There *had* been a naked man in the woods. Dammit! She'd seen him.

Her gaze fell on the front door. When she'd turned the lock, it had clicked. Right? She hurried over to check it again. Locked. She ran a shaky hand across her forehead. Safe. Nothing could get her.

Her gaze strayed toward the back of the house. Oh, God, the back door wasn't locked. She ran down the hall, slid around the kitchen table, grabbed the doorknob, and then clicked the lock, double checking to make sure. She breathed a sigh of relief. Now she was safe from naked men.

Like that's been a problem lately. Shintara's words dripped with sarcasm.

Ria grimaced. "I haven't wanted to date anyone, thank you very much." If she wanted a man, she could get one. There was a big difference between wanting one and needing one.

What if there was one already in the house? He could have sneaked inside while she was in the front room.

Goose bumps popped up on her arms. She grabbed the heavy flashlight off the kitchen counter. If anyone stepped out, she'd whack him over the head. Holding it in front of her like the Olympic torch, she tiptoed to the bedroom. She glanced inside, then hurried to the other side of the door, and did another quick scan.

It looked empty.

You're really being overly dramatic. I thought the naked guy was hot.

"Shush," Ria whispered as she eased along the bedroom wall and poked open the bathroom door with the toe of her tennis shoe.

Empty.

Behind the shower curtain? She swallowed hard. That's where all the killers hid; just waiting for some poor naked woman to pull the curtain back so she could take a shower.

Not this time!

She raised the flashlight, then flung the curtain open.

Nothing.

Thank God!

She set the flashlight on the counter, then sat on the toilet.

Everything she'd been through began to sink in. She'd survived a . . . an attack. He'd come at her, probably meaning to kill her, or worse, although she couldn't think of anything worse than being dead. But Ria had remembered the training she'd taken at summer camp when she was thirteen. A satisfied smirk lifted the corners of her mouth. She'd maced his butt.

Technically, you maced his face.

"Shut up."

Ria would do it again if she had to. Nobody better mess with this girl!

As she sat there, she stared at her bed. Had the dust ruffle just moved? There it was again. Her bravado quickly disappeared.

What if someone was under it? Killers hid there, too, just waiting for an unsuspecting woman clad in a lacy teddy. . . . Wow, maybe she did need to get laid. But not by a killer. She jumped to her feet, grabbed the flashlight and eased into the bedroom.

"If you're under there, you might as well come out," she said in a firm voice. Oh, yeah, that was really smart. If there was someone under her bed, did she really want them to come out? No, she wanted them to stay there until Heath arrived.

Drama queen, singsonged through her head.

Stupid voice.

But Ria couldn't resist checking under the bed. She could escape before anyone scrambled out. She flipped the bottom of the bedspread onto the bed, then backed far away, and squatted down until she could see under it.

"Ruffles, what are you doing under there?" She eyed the black-and-white cat.

"Meow." Her tail bumped where the dust ruffle would've been.

Ruffles pretty much stayed under the bed, hence the name. Shaking her head, Ria came to her feet, then went to the front window and peered out. No sign of the naked guy. What had he said? His name was Crisco, or something, and he was from another planet. An alien? More like a psycho on the loose.

But very sexy, the voice in her head said.

"Shut up," she automatically mumbled.

She was tempted to call and see where the deputy was but forced herself to wait a few more minutes. Tilly would blow everything Ria said out of proportion if she called again.

Okay, she might be just a little . . . excitable at times, but was that a crime? Besides, she'd had good reason in the past to call the sheriff's office. Like the time there had been a wolf in her backyard.

How the heck could she have known that Matt Jenson had bought a new show dog? It had looked like a wolf to her—sort of. And the big dog scared her when it came barreling around the corner while she was painting the back porch a pretty purple.

She actually thought the purple made the dog look very unusual . . . cute. And she had only gotten a little on his tail.

Matt hadn't agreed.

People in a small town just never seemed to forget things. Even giving Matt's dog a year of free grooming had only made things marginally better.

When she saw the patrol car pull up, her body sagged against the window frame. Tears threatened, but she rapidly blinked them away. Now she was truly safe. She unlocked the front door and hurried outside.

Heath climbed out of the patrol car with a tired sigh, and pushed his hat a little higher on his forehead. "What's this about a naked man? You know your momma will skin you alive if you have a naked man in your house."

She frowned. "I don't have a naked man in the house." She squared her shoulders. "Not that it would matter. I'm twenty-eight years old. If I want to have a naked man in my house, I will."

"And that's why I have to deal with your naked man, because you young kids don't listen to your folks. Marry the guy first, and you won't have nearly as many problems."

She stomped her foot. "I don't have a naked man in my house!"

"You don't have to get testy. I'm here because you called about him, not the other way around. If he's gone, then your problem is solved."

She opened her mouth, then snapped it closed. She should sell her shop and move far, far away. Right now, that sounded like a good idea.

After taking a deep breath, she tried again, speaking slowly and calmly. "I was out running. That's where I saw the naked man. In the woods."

Heath tensed, eyes narrowing, his police instincts going on full alert, hand moving toward his gun. "Why didn't you say that in the first place?" His gaze searched the wooded area for any movement.

"I did. At least, that's what I tried to tell the stupid dispatcher."

"I'll need a description." He pulled a pad and pencil out of his shirt pocket.

She thought back. "Tall." He was a lot taller than her. And tanned. "Dark." Wow, it was really hard to actually give a description of someone she had seen for a brief moment, and she really didn't think Heath would appreciate her saying the naked guy was . . . well endowed.

Heath cleared his throat.

All right already, she was thinking.

The naked guy had been nice looking, in a serial killer sort of way, though. "Handsome," she finished.

His pencil paused above the pad. "Tall, dark, and handsome?"

It sounded bad now that she thought about it. "Well, he was," she defended herself. Where was it in any rule book that serial killers had to be ugly?

He sighed. "What was he wearing?'

"He was naked. I told you that already."

"I guess you did." He studied her for a moment. "Maybe you'd better tell me exactly what happened." He motioned for her to go up on the porch.

Whatever. She walked up the steps and plopped down on the porch swing. Heath followed, then leaned against the railing.

"I was out running, and this hawk landed in front of me."

"A hawk?" His eyebrows drew together. "I thought you said it was a naked man."

"The first thing I saw was a hawk."

"That's not normal. I mean, having one land in front of you."

"I know. It was almost creepy the way the bird just stared at me. And then a heavy fog rolled in."

"Fog?" He looked at the blue sky, then back at her.

"Yeah, it was really weird."

"Go on."

"I heard someone groan."

"The hawk?"

She shook her head. "I thought it might be the hawk's owner or something. Then the fog sort of drifted away, and there was a man."

"The naked man?"

She sighed with relief. He was finally getting it. "Yes, the naked man."

"What did he say?"

"That his name was Crisco, and he was from another planet. I forget what name he called it. And that he was here to take me back with him. That's when I maced him and ran home."

He closed the pad and slipped it, along with his pencil, back in his pocket.

"Do you want me to show you where I saw him?"

"I don't think that will be necessary." He came to his feet and marched down the steps, heading toward his patrol car with purposeful strides.

"Where are you going?" She jumped up and followed.

He suddenly turned, and she had to skid to a halt to keep from plowing into him.

"Ria, if it wasn't for the fact that I've known your mom and dad for at least twenty years, I'd run your butt in for making a false report," he said with more than a touch of exasperation.

"But he was there."

"Think about what you're saying, girl." His eyes suddenly filled with pity. "A hawk lands in front of you, fog rolls in when the sun is out. Then, apparently, the bird turns into a naked man who tells you he's an alien and wants to take you back to his planet."

Okay, it did sound crazy. "But it happened."

"Do you want me to call your mother for you?"

She shoved her hands down deep inside her pockets. "No, I don't want you to call Mom. I'm not having a spell or anything."

"They have doctors in Dallas who might be able to help you, you know."

"I'm not crazy!" She turned on her heel and stomped back toward the house.

Of course you're not crazy.

"Shut up!"

"I was only trying to help," Heath said.

"I wasn't talking to you."

Silence.

Great. Dig the hole a little deeper.

She strode up the steps and into the house. Then it hit her. Everyone in Miller Bend had a police scanner. She supposed it would be all over town by this afternoon that she was seeing aliens—and talking to the voice in her head . . . again.

Another mark against her. At least it would give the townspeople something to talk about at the July Fourth festivities this weekend. Unless something out of the ordinary happened that would give everyone something better to talk about.

Yeah, right. What could top her seeing a hawk, then a thick fog, then a naked man who claimed to be an alien and wanted to whisk her off to his planet?

Nope, they'd definitely be talking about her.

Chapter 2

"Hey, Ria, seen any aliens lately?"

Ria froze in the process of unfolding her camp chair. She recognized the voice—Ben Dansworth. He was a real dweeb, and had been since third grade.

"Don't pay any attention to him," Ria's mother said as she settled into her chair. "He's an ass. Let's enjoy the parade. After all, it's the Fourth of July. We've been blessed with nice weather, and how often do we get to watch a good parade?"

In Miller Bend? Nearly every holiday was all. New Year's Day, Valentine's Day, Chinese New Year . . . name it, and they had a parade. And then there were the celebrations that went along with the parades. They even had an Old Settlers reunion celebration—and parade. And it was the same floats, with only minor changes to denote why they were celebrating.

But a flood of warmth settled around Ria as she watched her mother make herself comfortable, smiling as she looked around at the people she'd known since the day she was brought into this world.

Living forever in their small town suited Ria's mom. Maggie Lancaster was a slice of hot apple pie with a scoop of vanilla ice cream on a warm summer day. She was crocheted sweaters and homemade quilts.

And she'd gotten stuck with a defective kid.

Ria only wished she didn't have to screw up all the time. Or hear the voice inside her head.

I beg your pardon. I'm not just a voice inside your head. I happen to be part of you. If you would pay a little more attention, I could explain everything.

"Shut up."

"What, dear?" Her mother glanced Ria's way, the lines around her mouth and eyes deepening.

Great. Ria had told her mother she no longer heard the voice. It was just a small white lie so her mom wouldn't worry.

Ria smiled. "You know, *shut up*. Not shut up when you tell a person to shut up. I meant shut up, as in, look at the Women's League float. Pretty snazzy, huh? That kind of shut up. We-worked-pretty-hard-for-this-parade-and-it-shows kind of shut up." Great, now she sounded like an imbecile.

Maggie smiled. "It is quite nice, isn't it? I told you all those hours you helped would pay off, and I was right." She sat taller in her chair. "Look, there's your father. Doesn't he look handsome?"

Ria breathed a sigh of relief, glad she'd averted a possible disaster. Her mom had questioned Ria about what she'd seen in the woods, then asked if Ria was feeling okay. She could just imagine what people had been saying, and what her mother was thinking.

She drew in a deep breath. It was all behind them now. Well, almost. There were still people like Ben Dansworth, who liked nothing more than to make a big deal out of anything that happened to her. May he rot in hell.

No, Ria would make sure her mother didn't have any more worries. At least, not where her daughter was concerned. An army of naked men could run through town, and Ria wouldn't say a word.

If I see any sexy naked men running through town you can bet I won't stay quiet.

And Ria would ignore the voice.

Snort. You haven't been able to ignore me before. Why do you think you can now?

Nope, she wasn't going to even think about Shintara. Instead, she'd concentrate on the parade.

Her father was driving the fire truck, since he was the chief. He beamed, waving at the crowd. Pride threaded its way through her. She had the best-ever parents.

She put two fingers in her mouth and whistled. If she'd had a bullhorn, she couldn't have gotten his attention any better. She had a great whistle. Her father spotted them and waved. It wasn't very ladylike to whistle that loud, but she didn't care. He'd taught her to whistle like a guy, and she was quite proud she could.

Her gaze moved farther down the truck, past the firemen squeezed on top and all of them waving at the crowd. Sometimes she wondered if men ever grew up.

Her eyes grew round and she almost swallowed her tongue. Not that anyone really could, but it certainly felt like it as she began to cough and sputter.

"Are you okay?" Her mother patted her on the back.

She couldn't look away. It was him—the naked guy who'd stepped in front of her on the trail. He sat at the very back of the fire truck, on top, arms crossed in front of him, as if he owned the damned thing or something. At least he had on clothes today.

"That man . . ."

Her mother's gaze followed where Ria pointed. She smiled as she relaxed in her chair again. "You must mean Kristor Valkyir. We call him Kris. Isn't he handsome? He's from another country."

"You know him?" Her mother knew the serial killer?

"Yes, dear. He's very nice. We rented him your old room."

"You rented him my . . ." she stumbled over the words. It took a moment for her brain to connect the dots, but when she did, she thought her head would explode. "You rented him my room!"

Her mother's expression quickly changed to concern. Several people turned and stared. Ria lowered her voice. "You rented him my room?" Maybe she'd misunderstood.

"We really didn't think you'd mind. He's agreed to pay us five hundred dollars a week. That's a fortune! Of course, we told him it was too much, but he wouldn't hear of paying less. Your father and I are not getting any younger and, what with the economy, we just thought . . ." She shook her head, then patted Ria's hand. "It doesn't matter. We'll tell him he has to leave at the end of the week. We just didn't think it would upset you so much."

"But he's the alien," she blurted.

Her mother looked around, as if someone might rescue her daughter from her delusions. "Ria, I promise you that Kris is not an alien."

She rolled her eyes. "I know he's not an alien."

Her mother breathed a sigh of relief. "Good. I'm so glad that's settled."

"Nothing is settled. I know he's not an alien, but that's what he told me. This is the guy who stepped out in front of me the day I went running. He said he was from another planet."

"Oh, you must have been mistaken." She laughed lightly. "I'm sure he only meant he was from another country."

Could things get any more frustrating? She inhaled a slow deep breath, then exhaled. "Okay, I can buy that he might have meant he was from another country, but where were his clothes?"

"Well, you know how they are in some countries. Nudity means nothing to them. At least, not what it does to us, and I have to say that he hasn't walked around the house without clothes since he's been staying with us."

Oh, yeah, that made things a lot better. Not!

"He's a little rough around the edges," her mother continued. "But he only needs a bit of polishing. I think he's spent far too much time around other men. I believe he told us he was in the military." She eyed Ria with more than a trace of speculation. "He's quite handsome, don't you think?"

What? Did her mother want them to hook up or something? Ria bit back a laugh. This wasn't happening. It couldn't be. Maybe it was all a bad dream.

"Don't worry so, dear. They say it causes wrinkles, and the good face cream costs a fortune."

"But, Mom—"

"Why, just yesterday," her mother interrupted, "Alesha Campbell said Kris got her white kitten down from a tree. She said Kris was very gentle, and little Fluffy fell in love with him." She patted Ria's hand. "Everything will be fine, and once you get to know Kris, I'm sure you'll love him as much as we do."

Love him? How could they love him? They'd just freakin' met him!

But he is hot, Shintara broke into Ria's thoughts. *I certainly wouldn't mind getting a piece of that action.*

Cry. That's what she wanted to do. Go home, curl up on her bed, and let the tears flow. She sucked it up though. No way was she going to let the crazy serial killer murder her parents while they slept.

"Anyway, you'll get a chance to meet and talk to him tonight."

Her ears perked up. "What do you mean? What's happening tonight?"

"We're having a small get-together at the house. Your father wants to thank some of the volunteers who helped put together the Fourth of July activities. He is the president of the revitalization committee, after all."

And why they had a gazillion parades every year, but she kept her lips clamped together.

"Now that we have the money Kris is paying us to rent your room, well, it was fate. It's only right that your father thank everyone properly. I've been meaning to ask you to join us but kept forgetting. You will come, won't you?"

"I wouldn't miss it." She knew what she'd seen, and what she'd heard. Her eyes narrowed as the fire truck slowly passed. Her gaze suddenly locked with Kristor's. Something fluttered to awareness inside her as her gaze drifted over his broad shoulders, solid chest, massive arms.

And we already know what he looks like naked.

"Shut up."

He mother glanced her way.

Ria pointed toward the high school band that sounded like a rusty train going down even rustier tracks. "Shut up, they're really improving."

Her mother's forehead creased. "You really think so?"

Ria nodded. "Oh, yeah, much better than the last parade."

While her mother's attention was on the band, Ria glanced once more at Kristor. So maybe he was downright sexy. The only thing she cared about was her parents' safety. By tomorrow, Kristor would be locked away in jail. She'd make sure of it.

Kristor suddenly looked her way, capturing her gaze. Her mouth went dry and it was hard to breathe. Very slowly, he let his gaze travel over her. Heat flashed through her body, making her itch in places that hadn't itched in a while. Not that he would ever get the chance to scratch them. She raised her chin and pursed her lips, but he only smiled.

He taunted her! Well, they would just see who smiled last!

The fire truck passed, then turned the corner, but she could still feel the tingles that one look from him had left behind. Much to her chagrin, they stayed with her until the parade was almost over.

Ria wished she could drag Carly with her tonight, but her best friend had caught a summer cold and decided to forgo the activities. Not that Carly joined in that much. She was more content to stay in her own little world, away from the crowds. The girl really needed a dose of confidence.

"Oh, there's Vicky Jo." Maggie waved at her friend.

"Go ahead and join her," Ria said. "The parade is almost over."

Maggie nibbled her bottom lip.

"I'll put the chairs in the back of my car, and then probably wander around a bit. I'll be fine."

"I'll see you tonight." Her mother hurried to catch up with her friend as Ria stood, folded the camp chairs, and looped them over her arm. Maybe she would grab a funnel cake and take it by Carly's. Carly had a strange passion for them. Besides, she needed to talk to her about Kristor, and plan her next action against him.

When she got to her car, she juggled the chairs while reaching in her pocket for her keys, but lost her balance. The only thing that kept her from falling on her butt was a hard chest and strong arms.

"Thanks." She laughed as she untangled from the chairs, but her laughter quickly died when she turned and saw the man who'd helped save her from an embarassing moment. "You!"

"Now are you ready to leave?" Kristor asked.

She automatically reached for her can of mace, before realizing she hadn't brought it. She'd only been going to a parade, not jogging through the woods.

"Who are you?" Her eyes narrowed. He had his nerve standing there as if he owned the world looking all . . . all . . .

Sexy? Manly? Delicious? Shintara's sultry laughter rippled.

Like a dictator, Ria finished her own thought. She returned her attention back to the crazy guy.

"Why did you tell me you were from another planet? And why are you renting my old room? I want you out of my parents' house. And I refuse to go anywhere with you." She looked around for a cop but, of course, there wasn't one.

"Your adopted parents are very nice. It was good when they took you into their home and raised you." His gaze

raked over her. "Although, you don't have the same person-
ality. They're very friendly."

Goose bumps popped up on her arms. "What do you
know about me?" Someone had told him she was adopted.
They had to. It wasn't like it was a big secret, but her parents
rarely mentioned it.

"I know of your family, and where you come from."

Why was she listening to this garbage? No way could he
know about her biological family. He couldn't. Could he?
She needed to think. He was confusing her.

She pushed the button on her keychain and popped the
trunk of her car, but when she started to lift the chairs and
put them inside, he brushed her out of the way and did it for
her.

She watched him, wondering if he was telling the truth.
She had searched for information—what adopted child
wouldn't?—and had come up empty-handed. The woman at
the adoption agency told her it wasn't unusual to have a baby
placed on the doorstep of the orphanage. Unfortunately, the
child would never be able to find out anything about her
family. So, how did this stranger know about her parents?

She closed the lid of her trunk. "Why should I believe you?
Everyone knows I was adopted. It's not a big secret. You
could be making all this up."

He clamped his lips together, his face taking on a reddish
hue. Ria wondered if he was about to blow a gasket, but just
as suddenly, he calmed.

"I have no reason to lie," he said in a stilted voice.

You could at least listen to what he has to say, Shintara
said.

*Yeah, like I listened to you about the whoopee cushion? I
don't think so.*

*Are you ever going to forget about that? Give me a break!
At least hear the guy out.*

Nope, Ria had learned her lesson with that one. Her high
school teacher? During assembly? Sheesh! What had she

been thinking to go along with Shintara? Although, Ria might have gotten away with it if Donald Evans hadn't told on her.

But what if he did know something? "First, tell me why you were running around in the woods naked." Let him answer that one.

"It is our custom."

Just as her mother had said. So maybe she might have misunderstood when he'd said he was from another planet. Maybe he had meant country. It was possible.

She wavered. As much as she loved her parents, there was a hole inside her that only knowing about her biological parents could fill. Ron and Maggie Lancaster would always be her parents, no matter what she discovered.

"Okay, I'll listen, but not anywhere too private. I still don't trust you."

He planted his fists on his hips, feet apart, as if he was about to argue. He reminded her of a Viking warrior, except dark rather than blond. One who was apparently put out at the moment because she didn't just take off and go wherever he wanted. And that was so not going to happen.

"Where then?" He finally gave in.

"The park," she said. They would have booths and picnic tables, and there'd be a crowd. Plus, it was within walking distance.

She pocketed her keys and headed in that direction, not looking to see if he followed, but she was pretty sure he did. She could feel his gaze on her. Was he on the level about knowing where she came from? She'd wondered for so long. Why had her parents left her in the care of strangers? What had they been like? Had they loved her?

Panic set in and, for a moment, she considered telling him to forget the whole thing. What if her parents were serial killers locked away in prison?

Maybe that's why she didn't stop walking. Good or bad, she needed to know.

Kristor stayed a step behind Rianna. Stubborn, obstinate female. Women usually did whatever he asked. Why should this one be any different? His frown deepened. Maybe because she was only part Symtarian. That had to be it.

Rianna tensed when she was around him, showing her uneasiness, but she also wanted knowledge about her past. He admired her for facing her fear. But would she believe him when he told her that her ancestors were from another planet? Probably not. He had to admit, he hadn't made a good first impression.

Throw her over your shoulder. Force her to return to New Symtaria and be done with it.

Labrinon, I wondered when you would say something, Kristor told his animal guide. He *had* thought about throwing her over his shoulder, but his father had cautioned him to lean on the side of diplomacy, and his mother . . .

Ah, his mother. For such a delicate flower, she could easily bend her husband and children to her will. In her soft voice, she had begged him to be gentle. It was not in his nature, but he would try, at least, for a while.

I'm sure she has naked men jumping out in front of her every day, telling her they're from another planet and wanting her to leave with them, Labrinon continued, words dripping with sarcasm. *You shouldn't have spoken. It ruined the element of surprise. Before you could grab her, she ran. Not a very well-thought-out maneuver.*

Did you not hear anything my brother said when he returned with Callie? Exasperation laced Kristor's thoughts.

Of course, I heard Rogar.

Not very well, apparently. When Rogar had transformed from a jaguar to a human, Callie ran away screaming.

But he convinced her to return with him, Labrinon added.

After much wasted time.

Your tactics weren't any better.

Labrinon was right, but Kristor hadn't meant to scare Rianna. He'd only wanted to get his mission over and done, and return to New Symtaria, while trying to please the Queen Mother. He thought if he spoke to Rianna, she would remain calm.

By the gods, he was a warrior, not someone who should have to hunt impure offspring and bring them home. His father, the king, had bade him complete this mission. How could he say no? So now, he followed behind a mere slip of a woman as if she was the one in control.

He silently fumed as Rianna led him down a walkway, then cut across a grassy area. When they topped a small rise, he looked down upon what appeared to be a festival of sorts, with booths, and much laughter, and many people.

Rianna's father had said they would be celebrating the July Fourth festivities. Kristor would look up the word on his database when he returned to the dwelling where he was staying. These Earthlings were an odd race, and this mission tiresome.

His gaze dropped to the gentle curve of Rianna's hips. He watched them sway as he walked behind her toward the celebration. Something shifted inside him. She ignited his imagination. His blood stirred at the vision of naked, intertwined limbs, of her arms pulling him closer, begging for his touch, his mouth. . . .

She stopped, suddenly turning, then clearing her throat. When he raised his gaze, she didn't look happy that he'd been staring at her form. She should feel pleased that a warrior, and a prince, would honor her with his attention.

"We can sit here," she told him.

There was a hard edge in her voice. She could take lessons from the women of New Symtaria. They knew how to treat men of his standing.

The way Marane treated you?

Labrinon's laughter filled Kristor's senses. Anger flared inside him. *Marane doesn't count. She's a witch with a vile temper. Enough! We have business to attend.* He sat on the hard surface. A very uncomfortable seat, and not one he would have chosen.

Ria started to sit, but apparently had second thoughts, and moved to the other side of the table.

"You're very stubborn," he said.

Smart. I'm sure that will win her over.

Kristor ignored Labrinon.

"I like to think of myself as being cautious, rather than stubborn," Rianna said.

He would try to be more pleasant. "Stubborn can be a good quality. I have won many a battle by not admitting defeat, but pressing forward instead. It is a tactic that has worked well for me." He hadn't meant to encourage her behavior. "Except on a female. It does not sit well on them."

She raised an eyebrow. Definitely stubborn, but very nice to look upon. Her thick, dark brown hair was pulled away from her face. Although her features were delicate, there was a sensuous, earthy quality about her that was undeniable. Her Symtarian blood, no doubt.

"What do you mean, you're a warrior?" she asked.

The proud fighter in him sprang to the surface. "I defend my home from invading armies."

She seemed to absorb his words, although she didn't appear particularly impressed. Most women were. He had faced death many times and been victorious. He'd defended New Symtaria with his life, and would do so again.

"What do you know about my parents?"

Yes, she was very quick to dismiss his warrior status. Not that it overly concerned him. He was here only to complete his mission, and return with her to New Symtaria so she could embrace a culture as old as time.

And mate.

Possibly with him.

In fact, now that he thought about it, that was a good plan.

"My parents?" she prodded.

Stubborn, and in a hurry. She had been running when he'd first encountered her. She would not be the type who wasted time. "You come from a very prestigious lineage," he finally spoke. "There is royalty in your blood, but we are not related, so it will be okay if we mate."

She squared her shoulders. "I beg your pardon?"

He frowned. She did not seem to take to the idea very well. Maybe he wouldn't mate with her. Why should he let her have the pleasure of his body, when she didn't look as though the idea tempted her? This Earthling side of her was without passion.

He decided to ignore her response to the possibility of their one day mating, and continue explaining where she came from. "Your father had Symtarian blood. From what I've gathered, he was killed by one of the rogue Symtarians."

Which was happening to more impures than he wanted to count. Some rogues didn't like the thought of impures being brought back to New Symtaria and mixing with the pure bloods, but it was a necessity now. The Symtarian blood was too pure and, in a weaker mind, the animal guide was taking over the human side.

The animal guide's natural instinct was to hunt and kill. It was causing chaos among the different tribes. The impure's nature was more gentle, and the animal guide less dominant.

Except for Rianna. She did not appear that gentle to him.

"I'm of royal blood," she stated dryly.

He wasn't sure about the tone she used, but he would ignore it for now. "Yes."

"And my mother?"

"She too has passed. I believe the rogue Symtarian scared her so much that she left you to be raised in the institution. I'm sure for your own protection. She was later killed when the vehicle in which she was riding collided with another." It had taken much time to discover this information. He was ready to be done with it all.

She bit her bottom lip, blinking back the moisture that formed in her eyes. Kristor's heart beat faster inside his chest. Was she about to cry? Women who cried made him nervous. He probably shouldn't have delivered the information so bluntly, but what did he know about finesse? He left that to his brother. Rogar knew how to talk to women. It would be better to get Rianna back to Symtaria and let someone else handle her.

He cleared his throat. "Now, are you ready to leave?"

She shook her head, her expression puzzled. "Leave?"

"Yes, to go to New Symtaria."

"Why would I do that?"

"To be with your own kind."

"I don't even know where New Symtaria is."

"It's in another galaxy, but I have the means to take you there."

"The means . . ."

"Yes, in my spacecraft."

Now she worried him. Her face drained of color. What had he said? The fear returned to her eyes as she eased her legs from under the table.

"Is something wrong?"

"You just told me that you're an alien from another planet. What could possibly be wrong?"

Even though she said nothing was wrong, her actions were telling him something different. He reached for her hand. His sister had once told him women liked to hold hands. Except Rianna jerked away from him.

"Don't touch me! Stay away from me and my family!"

"I don't understand." He opened his hands out, palms up.

She shot to her feet, stumbling in her haste to put distance between them. "Of course, you don't. You're crazy!" She took off running before he could get his feet out from under the table. He turned sideways on the bench and watched her.

Rianna had a nice run. Long legs stretching out in front of her. She would make a good mating partner.

Except each time they talked, she ended up running away.

I don't blame her. You didn't handle that well, Labrinon said. *My plan is better. Throw her over your shoulder and let us leave this barbaric land.*

"Silence!"

Chapter 3

"He told me he was an alien from another planet," Ria explained to Heath.

Heath gave an exasperated sigh, but before he could open his mouth, Ria hurried on.

"And no, I don't think he's an alien, but I do think he's certifiable, and he's renting my old room from my parents. He could murder them in the middle of the night. I want you to lock him up. Put him in the state hospital . . . something."

"How about if I just talk to him for now?"

Just talk? That was all? He was a threat to her parents and possibly the whole community. She opened her mouth to tell him she wanted him to do more, but his expression said that was all he would do for now. It was a start, she supposed. "Fine. You'll see. The guy is off his rocker."

Heath scanned the park.

"There he is," she said, pointing Kristor out. He was looking quite unconcerned that he was about to be carted off to the loony bin. The guy probably didn't even know he was crazy. Heath would help rectify the situation, she was sure.

Heath started toward Kristor, or whatever his name was. It could be an alias for all she knew. Ria stayed right on Heath's heels.

He stopped, studying her for a moment. "Wait here."

"Wait here? But . . . but . . ." Of course. It made sense.

Heath had a gun and everything, and if there was a tussle, he couldn't concentrate on taking the stranger down if he was worried she'd get hurt.

"Okay, but be careful. He's pretty big."

"The bigger they are, the harder they fall," Heath said, without much conviction.

And Kristor was big. The guy had some serious muscles. Sexy muscles. Not that she was even remotely attracted to him. The guy was a nut case. The outside package tempted her, she wouldn't deny that. It was the inside that scared the hell out of her.

Ria tugged on the hem of her shorts, then twisted the material around her finger. If anything happened to Heath, her parents would disown her, the townspeople would probably kill her, and she was pretty sure Ruffles wouldn't like her, either.

Not that the cat had much to do with her now. The cat had always seemed fond of Heath, though. Most men actually. Ria had adopted a slutty cat.

But if the stranger hurt Heath, Ria would feel so guilty. Heath was practically an uncle. He'd given Ria her driving test. She frowned. Her first speeding ticket, too.

"You look deep in thought," Donald Evans said as he came to stand beside her.

She jumped, then quickly smoothed the hem of her shorts and stood straighter. She hadn't heard his approach.

Donald was looking as handsome as ever. They'd dated for a while. Nothing serious, although Donald would've liked to take it to the next level. But when it came to sleeping with him, she drew the line. Maybe she still secretly harbored a grudge because he'd told on her about the whoopee cushion.

But he was handsome, she couldn't deny that, and it was the reason she'd first started dating him. He was very *GQ*, with his thick blond hair and blue eyes.

She'd been on a self-improvement quest that month and thought dating him would help. It hadn't. She'd felt worse about herself. Nothing she had done was right. He always seemed to find fault.

And that coming from a man who didn't sweat. There was something really strange about a guy who didn't sweat.

Maybe she was being just as critical as Donald. He had a membership to the local gym, so she was pretty sure he sweated when he worked out. She'd just never seen him looking anything but perfect, and that bothered her.

"So, are you going to tell me what you're thinking so seriously about?" His gaze followed where she had been looking. His lips formed a straight, irritated line. "Or maybe I should say *whom*, rather than what."

"His name is Kristor, he's renting my old room, and the guy is certifiable."

His expression relaxed. "Is he the alien you saw?"

For a brief moment, she had a vision of herself screaming at the top of her lungs and pulling at her hair. The only thing stopping her from following through was the fact she didn't want to be in the same car as the one that would be taking the once naked man, who claimed to be an alien, off to the state hospital.

"I didn't see an alien," she ground out. "He told me he was an alien."

"Ahh . . ." He still looked skeptical.

Why should he believe her now? He never had in the past.

"I just want him out of my parents' house."

"Doesn't look like that's going to happen any time soon." Donald nodded toward the two men.

Heath shook the stranger's hand as though Kristor had just told Heath that he'd won the Texas lottery. What the hell? Heath was grinning when he started back toward her.

"Did he tell you he was an alien?" she asked when he joined them again.

"You must have misunderstood. He's from another country. Kris is a really great guy. He even agreed to play in the flag football game this afternoon. Good thing—we were short a man, and would've had to cancel." Heath cast a sour look in Donald's direction.

What?

No, no, no!

"Let me get this straight," Ria began as calmly as she could. "He won you over because he agreed to play in a stupid football game? And you're not taking him to the state hospital, not even after the game?"

Heath frowned. "It's not a stupid game, and I can't very well lock him up just because he's a foreigner. How would that look?"

"He said he wanted me to go to his planet, and he would take me there in his spaceship."

Heath chuckled. "Maybe that was his way of sweet-talking you?"

Beside her, Donald went rigor mortis. Sheesh, it wasn't as if they were still dating. He didn't own her. Then again, he could just be concerned the guy was a stranger. Doubtful, though. Donald still acted as if they were an item.

Her attention turned to Kristor. He was helping the Widow Simmons up a steep slope, and she was grinning like a young girl. Good Lord, she was at least eighty-five.

"You could do worse." Heath glanced at Donald again, then back to her. "And you're not getting any younger."

Ria bristled. "Twenty-eight is not that old."

Donald slipped his arm around Ria's shoulder. "I'm sure you'll check this new man out, Deputy. After all, it would be a shame if he was indeed a lunatic. I would rather believe one of our own, than someone you've known all of two minutes."

Heath squared his shoulders. "I'd already planned to do that, since it's my job. I don't think you have to worry that I don't know procedure. I signed on to protect the citizens, and that's exactly what I'll do." He tugged on the end of his hat, then turned and left.

"You can move your arm now," Ria told him. The heavy weight was like an anchor.

He took his time moving it. "Have lunch with me."

Donald had inherited the running of his parents' restaurant when they retired to Florida. It was a good place to eat. Not that they had many choices. It was either the restaurant, the Dairy Queen, or Sonic.

"I'm going to grab Carly a burger, and see how she's feeling." It was best not to start something else up with Donald. It had taken her too long to break free of his tight rein the last time.

"I'll have the cook fix her something special," he said.

"Donald, I . . ."

He smiled. "As old friends, nothing more. Carly would much rather have something from the restaurant, I'm sure."

She didn't see anything in his expression that would tell her otherwise, and it wasn't as though she hadn't known him all her life. "Okay, but I can't stay long."

He grinned, taking her hand in his. She looked across the park and caught Kristor watching her. He wore a dark scowl. She had a feeling he didn't care for Donald's touching her. What? Did he think she was *his* property? He might have fooled the deputy, but he didn't fool her for a second. She stepped closer to Donald just to prove she didn't belong to Kristor, either. Donald smiled down at her.

"I used to love it when you wore your hair down. It made you look more like a grown woman and less like a ragamuffin. I wish you'd wear it down more often."

For a moment she'd forgotten exactly what it was about Donald that irritated her. She was so glad he'd reminded her. "Then isn't it a good thing we're not dating because I love my hair up. It's so much cooler." She smiled.

"Stubborn woman." He laughed, but it sounded brittle.

"You're not the first person who's told me that," she said. Except when Kristor had said it, it hadn't sounded quite as condescending.

Lunch went by fairly quickly, mainly because Donald kept getting called away. His irritation was clearly visible. When he had to see about a malfunctioning dishwasher, she took the opportunity to escape.

Carly didn't live very far away. No one in town lived very far away, though. Ria could cross town in peak traffic, with the light red, and still be at Carly's in under five. They only had one red light, and a blinking caution light, and a few stop signs that people sort of stopped at.

She climbed the stairs to Carly's second-floor apartment and knocked on the door. A few moments later, the door was opened by a bad imitation of her friend. Carly sported a red nose, and watery, red-rimmed eyes.

"Oh, sweetie, you look awful."

Carly opened the door wider, then covered her mouth with a tissue when she began to cough. "I feel awful."

"I brought sustenance." She raised the white carton.

Carly puffed her cheeks out. "Blah. Food."

"You have to eat."

"I'd rather lie down and die." She moved to the sofa and collapsed on it. "How was the parade?"

Ria took the carton to the kitchen and put it in the fridge for later. "My alien was there," she said over her shoulder.

Carly sat up with a start, then grabbed her head, and lay back down. "I can't believe you sprang that on me."

"Sorry." Ria went back to the living room and curled up on the chair, keeping a safe distance from any germs floating in the air.

"This was the naked guy you saw in the woods? What happened? I want all the details."

She had already told Carly everything. Ria had known she could count on her friend to believe her. Now, she quickly related what happened in the park, what Kristor had told Ria about her parents, and then the lies he'd told Heath.

"I take it that you don't think he's using a new line to come on to women?"

Ria shook her head. "I think the guy is crazy. Mom doesn't though." She grimaced. "You should've seen her gush when she talked about him. You'd think he was a god or something. Apparently, he's casting a spell over the town. Well, at least my parents and Heath. I know why Heath thinks he's great. He agreed to play in their flag football game this afternoon. But my mom? She should know better."

"She'll come to her senses when the newness wears off."

"If she's still alive."

"So what are you going to do?"

Ria sighed. "I don't know."

"Know thy enemy."

"Huh?"

"Go to the football game."

Ria's stomach twisted in knots. "I have to. Remember? I'm a cheerleader." It was Mary Ann Proctor's fault. That, and the fact Ria had turned down a post on the Women's League board, which meant if she missed a meeting, she got volunteered for whatever everyone else didn't want to do. Drat, how could she have forgotten about the football game? It was a community event, and therefore, the league was obliged to participate.

Carly clutched her chest as deep hacking coughs wracked her body again. Ria's chest ached just watching her.

Carly waved her hand. "Go away before you catch my cold."

Ria hated leaving Carly, but she probably needed more rest anyway. After making sure Carly had a hot cup of soup, a glass of 7-Up over ice, and a new box of tissues, Ria left. Carly might be right. She was sure she could point out enough faults that people would start to despise Kristor. She nodded. It might just work.

Kristor looked around the locker room. Benches sat low to the floor making his back and legs ache, so he had chosen to stand. A distinct odor hung thick in the air, as though something had died, and they'd forgotten to bury the carcass. Not that he expected a room that housed warriors to smell sweet. He'd been around men long enough to know their body odor was not always pleasant.

That was something else that bothered him. These men did not look like warriors. Heath maybe, although he had gray running through his hair. His reflexes were sharp, though. When someone had tossed him an oddly-shaped, brown ball, he'd caught it.

And there was the man called Neil. He was younger. Heath said he was a deputy. Kristor understood most of the language and knew that probably meant second in charge.

But the others. He shook his head. They had let their bodies go. How did they expect to win a battle? Unless the ones they would battle were in worse condition.

These men came in different shapes and sizes: tall, skinny, short, fat. One man bent to tie the strings on his shoes and when he rose, his face was red, and he could barely draw in a deep breath. No, Kristor couldn't imagine them winning a battle.

"I want to introduce y'all to Kris. He'll be taking Smiley Wilson's place, since Smiley has that bug going around," Heath said.

"You ever play football?" a short, balding man asked.

"Play? I thought we were here to win a battle?" Kristor turned to Heath.

"Yeah! That's the kind of attitude we want on this team," another man yelled.

Kristor relaxed. Heath hadn't lied. He did not come to play, but to fight. He was a warrior.

"We're the shirtless team this year, guys, so take 'em off," Neil told them.

"Anybody bring sunblock?" a pale man asked.

"I got plenty," another answered.

Maybe they had powers since they could block the sun. The men began to remove their shirts. They must be braver than he'd first thought if they planned to go out on the field without armor. They earned a measure of his respect for their act of courage.

"Y'all ready to win?" someone called out.

"Yes."

"I can't hear you."

"Yes!" echoed through the room.

"Yes!" Kristor jerked his shirt open, buttons flying, material ripping, growling from the energy that burst from him. "Fight, kill, destroy!" He threw his shirt on the floor, raising his fists in the air and shaking them.

The men stilled.

It got deathly quiet.

"Can I put my shirt back on?" a scrawny man squeaked.

"Good Lord, man. I ain't never seen muscles like that. What do you lift?"

"Lift?" Kristor thought for a moment. "Anything I want."

The room exploded into laughter. Heath clapped him on the back. "I would imagine so."

Heath quickly explained the rules of football. Kristor was disappointed to hear they couldn't do anything more than steal a flag. A game of wits and speed. His brothers had often engaged in such sports.

This would at least pass the hours until he could convince Rianna it was time to go home to New Symtaria. The Queen Mother would be proud that he wasn't using force—yet.

Chapter 4

There were already a few spectators sitting in the bleachers when Ria made her way to the sidelines. She noticed several women in the stands were talking on their cell phones: hands waving in the air, eyes twinkling, laughter erupting. She knew the symptoms well. They must have something new to gossip about. That was fine with her as long as she was off the top of their lists.

Then again, they could still be talking about her. Nah, the Miller Bend grapevine moved faster than the speed of sound—meaning they only heard what they wanted to hear. That was life in a small town. On the other hand, people were quick to help when someone needed a hand. She figured you had to take the good with the bad.

She tugged on the hem of her short skirt, feeling ridiculous wearing the blue-and-white cheerleading uniform. One of the women in the Women's League had delivered it to her earlier in the week. As soon as she'd taken the skimpy, midriff-showing top out of the box, her heart sank.

It wasn't that she was a prude. She had a dozen or more thongs and a couple of bikinis in her dresser drawer. For some strange reason wearing the cheerleading outfit made her think about strippers, poles, and men shoving money into the waistband of her skirt.

Her eyes strayed to the field. Some of her tension eased.

She looked a hell of a lot better than the no-shirts team. Neil wasn't bad. She could certainly tell he owned a set of weights and used them.

And for an older guy, Heath looked in pretty good shape. Some of the others should've left their shirts on, though. The next time Ben Dansworth made a smart-assed remark about her seeing an alien, she was going to mention his beer gut. That should shut him up.

Her gaze skidded to a stop when it landed on Kristor. No shirt. Bulging muscles as he stretched and turned. God, he was tanned and delicious.

Oh, baby, stretch a little more to the right.

He did.

Her mouth watered.

Get a grip! He could quite possibly be a serial killer. Just because he'd gotten Fluffy out of a tree, and had helped a little old lady up a small hill, didn't mean he wasn't a murderer. That could be a cover.

But it was difficult for her to believe that when she was staring at hard . . . sweaty . . . sinewy muscles. Her breath caught in her throat. "Now more to the left," she murmured. "That's it. Right there. Yum."

So maybe he wasn't a serial killer. Just crazy. Was it horribly wrong to lust after a guy if he was just a little off kilter?

Kristor suddenly stopped stretching as though he sensed someone watching him. *Pffttt,* as if everyone wasn't. The guy had some seriously sexy moves.

Kristor scanned the area until his gaze stopped on her. He stared, apparently not caring that he was being rude. Yeah, right, why should someone who thought he was an alien care if he was being rude or not?

Turn away from him, she told herself. But it wasn't so easy when he looked at her as if she was an earthly body he wanted to explore and conquer. That wasn't going to happen.

His brain had probably been fried by too many *Star Wars*

movies, and she was not about to play close encounters of the sexy kind with him. She didn't want him pulling her against his strong chest, and she most certainly didn't want to run her hands over all those muscles or ... God, she couldn't stop staring at him! He was like a freakin' drug and she an addict looking for her next fix.

Heath pulled Kristor's attention away, and she could finally take a deep breath. What had just passed between them? A blast of electricity?

No, she'd only reacted to a gorgeous body. The guy was built, she wouldn't deny that.

Built? More like sculpted from fine marble, Shintara broke into her thoughts.

"Shut up!"

"Shut up is right," Mary Ann said as she stopped beside Ria. Her hungry gaze latched on to Kristor like a starving cougar.

This was not the plan. Ria was supposed to make people question Kristor, not drool all over him. Not that any woman wouldn't foam at the mouth. She sort of believed him about the warrior stuff. He had the broad shoulders of a man who would take command during a battle. But she refused to get the hots for a lunatic.

"I heard your mother rented your old room out to him." She delicately dabbed the corners of her mouth. "Lucky you."

Didn't anyone get anything around here? She dragged her eyes away from Kristor. "The man is a stranger, Mary Ann. We know nothing about him. He could be an escapee from a mental institution for all we know."

She was such a slut. When they were in high school, Mary Ann would go into heat every time a jock passed by. Nothing had changed.

Mary Ann turned, giving Ria the once-over. "I heard you saw an alien. They have great doctors in Dallas. One of them might be able to help you."

"I didn't see an alien."

"That's not what my sister told me. She heard from Tilly that you were all hysterical when you called the sheriff's office saying you'd seen a naked alien with hawk wings in the woods behind your house." Her gaze returned to Kristor as he did the warm-up exercises with the other men. "I wouldn't mind seeing *him* naked." Mary Ann raised her pom-poms and shook them.

Seeing Kristor that day in the woods was a vision Ria wouldn't soon forget. She shook her head, then looked at Mary Ann. "You wouldn't mind seeing any man naked."

The other woman sighed. "True."

Ria arched an eyebrow. "I wouldn't let your husband hear you say that."

"Oh, honey, Bobby Ray doesn't care where I get my appetite as long as I come home to eat."

She was probably right. Bobby Ray adored Mary Ann. She had him twisted around her little finger.

"Besides, I keep my man happy. Where do you think I came up with the design for these uniforms?" She gave a sly wink.

Eww.

"You comin' to the Women's League meeting Tuesday night?" Mary Ann asked. "We need to vote how we're going to raise money for the new x-ray machine at the hospital."

"Why not give blow jobs?" Ria smiled sweetly.

Mary Ann stooped to re-tie her tennis shoe. Her expression was thoughtful when she straightened. "That's an idea. You think Bobby Ray would mind?"

"I doubt it. He hasn't seemed to mind too much in the past."

"Ohh, good one." She chuckled. "You know, I've always liked you, even though we all know you're crazy." Her arm suddenly went up and she waved. "There's Becky, and Laura."

Bitch. Ria turned and smiled at the other two ladies. The last two arrived as the guys took the field.

"Wow, look at the crowd," Laura said.

What had started out as a few loyal, bored relatives in the bleachers had grown to overwhelming proportions. Ria had a feeling Kristor was the reason for the rise in popularity of the game today.

The next hour was filled with cheers and jeers. For an alien, Kristor had picked up the game pretty fast. Let him explain that.

Hmm, it might not be as easy as she'd hoped to convince people he was one crayon short of having a full box. The way everyone clapped him on the back, he apparently was making friends.

Her plan had backfired. No one wanted to hear that he might be a serial killer or even crazy. They were more interested in watching his moves on the field. Not fair. Kristor looked like he belonged more than she did.

"I do like the way they huddle," Mary Ann said.

Kristor's butt faced them. So what if he had a hot butt? It didn't make him any less mental.

Mary Ann's eyes widened. "Surely they aren't going to try for a field goal. It's insane. That has to be at least sixty-five yards. The record is what? Sixty-three?" She chunked her pom-poms on the ground in front of her and slapped her hands on her hips.

Mary Ann always amazed Ria. As slutty as she acted, the woman still knew her football. Which was probably because she *had* slept with every football player in high school.

"He is," Mary Ann said with disgust.

Now maybe Ria could convince people that Kristor was crazy. If they were pissed at him because he'd lost the game for the team, it wouldn't be that long of a stretch for them to believe the guy should be locked away. Texans took their football seriously.

Heath knelt, ready to catch the ball. Kristor walked back, knelt down, looked at the ball, and then the goalpost. Ria smiled. Victory was in the air, and it would soon be hers.

The ball was snapped. Heath caught it, and quickly placed it. Kristor was already running forward. When he was in back of the ball, he brought his right foot back and kicked. She watched the ball. It went higher and higher.

That wasn't possible. Was it?

She glanced at Kristor. He'd knelt on one knee, his arms stretched toward the ball as if he were willing it to cross between the goalposts. Her eyes narrowed. There was something really strange going on. She looked at the football again just as it sailed between the two posts.

The crowd erupted with screams of amazement flowing down the bleachers and onto the field.

Kristor stood, chest puffed out, and gave a battle cry. The other men surrounded him, clapping him on the back, and attempting to copy his victory cry but sounding more like a bunch of mice escaped from the lab.

Kristor met her gaze again and grinned.

Now she was pissed.

She would have to think of something else before her parents' party tonight. Something that would blackball Kristor. He was the crazy one, yet the town acted as if she was the mental case. Life was so not fair!

Chapter 5

Kristor eased his arm into the shirt, wincing as he dressed for Maggie and Ron's party. One of the men had barreled into him, hitting Kristor just where it would hurt. If one of his brothers saw him right now, they would laugh themselves silly. The man had been scrawny, his bones poking out, which is probably what caught him in the ribs.

You're out of shape, Labrinon commented.

Kristor glared at his reflection, and for a moment saw the eyes of a hawk staring back at him. *I have no war to fight. It isn't my fault.* It was actually. The borders of New Symtaria were secure. No one dared attack them.

Just don't let your body grow weak. It would be embarrassing.

"Silence," he growled.

You grow irritable. Maybe because you haven't had sex in a while.

I mated only days before I left.

Then you had to find Rianna. That has taken many weeks. Maybe if you mate with her, she will go with you to New Symtaria.

Silence! His guide made him weary.

But Labrinon was correct that Kristor grew irritable. The clothes he wore were uncomfortable. But it was what everyone in town chose to wear. Kristor had shifted into his animal guide, and Labrinon had flown over the town. Through the hawk's eyes, Kristor had seen how people acted, and what they wore.

It was easy to insert the information into his database when he returned to his craft, then punch in what he needed, and have everything appear.

Driving had been a little more difficult. Earth crafts weren't the same, very antiquated and cumbersome. He found he preferred the looks of the smaller craft so had searched until he found a picture of what the database called a motorcycle. He'd pushed another button and the motorcycle had appeared in front of him. He'd been right about it. Once he drove the machine, it reminded Kristor of when he flew with Labrinon.

Learning so many new things drained him. He would rather be home, protecting his planet. Sometimes, Kristor did not understand his father's commands.

He flung open the bedroom door and stalked down the hall. Labrinon could also be quite infuriating at times. He turned the corner, and ran into a soft feminine form. There was an *oomph* from her as she landed against his chest. He grabbed her arms to steady her, and looked down into the warm brown eyes of Rianna.

"Rianna, I'm sorry." But he didn't let go. Her skin was as soft as a rabbit's fur.

She quickly backed away, putting a few inches between them. "You're still here."

He grinned, liking the way her mouth turned down. She had fire burning inside her. Having spirit was always a good thing. Warriors had strong spirits; they would expect no less from the women they bedded.

And he was pleased with what she wore. The material of her black top hugged her body in a nice way, and dipped low enough in the front that he could see the roundness of her breasts. The snug-fitting pants, that he discovered were called jeans, rode her hips and fit close to her body. She stirred his blood like no other before her. Maybe she did have powers.

"Did you expect that I wouldn't be here?" he asked.

"No, but I did hope."

He held back his smile. Angry looked good on her. It made her eyes dance with a fire. "Are you upset with me?"

"Now, why should I be upset? The townspeople think you're the best thing since sliced bread just because you won a stupid football game for them. On the other hand, you tell me you're an alien. I tell the sheriff, and everyone thinks I'm the one who's crazy. I don't know. Should I be pissed? And why is it that I'm the only one you tell?"

"We need to protect who we are. It's not wise to let others know where we actually come from."

She nodded. "Oh, yeah, I forgot. We're from New Symtaria. Another planet in another galaxy."

"Yes. Are you ready to leave?" He would like to have her all to himself on his spacecraft. He could almost feel her soft body pressed against his.

She poked her finger against his chest. "I will never be ready to leave with you."

Passion filled her eyes. He grabbed her hand and pulled her close, his lips descending to hers. She tasted sweet and sensuous. Her body molded to his when she fell against him. She didn't resist his touch. A good sign.

Labrinon had been right. He would convince her to leave with him by kissing her into submission. But as she pressed closer, her sweet scent wrapped around his senses, filling him with a need to do more than kiss.

"Ria!" a man's voice loudly intruded.

Rianna jerked away from him, and he was left with empty arms.

"What?" She smoothed a trembling hand through her hair, her eyes wide as she turned to the man. Then she visibly relaxed. "Oh, Donald, it's just you."

Kristor glared. It was the same man from the park. The one who had possessively put his arm across Rianna's shoulders. He didn't like him. And now, more so. A few seconds were all he would have needed to convince Rianna to leave with him.

"I really doubt your mother would approve of you making out in her hallway."

This Donald person stood tall, but he was thin, and didn't look as though he had any muscles. His clothes were crisp and he wore a jacket, even though the temperature was warm. He didn't sweat, either, although he wore this extra layer of clothes. That was an oddity in itself. Kristor doubted the man knew the meaning of battle.

It was time for the other man to leave. "Go!" he commanded Donald.

The man took a step back. Kristor reached for Rianna, but she moved away, her cheeks bright red. "I was not making out. He kissed me." She glared at Kristor as if it was all his fault.

"It didn't look like you were fighting him off," Donald said, but took another step back as he warily eyed Kristor, his hands curling into fists at his sides.

"Did you want something?" Rianna asked.

"Your mother was looking for you. Shall I tell her you were kissing the . . . What did you call him? Oh, yes, the certifiably crazy man that you hoped Heath would lock up in the state hospital."

"Go suck an egg, Donald." She turned on her heel, marching down the hall away from both of them.

"She's out of your league," Donald told him, his gaze disdainfully sweeping over Kristor. "She likes the intellectual type, rather than . . . overblown muscles."

"Like you said, she wasn't fighting to get away. Maybe she just likes more passion in her men." Kristor walked past the other man, forcing Donald to press against the wall or get flattened.

This Donald was nothing. A mere annoyance, like a pesky insect flying around his face. If Donald bothered him again, he would crush him, but not until then. Kristor didn't want to draw attention to himself.

At least now, he had found a way to get Rianna to go with him to New Symtaria.

I told you seducing her was the way to get her to leave.

So you did.

Ria hadn't felt a thing when Kristor kissed her. Not a thing. He'd only taken her by surprise.

Boring. How many times are you going to repeat that mantra?

As many times as it took to make herself believe it. She grabbed a longneck out of the large tub of ice, twisted off the cap, and took a good long drink. The cold liquid slid down her throat. She could already feel herself begin to relax.

"Hey, Ria, heard you saw an alien flying around in the woods," Jamie Wilks said, then eyed the beer she was holding. "Maybe you ought to lay off the booze."

She bit her tongue before telling Jamie he could go screw himself. In a very calm—okay, irritated but calm—voice, she said, "I didn't see an alien flying around in the woods." She started to tell him it had been a naked guy claiming to be an alien, but decided against saying anything more. What good would it do? No one believed her. She was really close to throwing a pity party when Kristor stepped into the backyard.

All eyes turned toward him. Why not? He wore snug-fitting jeans and a maroon, button-down shirt. And boots. If he was a friggin' alien, where the hell did he get the boots?

"The hero," Jamie called out, and everyone began to clap.

"Hero, my ass," she muttered and took another long drink. "It was a stupid football game."

Jamie took a step back, slapping his hand over his heart.

"Wash your mouth out with soap, girl. You're talking about football here."

She snorted. "Yeah, right. A bunch of men, most of them retired, trying to run a ball to the other end of a field. I don't know about you, but it sounds kind of silly to me."

His eyebrows drew together. "You're acting really strange. You know, they have doctors in Dallas who could probably help you."

She opened her mouth to tell him what she thought about everyone and their Dallas doctors, but a strong arm slipped around her waist and pulled her close. Her face jerked up. How the hell had he moved across the yard without her seeing him?

Jamie nodded. "Ah, so that's the way the wind blows."

She tried to move away from Kristor, but his hand on her waist effectively kept her at his side. She glared at him.

"Y'all don't do nothin' I wouldn't do." Jamie grinned before he sauntered away.

Great, now what kind of gossip would be spread about her? She looked up again at Kristor. "Would you please remove your hand from my waist?"

He surprised her by doing as she requested. She only moved a few steps away from him, though. There was something about his body heat that soothed her. Oh, no, what did that mean? Suddenly nervous, she downed the rest of her beer, and went over to the tub and got another one, tossing her empty into the trash.

Kristor watched her. There was something in the way he watched her, though. It was as though he physically touched her: caressing her cheek, sliding down her neck, cupping her breasts, moving sensuously downward. Her stomach muscles tightened. A slow burn began to build inside her.

She brought the bottle to her lips and took a drink of the beer, grateful it had slivers of ice. It was all she could do to keep from running it over her face. When she met his gaze, there was a look in his eyes that said he knew the effect he had on her. Not that she cared.

And she was not returning to where he stood because she liked him or anything. No, she wanted answers. She gathered her courage, raised her chin, and joined him under the oak tree.

"How did you kick the football that far?" she asked.

He casually leaned against the tree. "I kicked, then I willed it to go between the poles. Isn't that what I was supposed to do—make it go between them? It seemed to please everyone."

"What do you mean, you willed it across?" The guy was getting stranger by the minute.

"I concentrated on the ball, and where I wanted it to go."

"Like telekinesis? When someone moves an object with their mind."

"Only small objects for short distances on New Symtaria. Rogar said the atmosphere is slightly different here and makes Symtarian men's powers stronger. Unusual. It's women who have stronger powers where I come from."

She chugged another drink. It didn't matter if he did move things with his mind, or that he was an alien, or that women had powers or not. No one would believe her. They only believed what they wanted.

"Leave with me and you may also find you have powers." He frowned. "Although Callie doesn't have any."

"Who's Callie?" She took another drink. She was starting to feel warm and fuzzy on the inside. And numb. She liked feeling numb.

"She's another impure. My brother brought her back after he finally convinced her she was part Symtarian."

Ria laughed. "Now I'm impure. Well, I never said I was a virgin, but that's something you won't be finding out for yourself."

"An impure is the offspring of Symtarians and another species. We are trying to bring them home to protect them."

"And I'm part Symtarian?"

He nodded.

She grinned. "And I need protecting?" If this was some kind of new pick up line, it was way over the top, and it was so not working.

"There are rogue Symtarians who would like to see all the impures dead."

"And that's what happened to my so-called father?"

"I don't think you believe any of this."

"You would be correct in your azz . . . azzumpshun. . . ." Her tongue did not want to cooperate. "You're right about that." She finished off the beer.

"Does your animal guide not talk to you? Explain things?"

"Ruffles doesn't do anything 'cept lay under the bed and sleep. Lazy cat."

"The animal guide is inside you. She is a part of you. You would hear her voice."

Told you so, Shintara said.

The world around Ria began to spin out of control. How did he know about the voice inside her head?

Chapter 6

"Someone told you about the . . . the voice that talks to me. Admit it. That's how you found out," Ria said, then quickly made sure there was no one within hearing distance.

Mary Ann was the only one remotely interested in them. At the moment, she was casting cat-in-heat looks toward Kristor, but she hadn't made a move yet. She couldn't possibly hear what they were talking about. And if she could, she certainly wouldn't be flirting with him. Maybe Ria should suggest Kristor take *her* to his planet.

"No one had to tell me," Kristor said, capturing her attention. "Every Symtarian has an animal guide."

No, he was lying. Of course he was lying. He had to be lying. Anything else was totally ridiculous. "There are no such things as aliens or animal guides or a planet called New Symtaria."

He's not lying. This is who you are. I've been trying to convince you all these years that I'm real. Except you wouldn't freakin' listen! And it's been driving me crazy! Now we both have answers.

"Shut up." Great, she'd spoken out loud. Kristor didn't seem to think anything out of the ordinary had happened.

Too much beer. That was it. It never took more than one-and-a-half longnecks to make her tipsy, and she'd downed two as if the Budweiser plants were filing for bankruptcy tomorrow.

"You are part Symtarian," Kristor reinforced.

"No, I'm not, because it would make me as crazy as you." She stomped to the tub and grabbed another beer. Maybe sinking into oblivion was what she needed. If she thought too much about what Kristor was saying, then she might start to believe him.

Set me free, Shintara cried out.

Go away! Ria chugged the beer, trying to drown out Shintara's voice.

I'm not schizophrenic, Ria silently screamed to herself. Then more quietly, she added *I'm not.*

But what if she was? Maybe there was a society of schizophrenics, and they searched each other out. There could be whole towns. Her forehead puckered. And you'd only need a few people to create one. One person could literally take on more than one role.

That is so not funny, Shintara said.

Ria didn't think so, either.

A couple of guys pulled out guitars, one a fiddle. Her dad set up the microphone. Good, she needed distraction.

Her parents lived on five acres on the outskirts of Miller Bend, and since the neighbors were at the party, no one worried about noise. Right now noise sounded good. Anything to drown out her thoughts.

She glanced around. The crowd of people had grown to over sixty and she suspected it would continue to grow as the night wore on. There was beer, hotdogs and chips, and boot-stompin' music. Half the town would probably end up in their backyard, bringing a couple of six packs, or something to eat, as their invitation.

Ria wanted to lose herself in the music, in the crowd, and keep her distance from Kristor. Mary Ann had finally made her way over to him. Her long dark hair swinging free, the strands like hissing snakes, her eyes laughing up at him as her claws casually rested on his arm. Her hubby was busy talking to some of the men, quite impervious to her slutty behavior. Not that Ria cared.

"Hey, pretty lady, dance with me," Jessie said as he sidled up next to her.

"That's the best offer I've had all day." Ria laughed, drained her beer, then tossed it toward the trash can, and almost made it, before wrapping her arms around his neck. His hold on her waist was loose and comfortable. She'd known Jessie most of her life, since his family had moved here from Henrietta, Texas. He was what people called "a good old boy." She just hadn't figured out what he was good for. That struck her as funny, so she laughed.

"I think someone has had too much to drink," Jessie said.

She shook her head. "Not nearly enough." To prove her point, she grabbed another beer as they danced past the tub.

The song ended, and Donald slipped in where Jessie had once been. She blinked twice as her vision changed from slicked back hair and dime-store aftershave to a very polished GQ guy, with only a light scent of the finest men's cologne.

"You're drunk," Donald said, smiling wide and showing his pearly whites, except his words were as sharp as barbed wire. He moved her around the yard in some semblance of a two-step. His movements were stiff and jerky. The man had absolutely no rhythm.

"Drunk? Not quite, but I'm getting there." Honey dripped from the smile she cast in his direction.

"You might think you're funny, but you're only making a spectacle of yourself. People talk about you enough as it is. You would think you'd at least attempt a lower profile."

She took another drink of beer, then belched like a sailor.

He curled his lip.

"I don't give a damn if they talk about me," she said.

"Can I cut in?" Neil asked.

Donald opened his mouth.

"Yes," she quickly spoke up, and moved smoothly into Neil's arms, well, until she tripped over something in the yard. But Neil caught her before she fell. That made her laugh, too.

Donald turned on his heel and was soon lost in the crowd. Good riddance. He'd always put a damper on her activities.

"Are you having fun?" Neil asked.

"The best ever."

"Uh . . . how's Carly?"

Even as looped as she was, she saw the spark of interest. "Why, Neil Jackson, are you sweet on my best friend?"

He blushed. "I just heard she was sick. Thought I'd ask about her."

"She's really sick."

His face fell. "So, she's not coming tonight?"

She shook her head and almost toppled over. He righted her. "Maybe no more beer," she mumbled.

"Carly?" he prodded.

Her eyebrows drew together. "How long have you liked her?" And why had Ria never noticed?

He gripped her a little tighter as they swayed to the music. "Since our freshman year. But she's never looked twice at me. The guys she usually goes out with are jerks. Why does she do that?"

"Maybe you should let her know how you feel. Then she might stop dating losers."

"Could you sort of test the waters?"

What was she now? A matchmaker. That is, besides being an alien. Correction: part alien. She frowned. "Does my skin tone look a little green to you?"

He held her at arm's length. "You're not about to toss your cookies, are you?"

"No."

"Good." He drew her back a little. "And you don't look green, either."

"Do I have anything poking out the top of my head?"

He examined the top of her head. "Like what?"

"Antennae."

"Why? Are you thinking about become a human transmitter?"

"No." She hadn't really thought she was part alien.

He suddenly smiled. "I bought some blue body paint a number of Halloweens ago. I thought I might look cool if I dressed like one of those blue guys that perform out in Las Vegas. Didn't think the junk was ever going to fade away. Went to the hospital when that old bull threw me and they wanted to put me on oxygen."

She chuckled.

"It wasn't that funny at the time." He blushed, then grinned. "I guess it is now, though."

She'd always liked Neil, in a sisterly sort of way. "Yeah, sure, I'll test the waters with Carly, but all you have to do is a little sweet talkin'. That's what a girl likes."

"Yeah, well, Carly isn't like other girls. She's special."

Neil dropped his arms from around her when the music ended, but before she could head for a place to sit, Kristor was standing in front of her.

"I've been watching how you move with each other," he said as Neil took off toward the food table. "The steps seem simple enough." Kristor pulled her into his arms.

There was something different about the way he held her from the way her last partners had held her. In his arms, she felt as though she danced on air. And if wind had a smell, it would be Kristor. The wind, the woods, the scent of a man.

"Why don't you go back to where you came from?" she asked, but her words came out on a sigh and didn't hold a lot of conviction.

"I have to protect you."

"From the rogue Symtarians? Wooo, I'm scared."

"You shouldn't be. I won't let harm come to you."

"I feel so much better now." She looked deep into his fathomless green eyes, but couldn't see even a little spark of insanity. Which meant zilch. "If you're an alien, why do you look like people from Earth? And where'd you get the clothes you're wearing?" Let him answer those questions.

"My database will create anything I need."

"How convenient."

"And I look like everyone else because our species is similar to yours."

"Anyone could have told you I've talked to a voice in my head, so that doesn't prove anything."

"I have a voice inside my head as well."

She missed a step, and he caught her closer to him. She rested her head against his chest, and let his warmth wrap around her. What the hell was she thinking? The guy was crazy. He had just admitted to hearing a voice.

Oh, wait, she had, too.

The song ended. She stepped away. Kristor looked as if he waited for her to do something.

"I'm hungry." She made a quick about-face and hurried to the table.

It practically bowed in the middle with the amount of food that had been piled on top of it. Texans rarely went hungry. She wasn't at the moment, but she needed to do something. Eating seemed like a good solution.

She grabbed a paper plate and a hot dog, chips, and then started to reach for a beer, but changed her mind and grabbed a Coke instead. As she passed the dessert end, she grabbed a thick slice of chocolate cake with fudge icing.

There were chairs and tables set up farther back in the yard. And if someone couldn't find a table or a chair, there were blankets spread out on the ground. Nothing formal here, just a good-old-boy backyard party.

With an alien or two.

She was so losing it.

There was a vacant table, so she grabbed it, only getting a little icing on her hotdog, which she was quite proud of since she was still feeling a buzz. A few seconds later, Kristor set his plate and drink down beside her.

"Don't you have anything better to do than stalk me?" she asked right before she licked the icing off her hotdog. Why did food always taste better when you were tipsy?

"I'm not stalking you. I'm only here to offer my protection."

"And try to talk me into going back to your planet with you."

He shrugged. "That, too."

She ate a chip, then swallowed it down with a drink of her Coke. "You don't think that sounds a little squirrely?"

"Squirrely?"

"You know, crazy."

"I'm sorry, but it's the truth."

She leaned back in her chair and really looked at him. "Okay, prove to me you're an alien. Where are your antennae?"

"Do people still believe all aliens are green and have antennae?"

Why did she suddenly feel as though she'd stereotyped a whole race of . . . of people? That was ridiculous. "Tell me why I should believe you."

He fingered a chip, then looked at her, his expression serious. "Because it's who you are. A part of yourself that you have denied far too long." He sat straighter. "We are a race capable of shapeshifting. Our animal guides are separate, yet we are one."

"Shapeshifting?" Wow, for just a second, she had sort of, only sort of, started to believe him. That should warn her away from any more alcohol for the rest of her life. His stories were getting more ridiculous by the minute. "You mean, you can take on an animal form?"

"As can you. My animal guide is the hawk."

"The one in the woods?"

"Correct."

She leaned closer.

He did the same.

"Bullshit," she whispered.

"Bullshit?"

"It means I don't believe you."

His eyes sparked with anger. She quickly moved back. Calling the guy a liar probably wasn't a good idea. The guy was mental, after all.

"You would deny your animal guide the right to be free?"

Why did she suddenly feel guilty? Why was she even having this conversation? She picked up her hotdog and took a humongous bite. Better that her mouth was full so she wouldn't tell Kristor just how crazy she thought he was. If she angered him too much, there was no telling what he would do.

"Has your guide never tried to get you to shift?"

"Into what?" she asked around the half of a hotdog that she was still trying to chew.

"You tell me."

A hawk, remember? Shintara's voice echoed through her mind.

"A hawk?" she said before she thought better about feeding Kristor's fantasy that he was a shapeshifting alien.

"A hawk." He nodded. "That is why I'm drawn to you."

"You're drawn to me?"

"As you are to me."

Before she got into a repetition of "am not, are, too", she said, "I was only talking out loud. Besides, I'm afraid of flying, so even if I could change into a hawk, I wouldn't."

"Ahh, so that has been the problem."

"There's no ahh, about it. I still think you're crazy."

"Concentrate on an animal. Your guide will help you to shift. It doesn't have to be anything that flies in the beginning."

"Yeah, right."

"Are you afraid to find out for sure?"

She came to her feet. "I'm not scared of anything." With a toss of her ponytail, she took her plate and carried it to the trash can. And she certainly wasn't going to concentrate on an animal. The idea was ridiculous.

Are you so sure about that? Shintara spoke up.

"Yes, I'm absolutely positive. I'm not part alien."

"Maybe you should go easy on the beer," her father said as he came up beside her.

She opened her mouth to tell him her buzz was already wearing off, but changed her mind. "You're right, Dad." She held up the Coke she hadn't quite finished. "Already switched over."

"Good girl."

Not much later, she kissed her mom good night, and got Neil to drive her home. Someone would drop her car off tomorrow. No biggie.

But once she was back at her house, she couldn't help wondering if some of what Kristor had told her just might be true. Did aliens actually exist? She didn't know why they couldn't.

Maybe that's what scared her the most.

Chapter 7

"**M**s. Miller is bringing Sukie in this morning," Jeanie said, hanging up the phone.

"Sukie?" Ria studied Jeanie to see if maybe she'd gotten her holidays confused and thought this was April Fool's Day.

Jeanie was a cute little redhead who'd been working for Ria a couple of years, and right now, she wore a serious expression. No, she didn't mix up the holidays. Teasing? Her lips didn't twitch, not even once.

She was telling the truth.

"You're not lying." Ria's bones dissolved into mush and she sank into the nearest chair.

Sukie was what everyone in town referred to as the "demon dog, psycho mutt"—a ten-pound fur ball of terror. She was a Pekinese with a bad temper, a pedigree longer than the distance from Ria's shop to the sun, and a wealthy owner who spoiled her unmercifully.

Ria would refuse to pamper Sukie except Ms. Miller's great, great, grandfather-in-law had established the town. He'd also started the first bank. The same bank that Ms. Miller's husband now ran. The same bank that held the mortgage on Ria's Pet Purr-Fect Grooming Salon.

Jeanie shook her head. "Sorry to be the bearer of bad news. She wants the works."

A hard shiver ran the length of Ria's body. "Oh, God."

"She'll be here in twenty minutes."

Ria sniffed. "But Sukie was just in here last week."

"They're going to the coast. She wants her to look pretty."

"Do you think it's too much to hope that she would fall into the ocean and get eaten by a shark?"

"Ms. Miller or Sukie?"

She waved her hand. "Either one. Both."

Jeanie was thoughtful. "Nah, I think I'd be more worried for the shark." She shuffled some papers around on her desk. "Uh, I've been meaning to ask if you'd mind if I took the rest of the day off."

Ria tilted her head and looked at Jeanie. "You're afraid of all the blood, admit it."

"Yeah, but well . . ." She blushed.

Ria sat straighter. "What?"

"Amy, over at the realty office, might have a house Lenny and I can afford. We're planning on a December wedding, nothing fancy, but we want to start marriage off right with our own place."

Ria reached across the desk and squeezed her hand. "I'm so happy for you. Why didn't you say something sooner?"

Jeanie laughed. "I am. I mean, I just did." She rested her arms on her desk. Her eyes sparkled like a Fourth of July firework display. "Have you ever been in love?"

Kristor's face immediately came to mind. He was the last man that she'd been around. That was the only reason she'd even thought of him. No, the guy was a nut, and since her mother had seen them talking and dancing at the party, she thought it was now okay to let him rent the room. Her mother had brushed away all Ria's protests.

Ria had never been so glad for Monday. She'd wanted to lose herself in work. Well, until she'd learned Sukie was on her way in. That was life.

"If you're going to look at that house, you'd better get over to Amy's office before she sells it to someone else."

Jeanie hesitated. "I hate to leave you alone with Sukie."

Ria planted her hands on her hips. "I refuse to let that snarling mass of shedding fur get the best of me this time."

"Be careful." Jeanie grabbed her purse and left.

"I am so not up for this." She hurried to the back to get ready, mentally checking off the things she would need. Heavy-duty thick gloves, towels . . . Valium. The last was for her, not the dog. So maybe she didn't have any, but it was a nice thought.

The bell over her door tinkled. She sagged against the deep tub where she bathed the animals.

"Oh, Ria!" Ms. Miller could've been an opera singer the way she always called as if she were onstage performing.

"Courage, you can do this. It's just a dog." Ria pasted a smile on her face as she pushed past the curtains that led to the front part of her shop, then came to an abrupt stop.

An apparition of Ms. Miller stood beside Jeanie's desk. At least, she thought it was Ms. Miller. She wore a wide-brimmed, red hat and a bright red dress with black polka dots, except she had no neck. The hat sort of floated on top of the dress and made her look headless.

"Oh, there you are dear." Ms. Miller raised her head and her face appeared. "I imagine Jeanie told you I would drop by with little Sukie."

Ria cleared her throat. "Ms. Miller, so nice to see you again so soon, and Sukie, of course."

"Say hello to Ria, Sukie." She jiggled her leash.

Sukie growled.

"No, no, Momma's little girl must be on her best behavior if she's going bye-bye this weekend."

Sukie didn't look as if she really cared. She was also minus the pink bows Ria had clipped on her ears last week. Ria figured they hadn't lasted the whole day. She was, however, wearing her pink neckerchief.

The dog was cute. Adorable, in fact. She just had a lousy disposition. Ria had tried to get the pooch into training early, but Ms. Miller didn't want Sukie upset. So, each time she brought the crabby canine in, there was a tug-of-war on who would win. Mostly, Ria thought Sukie came out ahead.

"Take good care of my baby," Ms. Miller said before handing Ria the leash.

Sukie snapped at Ria's feet, but Ria was ready and jumped out of the way. She smiled at the dog. First round—me. She sighed deeply. But there would be many more to come before she finished with little Sukie.

"I'll take good care of her, Ms. Miller."

"I know you will, dear. And I'll stop by after I finish shopping."

"Take your time."

Ms. Miller left. Ria looked at Sukie. "You're going to be good this time, right?"

Sukie curled her lip back and gave Ria the evil eye—and she did it very well.

Why did Ria get into this line of work, anyway? Oh, yeah, she'd mistakenly thought she had a way with animals. Had that been dumb or what?

She slipped on the gloves and picked up Sukie. The mangy mutt growled as Ria put her in the tub of water. The dog latched on to one of the gloved fingers, but Ria had purposefully left her finger out of that one. She'd learned. Sukie seemed satisfied to attack it, rather than her.

"Your mommy spoils you way too much," she told the dog.

The dog loved the water, getting soaped down, and washed. If a dog could have a rapt look, this one did. Sukie let go of the glove and stretched forward so Ria could reach that one particular spot.

"That's a good Sukie," she spoke softly.

Grrr.

"Sorry. Forgot." Sukie didn't like anyone talking to her when she was getting her bath.

The bell on her shop door jingled. Her next appointment wasn't due yet, but she did take walk-ins. Or maybe Jeanie had forgotten something.

"I'm in the back," she called out, squirting more soap on Sukie.

Sukie gave her the evil eye again.

"I'm running a business and I do have other customers besides you."

She looked toward the curtains as Kristor walked inside the grooming area. Great. He was the last person she wanted to see. But she couldn't stop the flutter of excitement that rippled through her.

"You're still in town," she said.

"Just until I can convince you to leave with me."

They were back on that. Then she remembered they were the only two people in the store. He could murder her and . . . She studied him. No, if he'd been going to kill her, he'd had his chance, and hadn't taken it.

He was still a nut.

Sukie suddenly latched on to a finger of the glove that actually contained a finger. Ria jumped.

"Sukie!" The pooch hadn't hurt, only startled her. The gloves were too thick for the dog to cause much damage.

"Are you okay?" Kristor stepped closer.

Sukie growled.

"Shhh!" He held up a hand. Sukie hunkered down and looked away.

Sukie backing off? That was a first. "How did you do that? Are you a dog whisperer or something? I mean, Sukie can be very aggressive."

"Once you connect with your guide, you'll be more in touch with other animals." He stepped up and began to rinse the soap from Sukie.

Ria held her breath, waiting for Sukie to take a chunk out of his hand. But after only a few seconds, she relaxed. This wasn't fair. First, he wins over the townspeople, and now

Demon Dog. He'd cast some sort of magic spell over the mutt.

"If you didn't talk all that crazy stuff about taking off for another planet, it would be nice having you around."

He looked up.

"That didn't come out exactly the way I meant. It's just that you seem nice enough, and you're good with animals. But then you start talking about being a shapeshifting alien and that's just crazy."

He smiled. A smile that reached out and touched. Some men were like that. They could smile at you and all of a sudden, you weren't able to think rationally.

He pulled the plug to drain the dirty water but kept rinsing Sukie. "Can you say truthfully you've never wondered if there were people living on other planets?"

She leaned against the wooden table. "Yeah, I can truthfully say I've never thought about it. I'm not a Trekie fan, either."

"Trekie?"

"*Star Trek*. Oh, that's right, you're from another planet so you wouldn't know about our TV shows."

He grabbed a towel and wrapped it around Sukie before he brought her over to the table and began drying her. Sukie seemed to enjoy the rubdown. Not that *she* would mind too much if Kristor was the one rubbing her down. No, she told herself, you have to stop thinking about him in that vein.

"I can shift," he told her. "It would prove to you I am an alien." He met her eyes.

He had beautiful eyes. So clear. Such an intense green. She mentally shook her head and reached for the blow-dryer and plugged it in. If she asked him to shift into a hawk, it would prove once and for all she was right.

But then, she remembered the last time, and the fact he'd been naked. She wasn't sure she was ready for another naked Kristor, or that she would be able to keep her hands to herself.

And then there was the fact she was probably dealing with a crazy. What if he stripped down and started flapping his arms? It probably wouldn't be good for business if someone walked in the store, especially Ms. Miller.

"I think I'll pass for now." She turned on the blow-dryer and grabbed a brush. Kristor kept Sukie entertained while Ria blow-dried and styled the mutt's hair. She clipped two pink bows above her ears, and refastened a new pink bandana. Sukie jumped up and barked when the bell above the front door jingled.

"There's Momma," Ria said and snapped the leash in place. But as she reached to set the dog down, Sukie snapped at her.

"Shhh!" Kristor commanded.

Sukie immediately downed her head. Kristor picked her up, but before he set her on the floor, Sukie licked his hand. He patted her on the head.

Ria gritted her teeth. So not fair. She was the one who bathed the dog, and all she ever came away with were teeth marks.

"Ria." Ms. Miller's voice singsonged again.

Ria took the leash and walked Sukie out. "Here she is."

"Oh, you look so sweet. Ria, you always do such a wonderful job with her. Some groomers have told me our little angel is a monster in disguise. They're wrong, of course." She reached down and picked Sukie up. Sukie rubbed her head against Ms. Miller. "Ah, baby wants to snuggle."

More than likely, Sukie was trying to dislodge the bows, but Ria didn't tell Ms. Miller that.

Ms. Miller's eyes widened when Kristor stepped from the back. "Oh, I didn't realize you had someone here with you."

"Ms. Miller, this is Kristor. He's renting my old room from Mom and Dad."

"Oh, I've heard of you."

No doubt she had. Nothing much got past Ms. Miller.

"You have an interesting dog," he said.

"I know. Sukie is our little darling." She held the dog a little tighter, but Sukie was having none of it. The dog began to squirm until Ms. Miller had to put her on the floor. Sukie immediately ran to Kristor. Kristor knelt down and began to pet her.

"Oh, she doesn't normally take to strangers."

Ria smiled. "Kristor has a way with animals."

"Apparently." She suddenly smiled. "If Sukie likes you, then I do, too. They say a dog has a natural instinct about humans, and dogs know if they're good or not. I guess you pass the test."

Ria wondered what that said about her.

Ms. Miller walked over and took Sukie's leash. "Come, sweetie. Daddy is waiting for us."

Kristor straightened as Ms. Miller left the shop. "She is a very strange person."

"I think we've finally found something we agree on."

He walked closer. "We would agree on a lot more if you would concentrate on shifting into an animal."

But then that would make Ria as crazy as him.

The bell above the door jingled again and Jeanie walked in.

"I thought you weren't coming back today."

Jeanie dumped her purse behind the desk. "Amy had a family emergency and had to leave. The house wasn't what we were looking for after all. We're going back out on Sunday. Amy promised to have more houses lined up for us to look at." She turned her attention to Kristor, then looked pointedly at Ria.

"This is Kristor. He's renting my old room from my parents."

"Hi," she said, but her gaze said a lot more.

Good grief, Jeanie was engaged. "Kristor was just leaving."

"It was nice to meet you," he told Jeanie, before turning back to Ria. "Think about what I said." He left, but Ria couldn't drag her gaze away from him as she watched him cross the street.

"Wow, you've been holding out." Jeanie picked up a manila folder and began to fan herself.

"Not at all. I'm not the least bit interested in him."

Jeanie stopped fanning. "You're kidding, right? I mean, the guy is seriously sexy."

"There's more to a man than his muscles."

"The way he looks, he doesn't even need a brain. He's great eye candy."

"And you're engaged so you might want to leave the sweets alone."

"You're right. He would definitely send any female into a diabetic coma from sugar overload." She studied Ria. "You, on the other hand, have been on a sugar-free diet way too long."

The bell jingled above the door, saving Ria from further conversation. The rest of the afternoon was busy with clipping hair and bathing animals. Thankfully, very well-behaved animals.

But she couldn't help thinking that Jeanie might be right, that Ria hadn't dated in a while. A very long while. Not since Donald. A sour taste formed in her mouth. That had been a huge mistake.

It also meant she hadn't had sex in a while. Not that the pickings in Miller Bend had been that great. The only guys left in town were the ones she had already dated, at least most of them. She wasn't that great at recycling.

Except now there was Kristor.

Chapter 8

Jeanie left right before Ria finished Bruno the beagle. Bruno sounded like a killer, but he was a sweetheart. As soon as the dog and owner left, Ria turned the sign around to CLOSED and went to the back to put things away. She was beat.

You should've listened to Kristor. He's right, you know. You're part alien. I've suspected for a long time, but you're too hardheaded to listen, Shintara said.

"I'm not crazy." Ria mumbled. "I'm not."

It was a conspiracy. Kristor was sent here to drive her crazy. Who disliked her enough to do that? Ms. Henderson had never forgiven her for the whoopee cushion incident. The teacher could really hold a grudge. What had ever happened to forgive and forget?

Then there was Matt Jenson and his purple dog, although she'd given his dog the free groomings so that should have exonerated her. The dog had even placed in a number of shows, thanks to her. Still, when he brought the dog in, Ria knew he did so grudgingly.

Donald? He had been a bit ticked off when she told him she only wanted to be friends. But then again, he had taken her out to lunch a few days ago, and it had gone fairly well. And he seemed okay with everything. The breakup had been a few months ago, too. Not that she'd seen him with anyone else. That didn't necessarily mean he wasn't dating.

Ria leaned against the wooden table. She needed to go running. That always cleared her head and helped her think straight. She kept something to wear at the shop, just in case the urge hit her.

She quickly changed, but rather than go straight home, she decided to run along the path in the park. Much less chance of running into a naked alien. She snorted. She couldn't believe she'd even come close to believing him.

The streets were quiet. Not unusual. The most excitement they'd ever had was when some of the high school seniors had stolen some signs and burned them in the bonfire after the football game.

She frowned. It had only been one stop sign, and a couple of those wooden barrier things. Boy, they had really gotten in trouble for that one. Come to think about it, she was pretty sure Donald had been the one who'd snitched on them.

She parked in one of the spaces and got out. After a few stretches, she took off at a slow pace. Soon, adrenaline released into her bloodstream, and she picked up speed.

Everything ceased to exist. She could feel the beat of her heart, smell the wind as it rushed past carrying the scent of pine trees in the air.

Except for a scout troop practicing skills, there was no one else around. She circled the small park, running until she felt all pressure leave. Nothing, nothing at all mattered. There was only the sound of her shoes hitting the concrete running trail. All her worries evaporated.

She ran until she could run no more, then stopped at one of the benches, dropping down onto the wooden seat. Sweat glistened on her skin, and she could almost feel the blood coursing through her veins. This was exactly what she'd needed to clear her head of any lingering crazy notions. Of course Kristor wasn't an alien, and the voice inside her head was just that—a voice. She stretched her arms above her head and took a deep breath, feeling her body relax.

Did you ever wonder that the reason you run is because

you're running away from who you are? Shintara killed the mood by popping into Ria's thoughts.

"Go away."

You can prove him wrong.

Ria opened her mouth, but then snapped it closed without saying anything. Shintara was right. She could prove it. He'd said to think of an animal. Okay, she would. What the hell.

But not a hawk. Not that she thought she would really change into anything. She just didn't want to think of one. An uneasy shiver swept over her at the mere thought of flying.

So what kind of animal should she think about?

A frog croaked. She chuckled. It was a sign. Yeah, sure. She closed her eyes. *Here, froggie. Big green frog. I will become a big green frog and terrorize Miller Bend,* Ria thought to herself. Ohh, when she shifted, maybe she would hop over to Donald's restaurant and scare the hell out of him. On second thought, frogs' legs were on his menu.

You have to concentrate. And . . . be . . . serious! Shintara was clearly exasperated.

Okay, okay.

She closed her eyes. Inhaled, then exhaled. She pictured a frog. Frogs weren't so bad. She'd had one as a pet once. Her mother had been thrilled when Ria lost her fascination with them.

Nothing happened, but just to prove her point, she kept her eyes closed and continued to concentrate. She visualized a frog, saw it jumping along the trail. Time passed. She thought about what it would feel like to become a frog. No problems, no worries. Just sit on a lily pad and watch the world go by, and occasionally croak. . . .

Her stomach began to burn. Ugh! No more nachos for lunch. This was awful. She opened her eyes, but she couldn't see. Oh, God, she'd gone blind. Her stomach began to cramp. She moaned, doubling over as the cramping worsened. The deep burning pain sucked at her insides. She fell off the bench, landing with a thud. Fear choked her, stealing her breath. She didn't want to die. She still had too much to do, like getting laid at least one more time. She was pretty sure angels didn't have sex.

"What's happening to me?" she screamed, but no words came from her mouth.

Oh, God, her voice had been stolen, too. She probably shouldn't have mentioned angels and sex in the same breath. Oh, no, what if one of the higher-ups had changed his mind and she was being sent in the other direction? Or maybe she had contracted a horrible disease. Kristor! It was all his fault. . . .

Everything suddenly grew quiet.

Ria immediately stilled.

The burning subsided. She could breathe again.

She cautiously opened her eyes. Blinked. She could see again, but it wasn't the same. Something had changed. She looked around. The scouts were still tying knots. Everything looked normal.

She tried to stand, but nothing seemed to move like it was supposed to. When she started forward, she bumped her butt. Ow! That had hurt.

Maybe the scouts could help her. She opened her mouth to call out, but what she heard was a heavy smoker's belching. She had a feeling it had come from her. Wow, those had been some really spicy nachos.

No, something wasn't right. She raised her arm. It was . . . green and slimy. Oh, yuck.

What the hell had they put in the nachos?

You're a frog. You could've been a hawk soaring through the air, but no, you had to think about a stupid frog, Shintara said with more than a touch of snarkiness.

No, no, this couldn't be happening. *I'm not a frog. I'm not a . . .*

"Hey, look at that frog, guys." One of the scouts pointed

toward her. "It's huge! If I can catch it, I'm going to take it home."

"We can make frog soup!"

Oh, fuck.

Ria quickly glanced around, then made a mad dash for the trees. For a frog, she could move pretty fast. But anyone would with several scouts chasing you, wanting to make frog soup.

Feet pounded on the ground, coming closer. Her heart slammed against her chest. She moved between the trees and wiggled under some green leaves, triing not to breathe.

Feet scurried over the ground. *Please don't step on me! I don't want to get mushed. Calm down,* she told herself. Everything would be all right. She just needed to stay nice and quiet.

"Boys, recess is over. Let's get back to tying knots, then we'll go for pizza," the scout leader spoke.

"Yeah, pizza."

"Lots better than frog soup."

Laughter erupted around her. They were leaving. Thank, God!

"Oh, wow, someone lost their clothes."

Ria peeked out long enough to see her underclothes being twirled around.

"Oh, man, these are sweet," an older scout said.

"Boys, those probably belong to a vagrant. Run and toss them in the trash can."

The kids took off, making a slingshot out of her thong.

Vagrant! Her thong alone had cost fifteen bucks! The lacy bra thirty-five. She opened her mouth to protest, but the only thing that came out was another loud belch. She hunkered down deeper under the leaves.

At least they were gone. Now what was she supposed to do?

Then it hit her: She was part alien. Everything Kristor had

told her was true. But she didn't want to be an alien. And she certainly didn't want to go to his planet. She had a women's meeting tomorrow night. And who would run her business while she was away? Besides, she was not about to get on anything that would leave the ground.

Bzzzzz.

Her tongue shot out and she snatched the fly.

Eww! She'd just eaten a fly. Yuck!

She sniffed. Or attempted to, at least. What if she stayed like this forever? Destined to live her life being chased by boy scouts or worse, ending up in someone's soup pot, or at Donald's restaurant.

"Come on, Trisha, no one will see us here. I just want to hold you in my arms."

Ria looked up. Was that Jeremy Harris? Just her luck. He was really mean. A senior with a chip on his shoulder. His parents had never been able to control him. Wild as a young bull.

She watched until they came into view. It was. He was what?—eighteen, and he was with Trish Simpson. And Trish was only fourteen. Well, almost fifteen, but way too young for the likes of him.

"I don't know, Jeremy. I don't think my mom would like knowing I was in the woods with you."

"I promise I won't hurt you. You said you liked me. And I just want to hold you."

"I do like you."

"Then prove it."

What a sleaze! Ria opened her mouth and croaked as loud as she could. Trisha jumped and screamed. Jeremy laughed.

"It's just an old bullfrog. He can't hurt anything. See." He removed the plastic lid from his drink and dumped ice and soda on Ria.

She sucked in a deep breath.

"Oh, leave it alone," Trisha cried.

Jeremy laughed. "It likes the cold, baby. Frogs can't feel anything."

Like hell I can't feel it!

Trisha pouted. "Are you sure?"

He pulled out a lighter. "Yeah, watch this." He flicked it and the flame shot out.

Ria shied away. Ohmygod, she'd gone from the soup pot to the fire!

"No!" Trisha grabbed his hand. "Jeremy, you're mean! Everyone is right about you. Don't ever call me again or I'll tell my mother!" She turned and stomped through the leaves, heading away from the trees.

Jeremy looked at her . . . the frog, then kicked a clod of dirt toward Ria before hurrying after Trisha.

Could frogs cry?

Ribbit . . . burruppa.

Ria didn't want to be a frog. She wanted to go home. If this was what it meant to be an alien, then she wanted no part of it. If . . .

Wait a second. If she could think herself a frog, then she should be able to think herself human again. She closed her eyes. *I want to go home. I want to . . . wait, that was a movie.* Deep breath. Try again. *I'm Ria, and I want to be me again. I want to run through the park. I want my life back. I want . . .*

A deep burning pain gripped her. She couldn't see, she couldn't breathe. The world swirled around her. She felt as if someone had her on a rack and stretched her limbs out. She was dying.

Who would tell her parents? Oh, God, no funeral or anything. What could they do? Have a froggie funeral? Kristor might realize she'd shifted, but her family wouldn't believe the lifeless frog was their daughter.

The burning pain stopped. She opened her eyes. Blinked. The trees were back. She raised an arm, wiggled her fingers.

Except for the sticky soda, and the dirt stuck to it, she was human again. She sat up. Yes, she was back. She jumped to her feet.

Yes!

She swung her arms out and twirled around before leaning against the tree as she tried to catch her breath. Then it dawned on her.

She was totally naked.

Chapter 9

Kristor spotted Rianna's car, and pulled in beside it. He'd worried about her since this afternoon at the pet store. He could see she was starting to have doubts. What if she decided to try shifting? He remembered his first time had been traumatic, although it had gotten easier with time.

It might have been wise if he'd mentioned the downside to shifting. Like the burning pain that would lessen the more times someone changed to animal form. And he probably should have told her that after one shifted back to human form, they wouldn't have their clothes.

We can only hope that she has attempted to shift and lost her clothes in the process, Labrinon said. *Think how much easier it would be to seduce her. Half the work would already be done.*

I don't wish her first time to be terrifying.

I'm almost positive she's not a virgin.

That's not what I was talking about.

His gaze scanned the park. It wasn't that big so it shouldn't be difficult to find her. He walked down the paved path. If she was running, then they should eventually meet.

"Pssst."

Kristor waved his hand in front of his face, but he didn't see the flying insect.

"Pssst," came louder this time.

He turned. Rianna poked her head around a tree.

"Why are you hiding behind a tree?" he asked.

Her bottom lip quivered. "Because I shifted into a frog, and the scouts chased me, and Jeremy threw his soda on me, then kicked dirt on me . . . and I'm naked! I want to go home."

Oh, no, she was about to start crying. He couldn't handle tears. Nor the sad eyes turned his way, or the pouting lower lip that looked very kissable right now.

He quickly looked away. "Where are your clothes?"

"The boys tossed them in the trash can."

This was exactly what he'd been afraid of. His mother would not be happy that he hadn't explained things well enough. He could only hope she wouldn't find out.

This is your chance! Labrinon screamed at Kristor. *She's begging you to comfort her. Go to her, put your arms around her. Then let everything happen naturally.*

Kristor ignored his guide and looked around. He spotted the can, and walked over to it. When he reached inside and pulled her top out, it was covered in food and drink. He retrieved her car keys from her pants pocket and walked back. "Your clothes are ruined. I can go to your house and get more."

"Don't leave me!"

What was he supposed to do? Even though the sun was going down, he didn't think she would want to run across the park naked, although the idea appealed to him. There was only one thing to do. He tugged his shirt over his head as he walked toward her.

"Stop! What are you doing?"

"I was going to give you my shirt."

"Oh."

He took another step closer.

"Wait."

Now what? "Do you want my shirt or not?"

"Yes, but toss it over."

Women. He tossed it toward her, but it got hung up on a bush. She leaned forward. Kristor caught a flash of tempting pale skin, and realized he was in a pretty good situation. Except she jumped back behind the tree.

"You did that on purpose."

"No, I didn't." But if he'd thought about it, he might have. But he hadn't, so her accusation was false. "It snagged on the bush. I'll untangle it."

"No!"

"Then what would you like me to do?" This was getting tiresome.

Throw her over your shoulder and be done with it, Kristor! You have the advantage.

Labrinon was right, but Kristor would still need to get her to his craft and he didn't think she would go quietly—naked or not.

"Turn around," she ordered.

"Let me at least get it out of the—"

"Turn around." Her teeth were gritted when she spoke and her eyes flashed fire. At least the tears were gone.

"Okay, but do you realize you're not in a position to give orders?" He turned his back to her, heard the bush rustle, and visions of a very naked Rianna filled his head. Sweat beaded his brow. "Do you need some help?"

"No!"

"I wouldn't mind."

"I just bet you wouldn't," she mumbled.

He grinned, admitting she was an interesting creature.

"You can turn around now."

He did. His gaze slowly worked down from her head, past the white T-shirt that didn't hide as much as she probably hoped it did, especially when she tugged on the hem. Then his gaze slipped down her long legs. A rush of heat infused his blood with sexual need.

"You can stop staring."

"Why?"

Her eyebrows drew together. "Because it makes me uncomfortable."

"It does me, too, but I think probably in a different way."

Her gaze dropped, then jerked back up, her cheeks turning a bright shade of red. "I need to get to my car," she ground out.

"And how do you propose we do that? Other than run very fast. Or shift into our animal guides."

"A hawk? I don't think so. Besides, once was enough."

Kristor had a feeling it would take a lot of convincing to make Rianna see her animal guide as an extension of herself, rather than a nuisance. Although sometimes he wondered about Labrinon.

I've saved your hide on more than one occasion, Kristor.

That you have, my friend. My apologies.

Accepted. Now throw her over your shoulder.

Enough! Unless you would be willing to explain to the Queen Mother why Rianna was taken against her will.

Good point.

Maybe that would shut up Labrinon, for a while at least. He looked around, seeing that the park visitors had left. "I think we can make it to the vehicles without being spotted."

She nodded, but then stopped before going out into the open.

"My keys," she said, reaching her hand toward him.

Kristor dropped them into her hand.

"Follow me home. I have questions." She strode past him, expecting him to follow.

A desirable woman, but also very demanding. And he did follow. The temptation was too great.

As soon as she cleared the cover of trees, Rianna began to run. Even though his shirt reached mid-thigh on her, when she ran, the hem kicked up in the back showing a nice portion of her buttocks. Labrinon was right about one thing: Kristor had gone too long without mating. He straddled the motorcycle and followed her car.

Her home was a bright canary yellow, different from the

others. He liked it. She hurried into the house, leaving the door open. He closed it after he went inside. When a door slammed in another room, disappointment filled him. He had a feeling she was putting on more clothes. A shame.

He wandered around her front room. It was comfortable, with pillows and rugs, a sofa, and a chair.

Meow.

He glanced down as a black-and-white cat came into the room. He reached down and scratched behind her ear. She in turn, rubbed against his leg. After a few moments, she curled up on the chair.

The house was small enough that he could hear when Ria turned the shower on. For a moment, he closed his eyes, indulging in a vision of water cascading over her naked body, and how she would take the soap and lather over her breasts, down her stomach.

He drew in a sharp breath. Being around Rianna was not going to be easy if all he could think about was mating with her.

Kristor sat on the sofa, thumbing through a book on the table in front of him to take his mind off what was happening in the other room. The book was a picture record of Rianna's life. He settled against the back of the sofa with it.

By the time she joined him, he'd caught up to her current life. He set the book down and stood. Her hair hung in damp tendrils.

She handed him his shirt. "Thanks for loaning me something to wear."

"Of course." He watched as her expression went from grateful to irritated.

"Do you think you might have mentioned that after I shifted back, I would be naked?"

"There's much I would like to tell you, but in the past you refused to listen. I believe you said I was crazy, a nut case. . . ."

She held up one hand. "Okay, okay, but what did you expect me to do? Jump at the chance to go off with a stranger?"

"Yes." As he pulled his shirt on, he noticed Rianna seemed particularly interested in watching him tug the hem down. As soon as he was covered, her shoulders relaxed. She was attracted to him, no matter how much she would deny it.

"Why are you looking at me like that?" she asked.

"Because you're beautiful and I want to mate with you."

She scooted farther away, tugging her hand free. "Mate with me?"

"I believe you would say 'making love.' "

"I barely know you."

"But you're attracted to me." He didn't understand her hesitation.

"On Earth we don't jump into bed with someone just because they ask us. We like to at least get to know the person first."

No, he would never understand this woman. "But you do know me."

"I know some things about you, but I don't know what kind of person you are."

"I'm a very good one." He moved closer. "Now we will mate."

"No, we won't. We need to know each other longer than a few days."

"Then we will mate?"

"We don't usually discuss a timeline, either. If it happens, it will happen."

That made absolutely no sense. Before he went off to battle, he released tension by mating, and it always helped. If all Earth people waited to mate until the time was right, he doubted any battles were won.

"If I'm part alien, why am I on Earth?" she finally asked. "What? Did my biological parents defect?" Her face lost some of its color and she sat hard on the sofa. "You didn't lie about them, either. They're dead."

He sat beside her and took her hand in his. It was small,

soft, and warm. There might be some advantages to holding hands. For once, it would seem, his sister had told the truth.

"I probably shouldn't be this upset. It's not as though I knew them or anything. It's just that I really did think you were crazy."

He let her remark pass about his being crazy. "I'm sure they would have loved getting to know you."

"You think so?"

He could easily get lost in the deep brown of her eyes. She was a beautiful woman. Most Symtarians were, but Rianna was different. Maybe it was the mixing of the blood.

"Tell me more about how my parents came to be on Earth."

Rianna didn't look as though she would change her mind tonight, so he settled back against the sofa cushions. "Symtaria was dying. There were poisonous gases in the air. Some of our people were relocated to different planets, while others searched for a new home. It took many years, but the old ruler and his advisors found New Symtaria."

"If this was many years ago, why weren't the others brought to their new home?"

He shifted positions. "They were accidentally forgotten in the process of rebuilding what had been lost."

"Forgotten? Forgotten! How the hell do you forget your own people?"

He came to his feet. "You have to understand it was not their intention to forget them. There were many things to do before they could send an expedition to find them. Then the old king joined his ancestors in the afterlife. . . ."

She came to her feet. "And everyone forgot about them again."

He was thoughtful. "You could say that."

She slapped her hands on her hips and glared at him. "I just did."

At least he no longer thought about mating with her. No,

now he was thinking about killing her and being done with his mission. Was it his fault they had been forgotten? He thought not.

She paced the room, then stopped and looked at him. "And you can change into any animal?" she asked.

"Some Symtarians can, not all. Once you connect with your true guide that is the form you take."

"And my guide is Shintara."

"Yes, it would seem so."

"And she's like another person sharing my body?"

"As you will share hers when you shift into your animal guide's form."

"Eww. I don't think I like the idea of sharing my body with someone. And sometimes she's a pain in the ass."

"I understand perfectly," Kristor said.

I do not find that humorous, Labrinon commented.

"If you concentrate, you'll be able to connect fully with your guide."

She hesitated before sitting back down. He noticed she chose the opposite end of the sofa.

"You mean if I concentrate on shifting into a hawk?"

"That is correct."

She shook her head. "Not going to happen. I've had all the shifting I want."

"You would deny your heritage?"

"Excuse me? And who was it that forgot about the ones sent to Earth?"

He chose to ignore her remark. "If you stay here, you'll be in danger."

"From the rogue aliens you were telling me about. The same ones who killed my father."

"Yes."

"And they want to kill me, too, because I'm of mixed blood."

"An impure. Your father was also an impure."

"I don't think I like being an impure. It makes me sound like I have a disease or something."

"To them, you do. They don't want you to return to New Symtaria. They think diluting our blood with a mixed race will make it tainted."

"Will it?"

"No, it will save our race. Our blood has become too pure. Our guides are becoming stronger than our human side. There has to be a blending of each without one becoming too strong."

"Or what?"

"Then the weaker side will die."

"But I'm stronger than my guide. So what will happen if I never shift into a hawk?"

He hesitated, then just came out with it. "Then your guide will cease to exist."

Chapter 10

Whoa now! I am not planning to die, so don't even think you can kill me off, Shintara quickly told Ria.

"The idea does have some merit," Ria told Kristor, but immediately regretted her words.

Shintara was silent long enough for guilt to start seeping into Ria.

You would really . . . let me die?

I'm scared of flying, Ria told her.

There's nothing to it.

How would you know? You've never done it, either.

Have you ever seen an unhappy bird?

Ria was so not ready for any of this. A throbbing started at her temples. She reached up and massaged them, but the ache was still there.

"No, I don't want Shintara to die," Ria finally said to him. "You just need to go back where you came from. Then my life will get back to normal."

"You know I can't do that," Kristor said.

"I don't really care what you can or cannot do. I just want you out of here." She jumped to her feet and strode to the door, flinging it open.

He sauntered toward her, but didn't walk out. His presence filled the room. The throbbing spread to the rest of her body, but changed and became a burning need that she found hard to suppress.

"We're meant to be together. You enjoyed my kiss." He brushed her hair behind her ear, caressing her cheek.

Her body leapt to awareness. Months had passed since she'd felt a need as strong as this one.

"I want to know you intimately," he leaned in and whispered close to her ear.

"Why?" Her words trembled.

"Does there have to be a reason for two people to enjoy each other's bodies?"

"But you're an alien."

"As are you." He lightly massaged her shoulders.

"Only part." She should tell him to stop, but when she opened her mouth, he covered her words with a gentle kiss. She tasted him as his tongue stroked across hers. He wasn't demanding, not forcing her, but giving her the choice to push away or pull closer.

Butterflies fluttered in her stomach, but quickly changed to a deep aching need when he slid his hands over her buttocks and pulled her against him. His need was evident.

What? Was she crazy? She didn't know this man. Hell, she apparently didn't know herself. But who could she talk to? Who, other than him, would believe her when she told them she'd shifted into a friggin' frog? Kristor was her only connection to who she really was.

Maybe she just wanted to relieve the tension building inside her. And maybe that's why she didn't push him away.

She shoved on the door, closing it.

He ended the kiss and moved back, studying her face. Then he reached for the hem of her shirt. It was almost as if she were having an out-of-body experience as she raised her arms above her head. He tugged the top off, then let it fall to the floor.

A shiver ran the length of her body. He didn't move, only

looked. Then he kissed one shoulder, running his fingers under her bra, sliding each strap down her shoulder before reaching behind her and unfastening the clasps. At the last second, she clutched her bra to her breasts, not letting him bare them.

He raised an eyebrow.

What was it about that one look? It told her that she was denying them both. And that wasn't what she wanted to do. She was tired of the lies she'd been telling herself. She wanted him, more than she'd ever wanted a man.

She let go. Her bra fell to the floor. She raised her chin, but knew her bravado wouldn't last long. Why hadn't she suggested wine first? Like a whole bottle. She'd never been this nervous before.

He pulled his T-shirt over his head and dropped it on the floor. The man really did have some serious muscles. She tentatively reached out and glided her hand across his chest. It was firm to her touch. Sinewy muscle, hard ridges. Battle scars. Not perfect, but she wasn't seeking perfection. She leaned forward, her lips pressing against one jagged scar.

Kristor sucked in a breath, but didn't say anything. It was as if he didn't want to break the spell any more than she did.

How far would he let her go? She reached down and unfastened his jeans, then slid the zipper down. She met his gaze. His eyes were glazed with desire. She wondered how difficult it was for him as he held the warrior inside at bay.

She pushed his jeans over his hips, down his thighs. He kicked out of them. She hesitated, took a deep breath, and reached for the waistband of his briefs. The material molded to his erection. He was large. Her gaze fastened on the bulge. She licked her lips.

He stayed her hand before she could tug them down. Disappointment swept over her—until he ran his knuckles across her stomach, stopping when he was at the waistband of her jeans. He tugged the button through the hole, slid the zipper down. Her jeans followed. Slowly, deliberately, as if he would extend the mounting pressure growing inside them both, he knelt in front of her, and tugged them over her hips.

A flood of heat rushed to her face. He was kneeling right in front of her. He'd see her . . . all of her. She quickly brought her hands in front and covered herself. "I'm not sure I'm ready for this."

He came to his feet. "Not ready for what?" He caressed her breast, drawing on the nipple, then lightly pinching it between his thumb and finger.

She moaned, leaning toward him. "This is only sex," she said. "Make sure you understand that this doesn't mean I'll be leaving with you. I like my life here. And—"

He lowered his mouth to hers, effectively stopping all conversation. Not that she minded. His hands left trails of fire as he caressed her back, cupped her buttocks, and brought her against him. His erection nudged her mound. The ache inside her made her weak with desire. Her legs trembled so hard that she could barely hold herself up. She needn't have worried. Kristor scooped her up in his arms.

All those muscles. This was nice. No one had ever carried her to bed before making love. She thought it only happened in the movies. He laid her on the bed, then joined her.

"Only sex," she repeated.

"Yes," he agreed, but she thought he was only partially paying attention. He seemed much more interested in running his hands over her breasts, down her abdomen, and lightly scraping through her curls.

She automatically raised her hips, wanting more. He didn't disappoint as he tugged on the fleshy part of her sex, then slid farther down, dipping one finger inside. She cried out. He immediately backed off. She stopped his hand from moving farther away from her heat.

"No, I like that."

"Most Symtarian women are passionate."

"I'm not . . ." She bit her bottom lip. "I'm not a . . . a . . ."

Hell, she couldn't think straight. Not that she really wanted to think right now. No, she only wanted to feel. And what he was doing felt so damn good.

He nibbled her neck, and swirled his tongue inside her ear. "A pure blood?"

"Yeah, that's it."

"But you are still very passionate."

"I haven't had sex in a while." She closed her eyes, moving her body to the rhythm of his finger.

"You're damp with need."

She bit back a groan, but couldn't stop it when his mouth moved to her breast and sucked on her nipple, rolling it around on his tongue. She wanted to touch him, to explore all those delicious muscles, but she was quickly losing her ability to think, to do anything except lose herself in the exquisite pleasure of what he was doing to her body.

She was vaguely aware when he moved over her. "Protection," she muttered.

"I've taken care of it," he said.

She'd been so lost in the sensations flooding her body, she hadn't noticed.

He entered her. Filled her. Then stroked her.

Slowly, he moved his body. She rose to meet him. Cried out for more. He increased the intensity. In and out. Deeper. A little harder.

She wrapped her legs around him, drawing him in tighter. Clenched her inner muscles. He sucked in a breath.

In and out.

He dragged a pillow over and placed it under her.

Deeper still.

Heat washed over her.

In and out.

Faster.

Plunging deeper.

In and out.

Filling her.

She closed her eyes, lost in the sensations spinning through her. He took her higher and higher until she felt as though she soared across the sky, and there was no fear. The world around her exploded into a million pieces of light.

She grabbed his shoulders. Her body quivered. She cried out, gasping for air.

He tightened, muscles straining as he came, growling from the force of his orgasm. Then he was falling into her, rolling them onto their sides, pulling her close.

Tears filled her eyes. She'd never felt such a connection. Never felt this much emotion flooding through her. Never felt this damned satisfied.

"What just happened?" she finally asked when she could catch a decent breath. "Is it always like this?"

He shook his head.

She leaned back, looking into his face. "Did you feel it, too?"

He nodded, pulling her close, burying his face in her hair, inhaling the scent of the shampoo she'd used.

He didn't speak. Now he was worrying her. "What?"

"I think I have found my lifemate."

Her forehead creased. "Who?"

He moved just enough so he could look at her. "You."

Before she could question him more about this lifemate stuff, he doubled over, groaning.

Ohmygod, she'd killed him. Maybe Symtarians weren't supposed to mate with people from Earth or something.

She quickly sat up. "Kristor, are you okay?"

A fog began to roll in. She looked around. What the hell was happening? She jumped out of bed, and bumped her knee on the chair. She grabbed the robe that was across the arm, and thrust her arms inside.

The fog was so thick that she couldn't see. "Kristor?" She needed to find the phone and call for an ambulance or something. Oh, Lord, what would she tell them? She might have killed a man during sex?

She could feel the blood drain from her face. What if she

had killed him? What if she never had sex like that again? She mentally shook her head to clear it. No, that was selfish thinking. She should be more worried about him.

The fog began to slowly fade away. She caught a glimpse of a black-tipped wing. Ria took a step back. The fog cleared.

There was a hawk on her bed.

His animal guide, Shintara said. *Yum. Even better than the man. Look at that wingspan.*

"Shut up," she mumbled. Now what was she supposed to do? Better yet, it was late, and she was tired. Where the hell was she going to sleep? The sofa was too uncomfortable. She'd once fallen asleep there watching a tear-jerker movie and awoke with a crick in her neck. It had been very painful.

She stared at the hawk before making a decision. "Don't hog the covers," she finally said and lay down on her side of the bed, tucking the cover under her chin. She only hoped hawks didn't snore. Hell, she was so tired, she didn't really care at this point. It would've been much nicer snuggling, though.

Her sleep was fitful at best.

The next morning, Ria rolled over, stretched, and opened her eyes. Kristor watched her. His lips curled upward. Warm tingles spread over her body.

"Morning," he said.

"You're back."

"It would seem so."

She hadn't dreamt last night. It had all happened. The lovemaking, his changing into a hawk. But right before he'd changed, Kristor had mentioned something about her being his lifemate. There was a sound of permanency to it. She wasn't so sure she was ready for that, no matter how good the sex.

"What exactly does 'lifemate' mean?" she asked.

"Lifemate. It means we are meant to be together."

Dread filled her. "For now, you mean. I mean, nothing

long-term. Right?" Although, she didn't care for the idea of his moving on to greener pastures for at least a few weeks.

He brushed her hair away from her face, tucking it behind her ear. "Forever. Once a Symtarian finds his lifemate, then they are together forever."

"But we only had sex."

"Sometimes a male Symtarian knows the very first time."

"I barely know you." That sounded really slutty since they'd had mindblowing sex last night. "I mean, maybe I don't feel the same way."

"You will be very frustrated when you can't reach the same heights as we climbed last night. The only way to experience this kind of fulfillment is with your lifemate."

She scooted away from him and off the bed, pulling the robe she'd put on last night closer to her. She'd known deep down inside that nothing good would come from their making love, but had she listened? Noooo . . .

She took a deep breath and looked at him. Big mistake. My God, he looked delicious lying on her bed completely exposed. She dragged her gaze away.

"I'm going to put some coffee on," she said before hurrying from the room. It was too much to take in all at once. She stumbled, slapping her hand on the wall for support when it hit her again. She was part alien. Her ancestors were full-blood aliens.

But she didn't want to be an alien.

Kristor swung his legs over the side of the bed. He felt more alive than he'd felt in a long time.

And what will happen if you can't convince her to leave with you? Labrinon asked.

I will.

But if you don't. Symtarians have been known to go crazy if they can't be with their lifemate. I don't particularly like the idea that one of us would be a drooling idiot.

She will leave with me.

The truth was, Kristor didn't want to think of what might happen if Rianna didn't leave with him. Yes, he had heard all the stories of Symtarians losing their minds.

But he would convince her. He had no choice.

Or you could throw her over your shoulder, Labrinon reminded Kristor.

Yes, there is always that.

He stood, went to the bathroom and took a quick shower. Not as refreshing as standing under a waterfall, but definitely warmer.

You're getting soft.

He almost told Labrinon to be silent, but it never seemed to do any good. He spoke what he wanted, and had the right to do so. His guide had been true and faithful. Labrinon had saved his life more than once by telling Kristor when the enemy drew close. A hawk had superior visual acuity. No, Kristor wouldn't tell Labrinon to be silent.

This time.

He stepped from the shower, dried off, then knotted a towel around his waist. When he came out of the smaller room, his clothes had been laid neatly across the bed. He walked past them and went to the kitchen. Rianna was drinking coffee at the table.

It must be an Earth custom because the people who'd raised her did the same thing each morning. Kristor had tried the drink, but didn't find it to his liking.

"Do you have orange juice?" he asked.

She jumped, looked up, then choked. "I laid your clothes on the bed," she said.

"I prefer fewer clothes in the morning." At home, he rarely wore clothes. It gave him more freedom.

"And you run around my parents' home like this every morning?"

"No, I wear what you call 'pajamas.' Just like your father." He went to her refrigerator, opened the door, and spotted a carton of orange drink and brought it out.

"Just make yourself at home."

"Thank you." He brought a glass down from the cabinet and poured some juice into it.

"You seem to know a lot about Earth."

He sat across from her. "I studied. That, and Rogar explained a lot of things to me."

"Rogar?"

"My brother."

"What did he tell you?"

He frowned. "Don't use something called a microwave." He downed the juice. "This is very good. We don't have oranges on New Symtaria."

"Ria, are you up yet?" Carly called out.

Rianna's face lost some of its color.

"Oh, no." Her gaze flew to Kristor. "It's Carly."

The woman Rianna had called Carly stepped into the room, then came to an abrupt stop, her mouth dropping open to her chin when she saw him.

Chapter 11

"I'm sorry," Carly sputtered. "I thought you'd be alone." Ria couldn't believe this was happening. She would swear Carly to silence.

Oh, Lord, what if her mother found out? Not after Ria had complained so loudly about Kristor's staying with them. Besides, last night had been just about sex. It wasn't as though they were going to become an item or anything. And she certainly wasn't going to become his lifemate. Just wasn't going to happen.

But the sex had been fantastic.

Kristor came to his feet. Carly's eyes almost popped out of her head as her gaze very slowly took in every inch of Kristor's exposed skin, and there was a lot of it exposed.

A flutter of irritation swept over Ria, but just as quickly disappeared as her gaze fixed on Kristor. The man was downright, mouthwatering sexy.

"I'll get dressed." As he left the room, the towel parted down one side exposing a good expanse of his muscled thigh, and the towel was snug enough that it outlined his butt.

Ria couldn't look away. She couldn't move, couldn't breathe, as the blood rushed to her head. She watched him as he went down the hall, then turned into the bedroom. For the first time since she had known Carly, she wished her friend hadn't stopped by.

Carly hurried over to the coffeepot and poured some coffee into a cup, before joining Ria at the kitchen table. "Oh . . . my . . . God! How the hell did you get so freakin' lucky?"

Ria nervously took a drink of her coffee, then set the cup back on the saucer. She bit her bottom lip and wondered how exactly to tell Carly. Finally, she just blurted it out. "He's the alien."

"You slept with the alien? What do you mean you slept with him? You mean you had"—she leaned forward—"sex?" she whispered.

"You could . . . uh . . . call it that." She looked down into the dark liquid inside her cup. Last night had been so much more than sex.

"I thought you wanted to turn everyone against him so your parents would kick him out?"

That had been her plan, hadn't it? Wow, that idea had quickly gotten lost in the shuffle.

"And what's all that stuff you told me about him being an alien?"

She looked at her friend and knew she wasn't ready to tell Carly all that had happened. "I . . . uh . . . guess I did misunderstand him. He's from another country. He's an alien to the United States. I mean, this is his first trip here."

"And the hawk?"

She shrugged. "Coincidence."

Carly took a drink, then nodded. "Has he got a brother?"

Ria relaxed. "Yes, but did you know Neil is sweet on you?"

Carly blushed. "Neil?" She snorted. "I doubt that. I mean, look at the guy. He's got the wow factor."

"Don't sell yourself short. Neil really does like you."

Carly shrugged. "A lot of people like me. I mean, I practically grew up here. Everyone knows me. You probably misunderstood."

Ria shook her head. "No, he was pretty straightforward. He asked if I would test the waters."

Carly smiled. "Really?"

Ria nodded. "Yes, really, and give yourself a little more credit. You're a beautiful woman. You just come from a big family and they sort of swallow you up."

"He really asked you to test the waters."

"Yes, so tell me, what should I tell Neil? No swimming allowed? Or come on in, the water's fine?"

Carly leaned back in her chair, both hands hugging her coffee. "I like him, too. I have since he socked Ben Dansworth for pulling my chair out from under me in the sixth grade. When everyone started to laugh, he gave them a look that almost peeled the paint off the walls." She sighed. "Then he helped me up."

Ria sat forward. "A true southern gentleman."

"And he's interested in me?"

"Yes."

"Then, yeah, but remember you'll always be my best friend." She blushed. "Not that anything will ever happen between Neil and me."

Ria laughed. "You can have more than one friend."

"Yeah, but you're different. I don't know what I would do if you stopped being there for me."

"As if that will ever happen."

"I guess you're right. No one could ever keep us apart." Carly glanced at the clock on the wall. "Gotta run, I'm opening the office this morning."

"My new assistant is opening for me," Ria told her.

"How's she working out?"

"Katie?"

Carly nodded.

"The girl has been a miracle. Of course, she hasn't had to groom Sukie, yet."

"The demon dog?"

Ria nodded. "If she can make it through that, and the grooming business continues as it has been, I'll put her on full-time."

Carly glanced toward the bedroom. "Call me later when we have more time to talk."

Ria walked her out, then watched as she drove away. A little niggle of guilt stabbed her. She hadn't told Carly that aliens do exist. What could she have said? "Oh, and by the way, Carly, I'm part alien. Isn't that just the darnedest thing?"

How could she tell her best friend anything, when she didn't fully comprehend it herself? No, she needed to get a lot more comfortable with it herself before she tried to explain it to anyone else.

She grimaced. Her mom and dad would have coronaries. How did one break the news to her parents that their daughter was part alien? Hmmm, something to think about.

She started back to the kitchen just as Kristor stepped out of the bedroom. Damn, the guy looked totally awesome, even dressed. Her body tingled to awareness.

"You have the look of a woman who wants to mate," he said, stepping closer.

She drew in a deep breath, trying to clear those thoughts. What did she know about Kristor? He was an alien. A warrior. She needed to put the brakes on their relationship. "And I have the checking account of a woman who needs to go to work."

"I'll go with you."

It was a tempting idea. "Not this time. I'm going to be really busy." And she was. She had to supervise Katie. She bit her bottom lip, knowing she lied to herself. "We can meet for lunch."

He smiled, as if he had known he would have victory.

Men: Everything was a competition to them. She shook her head and scooted into the bedroom to get her purse.

"Stay here as long as you want." She didn't look at him again as she hurried to her car. She was afraid if she did, she might call in sick this morning. Kristor had some seriously good moves when it came to making love.

She started her car and backed out of the driveway. When she saw her neighbor on the front porch, Ria's hand froze on the steering wheel. Maybe because the neighbor's attention had moved from Ria to Kristor, who was standing on the porch. He smiled and waved at the neighbor. She waved back, then practically tripped over her own feet as she hurried back inside. Not good. It would be all over town that Kristor had spent the night with Ria.

Her life was quickly going to hell in a handbag. She put the car in drive and hurried to the shop. As soon as Ria parked at the side, she grabbed her phone and speed dialed her mom.

"Hi, Mom," she said as soon as Maggie answered.

"Good morning, dear." Then: "Is everything all right?"

"Fine, fine." She hunkered down in the seat. "I just wanted to tell you that Kristor spent the night with me last night." She squenched her eyes closed waiting for her mother to say something.

"Yes, I know, dear."

She shot back up in the seat. "You know? Already?" She frowned. "Did Mrs. Wilton call you?"

"No, dear, your father and I were out driving last night and saw Kristor's motorcycle parked in your driveway. Then when he didn't come home, we assumed he'd stayed at your place."

Ria wondered if she could get by with telling her mother Kristor had slept on the sofa. Probably not. "You're not upset, are you?"

Her mother's laughter tinkled across the phone. "Rianna

Lancaster, you might be my daughter, but you're also a woman, and your father and I both like the young man a lot."

Great, she had her parents' approval to have sex with Kristor. She didn't want to have this conversation with her mom.

"I'm here at my shop so I'd better go."

"Have a good day. Oh, and something else."

"What's that?"

"Someone said they saw you running across the park with just a T-shirt on. Do you know anything about it?"

"Me?" Her laugh cracked. "The things some people think they see."

"You're right, of course. I told them it couldn't have been you."

They said their good-byes and hung up. Ria breathed a sigh of relief. This town would be the death of her.

Kristor looked up, then down the street. It was peaceful, quiet. He'd been over many roads in his search for Rianna. This one should be no different, but it was.

The town was smaller. More interesting. He hadn't taken the time to get to know the people while he'd been searching, but he liked the ones who lived in Miller Bend. Especially the men he'd played the game of flag football with.

He liked everyone except for the man called Donald. He smiled with his lips, but it went no farther. Kristor suspected there was evil inside him.

The door on a barber shop opened. "Hey, Kristor, come in and sit a spell."

Sit a *spell*? He didn't know anyone did spells on Earth. At least, not spells that would work. Maybe it was only a false saying. He was discovering that people said one thing, but meant something entirely different. Especially in this state called Texas.

Kristor went inside and saw some of the men who had

been on the football field. Heath was getting his hair cut. Now he understood this place of business.

He sniffed. A lingering aroma of oil and leather filled the small store. Kristor had his own groomer, and the man often smelled of the oils he brought with him, but not worn leather. He liked the combination.

It had been a while since he'd had a haircut. He felt the top of his head.

"Wanting a trim?" an older man asked. He was short, and didn't have a hair on his head.

"Yes, a trim," Kristor said.

"Well, have a seat." He finished with Heath.

Kristor took a seat in front of the mirror. But when the man came over, he was still too short to reach the top of Kristor's head, even after he lowered the chair. The men seemed to think this was funny, so he laughed, too.

"Just remember I'm the one with the clippers," the old man said. He walked over, grabbed a short stool, and brought it back. "What'd your momma feed you?"

He thought for a moment. "Everything."

"Yeah, that's what I'd already figured out." The old man began to trim Kristor's hair.

He listened while everyone else talked. It wasn't the same as when he spent time with other warriors. There was much loyalty in the ranks, but they always spoke about battles. This was different. More laughing. And they drew him into their circle, as if he was one of them.

He wasn't sure he liked the warm feeling that wrapped around him. Kristor's family told him that he needed to loosen up, relax more, but how could he when he needed to keep his planet safe from invading forces? Not that he had to worry much about that happening. He'd created a good defense system against anyone foolish enough to attack them.

"Finished," the old man said, interrupting Kristor's thoughts. "What do you think?"

Kristor turned his head one way, then the other. "It's good."

"Of course it is. I'm the best barber in town."

Heath snorted. "You're the only one."

"Well, if there was another one, I'd be a sight better'n him." He stepped off the stool and carried it back to the other side of the room.

Kristor stared at his reflection, really looking at it for the first time. Did Rianna like his looks? Or did she prefer those of someone like Donald? Anger flared inside him. He would squash Donald if he put his hands on Rianna.

"The girls will be beating down your door," Neil said.

Heath came up beside them. "No, I think there's only one girl that he cares about. Heard you spent the night at Ria's."

He met Heath's eyes in the mirror. "Yes." How did he know? Apparently, they had a good communication system in this town, even as small as it was.

Suddenly, there was a shift in the room temperature. Kristor felt a chill settle over him as he watched Heath.

"I've known Ria a long time. I'd hate to see her get hurt," Heath said.

Heath was protective. That was good. "I will make sure she doesn't get hurt. I will protect her from harm."

Heath was thoughtful for a moment as he studied Kristor. Then he smiled, visibly relaxing. "Yeah, I think you will take good care of her."

The bell over the door jingled and Donald walked in. The jovial mood dropped. Donald looked around. He hesitated when he saw Kristor, then squared his shoulders and strode over to one of the barber chairs. He glanced around again, then grabbed a white towel that hung on one of the carts, and dusted off the seat before tossing the towel to the side and sitting.

"Not as much off the sides as you did last time." Donald adjusted himself to a more comfortable position.

"I cut hair the way I see that it needs to be cut. Never have any complaints from no one else. Besides, if you don't like my work, you can go somewhere else."

Donald sniffed. "You know there's no one else in town who cuts men's hair."

"Then I guess you better shut up and let me do my job."

"Later, Albert," Heath and Neil said as they started for the door.

Kristor decided it was time for him to go, too. He dropped a twenty on the counter and walked out. He'd figured out the monetary system before he came to Earth. If he ran out, his database would produce more.

Once outside, he said good-bye to the other two men, and walked in the opposite direction. He knew he was going toward Rianna's shop, and that he was too early for lunch, but something pulled him in that direction.

A small feminine body suddenly crashed into him, stopping his forward movement. He grabbed her arms so she didn't fall. A sultry scent tickled his senses.

"Oops!" she said.

He looked down. It was Mary Ann from the party. "Careful."

She smiled up at him. "You just seem to be in the right place at the right time, now don't you?"

"You're okay?"

"I am now, honey. And just about shopped out. I sure could use something to drink."

"There's a place near here where you can get food and drink?" he asked.

Her hands fluttered in front of her face. "As a matter of fact, I know the perfect place. A little restaurant right around the corner. I don't suppose it's too early to get something to eat. I mean, a guy like you would certainly want to keep up his strength."

"It's good that it's near. I'm taking Ria to lunch today."

"Oh, but I thought . . ." She sighed deeply. "I guess it

doesn't really matter. Maybe I can talk that overworked husband of mine into going to lunch with me. Tell Ria not to forget about the meeting."

A strange woman. Kristor watched as she walked away. There was an exaggerated sway in her hips. He was surprised she didn't throw something out of joint. He shook his head and continued down the street. This time, he didn't stop until he was standing in front of Ria's shop. She wasn't alone. There were two other women with her. He watched as she laughed at something one of them said. Her eyes sparkled and her face glowed. His heart ached to hold her close.

You've fallen in love, Labrinon said. *I'm always surprised how quickly Symtarian men can do that.*

She's beautiful, and Rianna will make the perfect lifemate.

You only need to convince her.

She's very stubborn, Kristor agreed.

Stubborn? I'd say it's a little more than that.

Rianna looked up and caught him staring at her. A softness entered her eyes. Yes, he would carry her back to his planet, if need be. He wouldn't take no for an answer.

It's about time!

But only if I can't convince her to travel back to New Symtaria with me.

That might take forever.

Have you so little faith in me?

With this woman? Yes.

Ria opened the door to her shop and stepped out. "I thought you were going to be here at lunch time?"

"I couldn't wait to see you."

She looked through the glass wall at the other two women. They waved her away. Ria grinned.

"Okay, I guess I can show you some of the town. If you haven't already seen all of it, that is."

"No, and yes, I'd like that."

She studied him for a moment. "Did you get your hair cut?"

"Yes, so we don't need to see the barber shop." The last thing he wanted was to cross paths with Donald again. He sensed the man wanted Rianna all to himself. Kristor wasn't about to let that happen.

Chapter 12

When Kristor took her hand, Ria didn't pull away. The slight roughness of his palm sent a spiral of heat to pool low in her belly, even though it was something as innocent as just holding hands. Oh, man, she was in really bad shape.

"This is pretty much Miller Bend," she told him. "The abstract office, the lawyer's office, water department, post office, flower shop, antique store, and the pharmacy. The library is around the corner." She chuckled when she saw the confusion on his face. "I guess you don't have all this on New Symtaria."

His expression showed his confusion. "What is a library?"

"A building that stores books. People go there to borrow them. You know, to read."

"I don't read much. I'm a warrior."

She hadn't really pictured him kicked back in a recliner and reading a book. "Do you have stores on New Symtaria?"

"We have tradespeople, yes, or we can get items we need with our database."

"Your database sounds a lot like Internet shopping. I think I'd rather go into a store."

"But if you could have everything with a click of a button, wouldn't that be better?"

"No, I think it's the thrill of finding a bargain that I enjoy. Clicking a button wouldn't really do it for me."

"That is the way it is during a battle. The victory makes the blood race through my veins." He stood taller, looking around as if he would love to battle now.

"That's exactly the way I feel when I go to a going-out-of-business sale," she said, drawing his attention back to her. Heaven forbid he start a ruckus with one of the townspeople. She didn't need any more gossip started about her. But she didn't need to worry as she watched his shoulders relax.

"When you connect with your hawk guide, you will feel that same rush," he said.

They were back to that again. Drat! And the morning had been going so well. "I think shifting once was more than enough for me. I'd just as soon not be terrorized again. Those scouts almost threw me in a soup pot. And getting ice and Coke dumped on me, then dirt kicked in my face was an experience I would rather not go through again."

"Your guide needs you."

Guilt swarmed around her like angry insects. "I'm not ready. Maybe in time I . . . I will be able to shift, but not right now. This is all too new to me."

"You can only gain strength through connecting. You might have need of this strength if the rogue Symtarians discover where you live."

"But you said you were here to protect me."

He stopped, forcing her to stop as well. "I can't stay forever."

This was Kristor's first indication that he would return to his own home. A cold feeling of dread landed with a thud in the pit of her stomach. She hadn't thought that one day he would leave, but it made sense. Of course, he couldn't hang around for the rest of her life. He had his own to get back to. The man was a prince.

But could she shift into a hawk when she was terrified of flying? And look at what had happened to her the last time.

Not only had she felt an incredible burning sensation, but she had thought she would die.

"I can't," she finally said. "Not right now."

He hesitated, watching her closely. "I'll give you more time."

Carly looked up when Donald came inside the travel agency. She pasted a smile on her face, even though there was something about the guy she just didn't like. He was a tattle-tale for one thing. He'd told on Ria when she had put the whoopee cushion under Ms. Henderson's chair. It had really been pretty funny, until he'd told.

And Donald was just too darn pretty. Men shouldn't be pretty. Even now, every blond hair was in place. It made her wonder how much he spent on hairspray.

But the motto of this agency was to make the customer happy and she would like to keep her job.

"Hello, Donald. Were you thinking about going some-where?" Far, far away, she hoped.

He wandered over to a rack of brochures. She came to her feet and joined him.

"Wanderlust, I guess. I feel the need to take a vacation somewhere exotic." He flashed a smile.

Carly relaxed. Donald wasn't her favorite person in town, but he wasn't so bad. And the whoopee cushion incident had happened when she and Ria were still in high school.

"The Caribbean? Barbados?" she asked.

"Yes, Barbados, maybe. Ocean breezes and piña coladas."

"It sounds great," she told him.

"I've always wondered why you work here but you've never gone anywhere exciting."

"I guess I enjoy living vicariously through my customers. I'm a nervous traveler." And she wished he hadn't mentioned that she never went anywhere. She certainly didn't need any-one reminding her. "Ria and I are planning to take a trip. She hired Katie as her new assistant. I'm sure she'll have her trained by the time fall gets here." Then Carly would have someone to go with and she'd finally get to travel. They could take a cruise somewhere. She closed her eyes and for a moment, pictured them landing in an exotic port filled with sexy, half-naked, male bodies.

Donald cast a look of pity in her direction.

"What?" She suddenly had a strange feeling in the pit of her stomach that she wasn't going to like what he was about to tell her.

He pointed out the window as Ria and Kristor passed. Ria looked up, and Carly waved. Ria waved back and smiled, but they didn't stop. Kristor frowned at Donald, who took a step back.

"It would seem Ria might be planning a trip with someone else."

Carly stiffened. "I doubt it. She just met the guy." But he had spent last night with her, and that never happened. Not that she could blame Ria. Kristor was damned good looking. But anything permanent? No, Carly didn't think so.

"Wasn't it just a day or so ago that Ria claimed the guy was crazy?" Donald laughed. "An alien?"

Ria *had* done a quick about-face. Carly's stomach rumbled. She watched until they turned the corner. They seemed awfully chummy. Holding hands and all.

"More friendships have broken up over a man," Donald said.

She straightened. Why was she even listening to him? "Well, it won't happen between us. We've been friends since almost forever. Even if Ria does fall in love with someone, we'll still be friends."

He shrugged. "I don't know. Ria seems to be getting pretty close with the guy. But don't worry, even if they went back to his country, or wherever he came from, there are always e-mails. If his country has the Internet, that is." He glanced at the brochures he held. "I think I'll just take these with me. I'm not exactly sure where I want to go."

"Yeah, that's fine." Please leave quickly. Her stomach had gone from rumbling to churning.

As Donald walked out the door, Carly went back to her desk. She'd never really thought about Ria getting married and leaving town. Carly had always thought they would fall in love with the perfect men, marry, and settle down in Miller Bend to raise two children each.

Had she really been that naive? Apparently.

Was Kristor the one who would steal Ria away? Whisk her off to another country? Ria was her only friend. They always shared everything.

But she hadn't told her anything about Kristor except that she was trying to blackball him. She'd been afraid of the man. Apparently, that was no longer the case.

And then there was this morning. She'd sensed Ria wasn't telling her everything. Just as quickly Carly dismissed the idea that Ria wouldn't confide something to her very best friend.

But what if Ria was already pulling away? A cold chill of dread wrapped around her. What would she do without her very best friend in her life?

She slumped down in her chair, and stared out the plate-glass window until the bell over the door jangled, alerting her to a customer.

Carly painted a false smile on her face and pretended nothing at all was wrong. But it took every ounce of her sagging energy to pull it off.

Ria flattened the Dairy Queen sack the burgers had come in, and dumped all the fries on top of it. "Community fries," she said.

He raised an eyebrow.

She grinned. "That means we share."

"I was going to take you somewhere nice," he told her. "I have money." His brother had told him people from Earth held the paper in high regard, although Kristor still hadn't figured out why.

"Isn't this nice?" She waved her arm, encompassing everything around her. "We have the whole park to ourselves. Besides, Donald owns the only nice restaurant in town. I don't think you two get along."

"It's very nice here."

She laughed. "Yeah, I kind of thought you would feel that way." She took a bite of her burger and chewed, then followed it with a drink of her soda. "Donald isn't so bad."

"Yes, he is. I think he could be very cruel if he doesn't like someone. You should be careful around him."

"Trust me, I've known Donald all my life. He's a little prissy. . . ." She caught his expression. "Okay, he's a lot prissy, but he's mostly talk. If cornered, he'll run the other way."

"I think he would lash out as he ran."

How often had she thought the same thing? Ria had never spoken the words out loud though.

"We have parks on New Symtaria," he said, changing the subject.

"Like this one?"

"There are more people outside enjoying the day on New Symtaria. When Old Symtaria released poisonous gasses into the air, it was said everyone stayed indoors or only went out with air-supplied masks. When New Symtaria was discovered, it was ordained by the old ruler that part of each day would be spent outdoors enjoying the fresh air."

"We don't spend enough time outside," she sighed. "It's the age of technology and I'm afraid when people do go outside, they're still busy talking on the phone or texting someone."

"Is that why you run? To enjoy the day?"

She picked up a fry, but it had already grown cold so she put it back down. "Partly," she told him. "I like to feel the wind on my face. I feel free when I'm running. As though I have no troubles in the world."

"It is the same when I shift and Labrinon soars through the sky."

"You can feel it, then?"

"Yes."

"Then does he feel what you feel?"

"Yes."

"Even when we . . ." She felt the heat rise up her face.

"He sleeps, giving me the privacy I need."

She let out her breath. She was so not into threesomes, especially when one of the partners was a bird.

They finished eating in silence. She bagged up their trash and they walked it over to the barrel, dropping it inside.

"Look." Kristor pointed to a hawk flying high in the sky.

"Someone you know?"

"Only a hawk, but watch it."

She did, wondering what it was he wanted her to see. After a moment, her neck began to ache. "What am I supposed to get out of this?"

"Just watch."

The bird seemed to lazily float in the air, slowly circling in the sky. No cares, no worries. "Okay, it's beautiful." She'd give him that, at least.

"You could be flying right now."

"No thank you. Not on a full stomach." Or any stomach as far as she was concerned.

"I will stay with you the next time you shift. I would fly with you."

"I'm not ready." She glanced in his direction, then quickly looked at the hawk again. It would be too easy for him to sway her into doing something she wasn't ready to do. "But it's a beautiful bird."

The hawk suddenly swooped down like a bomber plane. For a moment it was lost in the trees. What the hell was it doing? Had it crashed? When it reemerged, there was a wiggling tail dangling from its mouth.

"Eww."

"The hawk has great visual acuity. It can spot prey from a long distance."

"I don't want to talk about it. I *really* don't want to talk about it. And if you continue to talk about it, my lunch will come back up."

He laughed. A deep baritone sound that wrapped around her, singing to her soul. She met his gaze, and something passed between them. He leaned closer, his lips brushing against hers. His touch was nice and, all too soon, he pulled back. Oh, jeez, she really needed to think about something else.

"Do you swim?" she suddenly asked.

"Swim?"

"You know, in the water."

He opened his mouth, paused, then shook his head. "I don't know this."

She grabbed his hand and pulled him along with her. "I know the perfect place: Miller Crossing."

But when he aimed her toward his bike, rather than her car, she wasn't so sure.

"I've never thought motorcycles were safe," she told him.

"Are you going to play everything safe?" he asked.

She cocked an eyebrow. "I do not play everything safe. I took a chance borrowing the money to open my animal grooming shop. I could've fallen flat on my face."

He didn't say anything, only stared.

"Okay, fine, but if I die, you're going to have to tell my parents."

He straddled the seat and she climbed on awkwardly behind him. He handed her his helmet.

"You have motorcycles on New Symtaria?" she asked.

"No."

She frowned. "But you have cars and trucks."

"No."

The bike roared to life.

"How long have you been driving?"

"Your time?"

"Yes."

He pulled out onto the road, but yelled over his shoulder, "Two weeks. Maybe a little less."

She was going to die. Why did she go against everything she believed in to get on a dangerous machine like this with an inexperienced driver?

"Which way?"

"My house first." She wrapped her arms around his waist, closed her eyes, and hung on for dear life.

She had to admit on the ride over he seemed to be a skilled driver. Had he been lying? She had a feeling he was. Maybe to get her to hold on a little tighter. She would have done that anyway. She liked holding tightly to him.

She had a feeling her heart was in trouble.

All too soon, he pulled in her driveway and they climbed off.

"I thought you said you didn't have vehicles where you're from?"

"Not like this."

He grinned, and she knew he'd teased her. He always seemed so serious that she hadn't suspected him of having a sense of humor.

"Well, do you have shorts or something you can wear to swim in?"

"I have a database."

As they walked inside, he pulled what looked like an IPod of sorts out of his back pocket. As tempting as the thought of his only wearing the Ipod and nothing else, he might cause someone to have a heart attack if they walked up on a naked alien. Especially an alien built as well as Kristor.

"I mean something to wear swimming. You'll need a swim suit."

He punched around on the keys, a swirl of lights appeared, and in the center was a pair of swim trunks.

"How did you do that?"

He held up the little computer. "Database. I told you about it."

"Yeah, but I didn't think it would do this." She waved her arm toward the suit. "Can you make anything appear?"

"Most anything." He punched in some numbers, then smiled. More lights appeared and in the center was the skimpiest string bikini she'd ever seen.

"Funny, but I don't think so."

He punched around some more, and the suit disappeared. Before he could bring something else up, she said, "I have my own suit. You can change out here. I'll use the bedroom."

But when she went to her bedroom, she didn't choose the most conservative suit that she owned. Her choice wasn't a string bikini, but a pretty yellow swimsuit just the same, and one that flattered her figure.

She gave him what she thought was plenty of time, then walked into the living room. She'd slipped on a pair of blue-jean cutoffs over her swimsuit bottom, but the look he gave her told her he remembered what she looked like without clothes, and it took her breath away.

Not that she wasn't doing the same thing to him. If they didn't leave soon, they might not leave at all, and there was a lot more she wanted to know about New Symtaria. And Kristor.

"I'll just grab a couple of water bottles and some towels." She abruptly turned and went to gather everything they might need. But when she went inside the kitchen, she took a long, slow, deep breath as she tried to get her raging hormones under control.

Hell, it wasn't every day that she had the equivalent of a male cover model in her house, or in her bed. She had to stop thinking so much about him in that way. She could spend a nice afternoon alone with him without jumping his bones. Surely, it wouldn't be that hard.

Hard?

Get your mind out of the gutter. Ria repeated over and over to herself as she hurried outside.

Kristor was already at the bike. He took the things from her and put everything in the black leather bags that hung on each side of the motorcycle. She gave him directions, telling him the turns as they came up to them. Her fear of riding on the motorcycle quickly changed to exhilaration. It was a lot more fun than she'd expected. There was a freedom, much like when she ran, except she didn't have to work for the rush. She had a feeling this would turn out to be a nice day.

Miller Crossing was where she and Carly had spent most of their summers. It was a great place to swim. You couldn't cross it, though. It was too big, so you had to go around it. That made it more private and, most of the time, anyone could find a secluded spot.

She directed Kristor around to the far side. It was the best place, and she knew it was more concealed than some of the other areas. She didn't even attempt to question her motives.

He slowed, then turned off onto a narrow trail only wide enough for a motorcycle, bringing the bike almost to a crawl. Ria kept her knees in tight against the hard muscles of his thighs. When the water was in sight, he stopped the motorcycle, turning off the engine, and dropping the kickstand.

It was as though they were the only ones in the world, surrounded by the silence of the pine trees. For a moment, they sat looking at the clear slate of blue water. Perfect, unblemished. Begging for them to jump in.

She quickly climbed off and removed her helmet. Kristor climbed off as well.

"Now, do you have a view like this on New Symtaria?" she asked.

"Better."

She tilted her head and looked at him. How rude. "I doubt that. This would be pretty hard to beat."

"Come back with me and I'll prove we have the better views."

"Funny." She slipped off her shorts and laid them across the seat. "I'll race you to the water." Without waiting to see if he followed, she took off.

Kristor watched, knowing he would let her win—this time. A smart warrior knew which battles he needed to win. Not that he minded letting her go first. She was right, the view of her in that tiny yellow bikini could not be beat.

He followed at a slower pace. She screamed when she ran into the water. He laughed.

You'll miss her when you leave, Labrinon said.

I told you, I won't leave without her. Have I ever lost a battle?

But there may be many battles before a war is won.

I think I will enjoy winning each one, too.

I don't doubt it.

"It's cold."

Kristor smiled. The water might be cold, but it didn't stop her from diving in headfirst. He held his breath when she didn't immediately emerge. Just when he would have jumped in, she shot out of the water.

"Come on. I promise I won't let you drown."

Maybe he shouldn't have lied when he told her he couldn't swim. That had been wrong. He only hoped it took her a very long time to figure it out.

He waded in. She was right. The water was cool, refreshing after having the sun beat down on them. He walked to where she stood, the water to her shoulders. It was much lower on him.

"You have to get your head wet." She placed her hands on top of his head and pushed.

He didn't move. Why would he? Her breasts were in his face.

"You're supposed to go under," she complained.

He laughed, then obliged, although he rather enjoyed the proximity of her body next to his.

"There, now I'll teach you to swim. One arm, then the other." She demonstrated.

Kristor made sure his movements were awkward. In truth, he was a strong swimmer.

She shook her head. "Not like that."

She took his arm and made the motion again, then stood behind him, her chest pressed against his back. He closed his eyes, enjoying the moment.

"Are you paying attention?" she asked.

"Of course."

"I don't think you are."

"It's hard to move my arms correctly with you standing behind me. Try moving to the front."

She was so intent on teaching him to swim that she complied with his request, snuggling in front of him.

"Try putting your arms on top of mine and you can follow my movements."

He enjoyed the way she wiggled her bottom. He could follow her movements until the sun slipped beneath the horizon, or until he mated with her again. But then, she abruptly moved away.

"Okay, now watch me." She swam a short distance, then turned and came back. "Do you think you can do that?"

"I'll try." He swam out a ways, then dove beneath the water, coming up in front of her. He took her in his arms, pulling her close to him.

"You know how to swim," she accused.

"I'm a fast learner."

"Very funny."

"Are you mad?"

She tried not to smile, but it broke through anyway. "Furious." She leaned forward, planting her mouth on his.

When the kiss ended, they were both gasping for air. "I want to mate."

"In the water?"

"Good idea." He reached for her top.

"No, I wasn't agreeing."

"Then you don't want to mate?"

"I do, but not here, not now. I want to get to know you better. I think we rushed things a little last night."

He sighed, but gave in to her wishes. He would never understand women. They were almost the same on New Symtaria. "So what will we do?"

"Talk."

Yes, Earth women and Symtarian women were alike in many ways. A woman was a woman, no matter where she was from. Which made them even more interesting.

Chapter 13

Ria spread her towel on the ground and lay down. The sun was hot, but the leafy branches of an old and gnarled oak tree spread out, giving them plenty of shade. She closed her eyes and sighed. Kristor spread his towel next to hers, dripping water across her back.

She gave him her evil-eye glare. "You did that on purpose."

"Me?"

"Yes, you."

He lay down beside her. "I'm sorry."

"I don't think you are." His eyes twinkled with mischief. No, he'd definitely meant to drip water on her. Damn, he was just too sexy. Bare, tanned chest, rock-hard muscles, and all of it exposed for her pleasure. This had to be what heaven was like, or at least pretty darn close.

"So you do want to mate," he said.

It took a moment for his words to sink in. When they did, she quickly looked away, turning on her back and draping her arm across her eyes to block the glare of the sun, and the temptation to look a little longer at Kristor's delicious body. She'd meant it when she told him she wanted to slow down their relationship. She barely knew him.

And it was time to face the facts. As much as she'd like to think she had dreamed everything, she hadn't. She had really shifted into a frog. She really did have an animal guide. She really was part alien.

"Tell me about New Symtaria," she said. "Tell me about who I am, where I come from."

He was silent for a moment as though carefully choosing his words. "Symtarians are a proud people, but our ancestors were brought to their knees when Symtaria was dying. They had worn out the planet, polluted its resources. When they went in search of a new one, they vowed to learn from the mistakes of the past. We live a more simple life now."

"How so?" she asked.

"We're very careful with waste. We've learned to enjoy the simple things."

She rolled onto her side and looked at him. He'd turned onto his back, staring up at the sky. She loved watching him, and she loved hearing him talk about New Symtaria.

"And how did you become shapeshifters?" she asked.

"Long ago, gods and goddesses walked the land. They were one with the people. Part human, part animal. Their powers were great, and helped the people. Then they mated with some of the chosen. The offspring were not human, nor were they animal. Two living as one, they were both. One cannot truly survive without the other. Eventually, everyone had their own animal guide to help them when they were needed."

"It sounds like a fairy tale—a fantasy."

"Not quite. We angered the gods when we destroyed our planet through our carelessness. That is why we had to search for many years until we found this one."

"And now you're trying to make everything right by bringing the impures home."

"Yes."

"And what if they don't want to return?"

Silence.

"Kristor?"

"It is in your best interest to return with me."

She sat up. "And if I don't?"

He sat up as well, watching her. "I hope you will want to return on your own. The Queen Mother bade me exercise diplomacy."

The Queen Mother. Wait, hadn't he told her he was a prince? "This wouldn't happen to be your mother?"

"Yes, my mother."

She was going to throw up. He was a prince. A real true prince. She almost laughed out loud at the irony—and she'd been a frog.

"Now we will mate." He pulled her against him, his lips finding hers.

For a moment, she lost herself in the sensation of his body heat as it wrapped around her, enclosing her in a cocoon of sensual desire. His tongue stroked hers. His hands caressed her back, untying her top.

She jerked away, holding the little slip of yellow material against her chest. "No, we can't do this." She jumped up and turned her back, re-tying her top.

"Why not?" He came up behind her, pulling her close, lightly running his fingers over her bare stomach.

For a moment, she forgot why they couldn't make love. She lost herself in the sensations he stirred inside her. His fingers tickled over her flesh, dipping lower and lower.

A small animal rustled in the underbrush, drawing her out of the web of pleasure he was weaving around her. She remembered exactly why they couldn't make love, and stepped out of his arms.

"You're a prince." She turned around and faced him.

His forehead wrinkled. "What does that matter?"

"You're of royal blood."

"As are you. A princess."

She opened her mouth to refute his words, then shut it without saying a word. That was right. She remembered his telling her.

"You were serious?"

"Your lineage can be traced as far back as mine. Your ancestors have also been rulers."

Something fluttered inside her. She was a princess. Like Cinderella. Well, except she used a Swiffer to mop her floor so she was pretty certain it wasn't quite like scrubbing. And she'd never cleaned out a fireplace in her life.

Fred had talked to her, though. Her parakeet from childhood had communicated its thoughts.

Wow, her life was almost parallel to the fairy tale. How weird was that? Except she'd had loving parents. And no prince had . . . Okay, scratch that. Her prince had arrived to carry her off to his castle, even if it was on another planet.

No, it didn't matter. She was not going to fly off to another planet and play dress-up. "But you know how to be . . . to be royal and everything," she told him. "You're a prince."

"And you're a princess."

She shook her head. "But I don't know how to be a princess, and the next verse is that I don't want to be a princess. I don't know the first thing about being one."

"It's only a title."

"Only a title. Easy for you to say, you didn't grow up in Miller Bend. We don't have royalty here. I'm just small town. I'm jeans and boots, longneck beer, and burgers from Dairy Queen." She shook her head. "I don't know how to be a princess. I can't leave with you. Ever. I need to go home now, please." The sooner she left, the better.

But when she moved to gather up their towels, Kristor pulled her into his arms. "I can show you everything you need to know."

"But it still doesn't change the fact I refuse to shift again."

So you will let me die. Shintara's thoughts filled Ria's head, followed by sniffles.

Was Shintara crying? Oh, God, more guilt heaped on Ria's shoulders. It wasn't fair. "I mean, I'm not sure I can," she said, breaking. How could she not shift? Her animal guide was a part of her. Ria didn't want her to die and, worse, knowing she had caused her death. "I've never even been on a plane," she whimpered.

"You won't have to fly if you shift," Kristor said.

She studied his face. "I wouldn't?"

He placed his hands on her shoulders and looked deeply into her eyes. "No. You don't have to do anything you don't want to," he said.

He looked as though he was telling the truth. "I could shift, and not fly?" She wanted to be perfectly clear.

"Yes."

She still didn't trust him, but she forgot everything when his mouth covered hers. Sweet Jesus, this was what she'd been missing all her life. Heat ignited inside her as desire swirled around her stomach. His hands cupped her butt, pulling her closer until she could feel his need.

Ria didn't protest when he guided her back down to the towels. Why would she, when she wanted him as much as he wanted her? Rather than let him control the situation, she took charge, pushing him onto his back. She ran her tongue across his nipples and over his abdomen, nipping, then kissing.

She straightened, tugging at his swim trunks. He raised his hips to accommodate her desire to have him exposed and stretched out in front of her.

Slowly, she peeled his trunks down. Her throat went dry, and it was all she could do to take a breath, as memories flooded her mind. She remembered last night, when he'd plunged inside her, filling her, making her come again and again.

She stroked her fingers down the side of his erection. He drew in a sharp breath. She encircled it, squeezing lightly, sliding the foreskin down.

"You're magnificent," she breathed. Leaning forward, she licked down him, then back up. He grabbed her shoulders, squeezing lightly, massaging, hips raising. He needed more from her, and silently begged for more.

Ria wouldn't hold back. She drew him inside her mouth, tasting the man. Her tongue caressed the soft tip, swirled around, then sucked him deeper inside her mouth. Her nipples strained against the material of her top, and she grew damp with her own need.

With his free hand, he pulled at her top, as if he guessed her thoughts. It came loose, and he tossed it away. Then his hand was touching her, tugging on the nipple closest to him. Heat flooded her body, settling between her legs as small spasms erupted inside her.

"Don't stop," he said.

Stop? Not a chance. She liked what she was doing to him. The taste, the feel of him inside her mouth. No, she wasn't about to stop.

He raised enough to grab her waist and move her so that her legs straddled his face. Then he untied the strings on each side of her bikini. The warm air caressed between her legs, causing the most incredible sensations to wash over her, but it was nothing compared to when he sucked her inside his mouth.

She closed her eyes for a moment, unable to move, to breathe as she came from just one touch of his mouth, but he didn't stop as he continued his assault.

Nor did Ria as she brought him back inside her mouth, sucking and licking, cupping his balls, massaging with her free hand.

The inner muscles of her legs tightened as she tried to hold on to each spasm that assaulted her body with unbelievable pleasure.

She closed her eyes, and cried out, unable to think straight as her body began to quiver. She'd never . . . It was so . . .

"Enough," he moaned. Kristor nudged her head and she stopped. He continued to massage with his finger, though.

He moved her body so that she straddled him, but rather than enter her, he moved so that her sex was nestled against him.

Ria didn't think there was anything left inside her until he moved her sex against his erection. Her body tingled to awareness. She began to rub against him, the fire inside her building to a fever pitch. He held her in place, making the contact complete.

"I love watching you in the throes of passion," he whispered. "Seeing the desire burning in your eyes as you rub yourself against me. Knowing I have tasted the essence of the woman you are. The little bounce in your breasts, the curls between your legs covering you. But I have seen what hides beneath."

Oh, God, he was killing her with words. She couldn't see through the haze of her desire. She could only feel the friction building between them. She moved against him faster and faster. Harder and harder. Her body clenched, but she didn't stop. She wanted him to come. Through the fog of her desire, she watched his face, saw his need.

"Did you like it when I sucked you inside my mouth?" she asked, gazing down on his face and seeing how tightly he kept his own passion in check. "When I ran my tongue down your length? Did you like that? I loved tasting you, feeling you inside my mouth."

He jerked to a sitting position, pulling her tight against him as he came. Growling.

She wrapped her arms around him, holding on, panting as she sought air. She continued to move against him, the heat inside her building until she stiffened and cried out her own release.

Their ragged breathing was the only sound. As that quieted, everything around them grew still, their world coming back into focus.

"That was good," he said. "Very good."

"Messy, though."

He laughed close to her ear.

This was what they'd meant by pushing the boundaries. She'd read about it in a magazine. Ria had a feeling she'd pushed a lot of boundaries and tried something new today. This was the first time she'd had sex outdoors. The first time she'd had sex when the man didn't come inside her.

Did that make her bad? If it did, she had a feeling she liked being bad.

She suddenly frowned. "This is not taking our relationship slow."

"I thought we mated slower than the first time."

She leaned back and looked into his face. "That is not what I meant."

He sighed dramatically. "I thought as much. But you enjoyed it."

She leaned her head on his shoulder. "Yes, very much." Probably too much.

He suddenly groaned and doubled over. She knew what it meant. Great, now she would be stuck out here until he shifted back. She wondered how long that would be. As she looked up at the sun beating down on her, she wished she'd brought some sunscreen.

Crap! The Women's League meeting was tonight. If she missed it, there was no telling what she would get volunteered for.

Chapter 14

Ria took a quick shower, then slapped on the minimal amount of makeup that was allowed when going to one of the Women's League meetings. They were such sticklers for protocol. Sheesh! She pulled on a pair of jeans, heels, and a strappy little blue top. She glanced at her watch. If nothing happened, she should make it to the meeting right on time. One last look in the mirror and . . .

She paused, noting the twinkle in her eyes, the look of satisfaction on her face. Crap!

It was the look of a woman who'd been making love all afternoon. That wasn't good. Be serious! She wrinkled her forehead and frowned.

Great. Now she looked as if she hadn't had an orgasm in years.

This was nonsense. When had she ever cared what people thought about her?

Truthfully?

Okay, maybe she did care, but she wouldn't lose any sleep over what anyone at the Women's League thought, or the other townspeople for that matter. If she worried about every little thing, Ria would have been losing a lot of sleep in her lifetime.

A horn honked. That would be Carly. Since Ria's car was

still at Pet Purr-fect Grooming, she'd bummed a ride from her friend. They usually rode together anyway. Carly hated going alone.

Ria hurried down the stairs and opened the passenger door. "Hi, sorry I was running late."

"No problem," Carly said, but she kept looking at Ria, rather than putting the car in drive.

"Did I smear my mascara?"

"No, but you look different." She worried her lower lip as she drove away. "Relaxed, happy . . . I'm not exactly sure."

Ria lowered her window, letting the breeze rustle through her hair. "I spent the afternoon with Kristor."

"Apparently, you enjoyed yourself."

"We went to Miller Crossing. The place where we used to go all the time. We swam and lay in the sun." For some reason she didn't really want to talk about how they'd also had fantastic sex. It had never really stopped her before, but this time was different.

"You took him to our secret place?" Carly asked.

Ria sat a little straighter when she heard the hurt in Carly's voice. With Carly being sick, then meeting Kristor, Ria realized she'd neglected her friend.

"Why don't you come over for supper tomorrow night? I've missed hanging out with you."

Carly relaxed, smiling at her. But just as quickly, her smile vanished. "Won't Kristor mind?"

"Carly, you'll always be my best friend. You do know that will never change."

"You're right. I guess I'm just hormonal." She snagged a parking place in front of the library, and after she cut off the engine, they got out and went inside. It looked like everyone was already there. Most of the chairs were taken. They found a couple of empty ones at the back and slid into them.

"I was wondering if you two were going to show." Mary Ann's thick southern drawl rang across the room. "We were about to start without you, and you know what happened the last time you missed a meeting."

"And I do not plan on getting volunteered for another thing that I don't want to do, so yes, Carly and I are here." Ria was smug, she didn't care. No more skimpy cheerleading uniforms for her!

"Carly got lucky last time," Mary Ann said.

"I was at death's door. I really wouldn't call that lucky," Carly whispered.

"At least you didn't have to put on the outfit that Mary Ann designed. Sheesh, I felt like a stripper."

"Was it really that bad?"

"Worse than you can imagine," Ria said.

"Eww, I wonder if she wore it for Bobby Ray first?"

"Probably."

Mary Ann brought the gavel down on the desk, drawing their attention back to her. "I hereby call to order the Women's League meeting. The first order of business will be ideas to raise money to buy the new x-ray machine for the hospital. Are there any suggestions?"

"We could do a cookbook," Amy said.

Ria groaned and scooted down in her seat. Carly followed suit. She and Carly had chaired the last committee that did a cookbook and it was a hell of a lot of work. There was no way she had time this year. It was hard enough trying to figure out who she was.

The meeting droned on. Ria smiled in all the right places, and offered suggestions in others. She laughed at some of the things Carly said that were sarcastic, and they both got called on the carpet for giggling.

"I enjoyed tonight," Carly said after the meeting. She was driving Ria to her shop so she could get her car.

"I had fun, too. Did you see Rayann?"

"Ohmygod, I couldn't believe she actually wore a miniskirt to the meeting. She's got to be at least sixty-five."

"Fifty-seven," Ria said.

"Is that all? Good Lord, she must have had a hard life. Her face has so many wrinkles that if she had a facelift her eyeballs would be on her butt."

"Look who she's married to," Ria reminded her.

Carly grimaced. "Oh, that's right. I take back all I said about her. I heard Amos forgot where he lived one night because he's slept around so much." Carly pulled in next to Ria's car, and shifted into park before turning in her seat. "Why the hell does she put up with him?"

Ria rubbed two fingers together. "The man has money. And don't feel too sorry for her. Rayann isn't quite what anyone could call true blue."

"Then they deserve each other."

A comfortable quiet settled inside the car that comes only when two longtime friends share something together.

"I had a good time tonight," Ria broke the silence.

"Me, too."

"See you tomorrow for supper?"

"Yes, tomorrow."

Ria got out of the car and unlocked hers, sliding into the seat. Carly waved, then backed out as Ria started her car.

It had been fun tonight.

Then why did she feel just a pinch of guilt?

Maybe because the whole time, Ria had thought about Kristor, and wondered what he was doing.

You lied to her, Labrinon told Kristor.

I was forced to lie.

How could he tell Rianna that if she shifted into her animal guide, the guide would have control, and Rianna would have no say in what happened? She would never shift, and her animal guide would die.

He couldn't let that happen. He knew Rianna well enough to know that she was a kind and gentle person. To kill anything would also kill her.

I did what I had to do. He increased the cycle's speed, but still it was not enough. He needed to rid himself of the guilt he felt. By the gods, he had done what he thought was best.

Kristor pulled off the side of the road, hiding the cycle behind trees. He raised his face toward the night sky, as if to worship the stars. And maybe he was. Many of their gods had chosen to dwell with celestial beings. Maybe they would look down upon him with pity, and help him accomplish his mission successfully.

Tonight he would pay homage to the gods and soar the skies with Labrinon. Kristor took a deep breath, then exhaled as the shift began. The burning sensation had eased over time and the many shifts that had occurred but, still, changing was not always a simple matter.

He groaned, slumping to the ground. A thick fog wrapped around him. Nose became beak. Feet became talons that could slice the hide off a man. Kristor stretched his arms toward the sky. They became black-tipped wings that opened, lofting on the wind.

Kristor blinked and saw through new eyes. *Hello, old friend.*

Not so very old. I still have eyes as sharp as a young hawk's. Now, let us glide through the air, feel the wind on our face, because for now, we own the sky.

Kristor saw through Labrinon's eyes, and saw the ground below. They shared each sensation. He felt the wind on his face, smelled the heady scent of the pine trees, heard the cries of other birds. He had no cares, no worries.

Sometimes he wondered what it would be like to give up his human form and go through life living with his animal guide as the dominating force. There would be no wars, no more fighting, no cares.

You would not want that. Only living on the edge of life? You would die, and then I would be the only one left, Labrinon told him.

Are you saying you would miss me?

Do not let it go to your head.

Warmth flooded through Kristor. *As I would miss you if you ever left me. We are one, even though we are separate. You are a part of me as much as I am a part of you. I doubt the other could survive if one were gone.*

I didn't say I couldn't survive without you. I only said I wouldn't enjoy it as much.

Kristor was smiling when he closed his eyes, going deeper into Labrinon and only letting the sensations go through him. He felt the dips and the rises as Labrinon flew over the land. Then he slept as Labrinon traveled across the night, hunting, watching.

It was early morning when Kristor awakened, sensing he was back where he started. The change began: Wings became arms, the beak his nose, talons were now feet.

"It's cold," he mumbled. The sun was just rising above the horizon.

Next time, shift inside the warmth of a dwelling. Then I will return there. I thought you would want to be close to your conveyance, although it's a poor substitute for flying.

"It's better than running." He quickly dressed, then started the cycle. He liked this form of transportation. He had already input the information into his database. It would be good to recreate it on New Symtaria.

As long as you don't substitute it for me.

"Never." The cycle roared out onto the road.

Did you watch her during the night? Kristor asked.

She met with other women, then retired early. There was a light from her home so she is awake. Do you go to her?

Yes. Kristor felt a strong need to see her again. It was as though he had no choice. And when he pulled into her driveway, he felt a sense that this was where he was supposed to be. But then, he already knew Rianna was his lifemate. He only had to convince her of that fact, and she could be very stubborn.

* * *

Ria walked to the living room when she heard the roar of a motorcycle, but she already knew who would be in her driveway. Her heart fluttered wildly inside her chest, and her palms were damp with perspiration.

She opened the door and stared. My God, he was beautiful. If a man could actually be called beautiful. Sexy, oh, yes, he was that. Broad shoulders, slim hips, muscled thighs. The description she'd given Heath that morning she'd seen Kristor naked in the woods had been accurate. Kristor was definitely tall, dark, and handsome—and then some.

He still wore the same clothes he'd worn yesterday: T-shirt and swim trunks, sandals on his feet. Where had he been?

He placed his helmet on the seat, then looked up as she opened the front door. She stared at him through the dark screen. Their gazes met, held, then he smiled.

Her stomach did flip-flops. "I have orange juice."

"I need to shower." His gaze traveled over her. "Shower with me. Then we'll have orange juice." He strode up the steps, then opened her screen door, and took her into his arms. His mouth closed over hers. Then he was picking her up. She gasped, holding on tight as he carried her toward the bathroom.

She didn't protest. The thought never even crossed her mind. No, all that she thought about was the way it felt to be held in his arms, to have his mouth on hers, to feel his touch bringing her body to life.

He flung open the shower curtain and set her on her feet before reaching for the faucets. While the water warmed, he tugged at the belt on her robe. It came loose, and she shrugged out of it. She was just as eager as Kristor, and wondered if they'd even make it inside the shower.

He removed his shirt as she pulled her gown over her head. His movements stopped as he stared at her nakedness. No man had ever looked at her with so much hunger, so much need. Her body burned in response.

Without taking the time to remove his trunks, he grabbed her to him, fastening his mouth on her breast, sucking the nipple inside, rolling it around on his tongue.

She gasped, then cried out as she flung her head back.

He shoved her things off the counter and into the sink. There were small crashes when her makeup fell to the floor. She didn't care.

Kristor picked her up and set her on the counter, pushing her legs apart, and only then did he step back to remove the rest of his clothes.

Ria wanted to bring her legs together, hide what his eyes feasted on. But maybe she was an exhibitionist at heart, because she forced her legs to stay open. She had a feast of her own as she looked at him, now naked.

"I've never wanted a woman like I want you," he said.

"Nor I a man like I want you."

He scraped his fingers through the tight curls nestled between her legs, then slipped a finger inside her heat. She gasped, arching her back, wanting more.

"Do I please you?"

She bit her bottom lip. "Yes."

"You're wet with passion."

"Then mate with me."

He growled, brought her hips to the edge, then entered her. He arched his back, filling her, grasping her hips, then brought her up so that he held her in place. She wrapped her legs around his waist. He sank deeper, staying in that one spot.

She closed her eyes, and clenched her inner muscles. "I love the way it feels when you're inside me."

"Look at me," he spoke softly. "I want to see when you come."

Fire blazed through her. She opened her eyes when he began to thrust inside her.

In and out.

Deeper, harder.

He groaned. "Ah, by the gods, this is what I've needed all my life, but hadn't known." He stared into her eyes. "You are what I've needed."

Ria didn't have time to think about his words as the heat built inside her. She could feel the blood pounding through her veins.

He set her on the counter again. She leaned back on her hands. He held her in place with one hand, and massaged her breast with the other.

"Now, now," she cried, barely able to keep her eyes open as he'd wanted.

Then her world exploded around her as spasms ripped through her. It was so damned good. Each time with him it was better than the last. She clenched her inner muscles, wanting to feel every inch of him as he continued to stroke her.

Kristor threw his head back and yelled a warrior's cry, holding her tight as he came. She watched his face and saw the effect their lovemaking had on him. Excitement surged through her to know that she had given someone so much pleasure.

Their raspy breathing filled the room. Then she began to laugh. He looked at her, and joined in.

"Good morning," she said.

He grinned, then eased from her body and adjusted the water in the shower. She looked around at her makeup that littered the floor and sink. It was so worth the mess.

He suddenly groaned and went to the floor. It became harder to see as the thick fog filled the room. So much for showering after making love. When the fog cleared, the hawk stared back at her. For some strange reason that made her a little uncomfortable. She grabbed a towel and wrapped it around her as she slipped off the counter.

This was so not cool.

When she opened the bathroom door, the hawk hopped

out. She shut the door and dropped the towel. She could still feel Kristor's warmth. For a moment, she closed her eyes and held it close. God, he made her feel so alive.

She stepped into the shower. The water was just right. It could've been a lot more fun with the two of them.

As soon as she'd showered and dressed, Ria headed for the kitchen. The bird was nowhere around, but she was learning to leave her bedroom window open. The hawk had probably left that way.

She started the coffee and had finished her first cup when she heard a rattle in the bathroom, then the shower running. For a moment, she visualized the water cascading over Kristor's naked body.

The water stopped. She got up and poured a tall glass of orange juice, and herself another cup of coffee. He was dressed in jeans and a gray T-shirt when he joined her. No shoes. There was something a little rumpled about him. The look was sexy as hell.

He downed half the juice in his glass before setting it back down on the table and sitting across from her.

"Do you always shift after having sex?" she asked.

"Most Symtarian males do. We can't help it. It's the intense emotions that come with our release."

"I don't shift." Wouldn't that have surprised the men she'd been with? Talk about giving them the bird.

"It isn't the same with women."

"I don't know. I thought it was pretty intense for me."

He grinned.

She felt the heat rise up her face. No one would think anything could embarrass her after their lovemaking, but the way he looked at her did exactly that. "I need to go into work today," she finally said.

He reached out and took her hand. "I know you haven't come to terms with who you are. It will take time. I will be here to help you find your way."

"And if I never do?"

"You will."

She didn't want to push. Probably because she was afraid of what he might say. Could he force her to return? And what would she do if he did?

Carly had known Donald was wrong. Ria was still her best friend. Kristor was just a passing fancy. When he left, their lives would return to normal. *Pffft*, she and Ria had been friends for practically forever. Nothing would ever change between them. And Donald liked making trouble for people. Sometimes, she thought it was his goal in life.

Carly slowed as she turned the corner. Her smile faded. Kristor's motorcycle was parked in the driveway. This was the second time he'd spent the night with Ria. As long as she'd known her friend, no man had ever spent the night once, let alone twice.

She took a deep, calming breath. It didn't matter. Ria had said they would always be friends, and Carly had never known Ria to lie. Why would she start now?

But Donald's words came back to haunt her. Kristor was from another country. Would Ria fall so much in love with him that she would leave everything to go live wherever the hell he lived?

Icy chills raced up and down her spine at the mere thought of Ria's moving to a foreign country.

Carly continued past Ria's house, and turned another corner. Her hands trembled and she couldn't take a deep breath. If it wasn't for Ria, she would have no friends. If Ria left, she would be all alone.

No! That wouldn't happen. But no matter how many times she repeated that to herself, she couldn't stop the rising panic that clogged her throat.

Carly had no life without Ria, and she knew it. They had been friends for as long as Carly could remember. Ria was the outgoing one, the one who stepped out of her comfort zone, the one who wasn't afraid to try new things, except flying. Ria was the one who made life more interesting, and without her, Carly would die a slow death.

And Carly knew just how pathetic that made her.

Chapter 15

Saying one thing, and doing something else was another. Ria had told Kristor she had to work today, and she did. She might own her own business, but that didn't mean she could take off whenever she wanted. Most of the time, she put in long hours at her shop. And until she'd hired Jeanie and Katie, she rarely took any time off.

Not that she was complaining. She enjoyed grooming. It was all Ria had ever wanted to do. She loved animals, even tiny terror Sukie.

So why was she bored today?

Granted, keeping up with the books was not her favorite thing to do. She looked at the open ledger, and the numbers ran together. She closed her eyes for a moment and massaged her temples.

Maybe she needed to open the window. Her tiny office was located at the back of the shop and it was the size of a small walk-in closet. From here, she ordered supplies and tallied receipts.

The office was dark and dismal as the walls closed in around her. Why hadn't she at least painted it a pretty yellow? She hated looking at the dull brown wall color. It was enough to make anyone depressed.

Deep down, she knew that wasn't her problem. She had

sort of hoped Kristor would drop by. There, she had finally admitted it to herself. She missed him.

But had he stopped by?

Nope, he'd stayed away, and she was surprised at how much she did miss him. Oh, Lord, how could she let him worm his way into her heart? Was this what he meant when he said she would change her mind about going back with him?

No, she hated heights. She had a fear of flying. Flying! Ha! It was a hell of a lot more than that! He was talking about zipping through outer space, and that was so not going to happen. Not just no, but hell no!

It was the sex. That's the only thing she was interested in. Had to be.

She leaned forward and rested her head on the desk and closed her eyes. The sex had been really good. She'd never had multiple orgasms before Kristor came into her life.

You mean you actually did have orgasms before him? Wow, how did I miss that? Shintara interrupted Ria's thoughts.

"I had plenty of orgasms, thank you very much," she said without moving.

You could've fooled me.

"If you're trying your hand at being funny, I'm not laughing."

"Uh, Ria, who are you talking to?" Carly spoke from the doorway.

Ria jerked to a sitting position. "Carly, I didn't hear you." Her laugh came off worse than weak. "I was just thinking out loud."

"Sounded more like you were carrying on a conversation."

Now would be a good time to change the subject. "I thought you were coming over to my house tonight?" Ria came to her feet, smoothing the wrinkles out of her shirt.

"I thought we could run by the grocery store and grab what we needed. Maybe a pizza, and I have a bottle of wine. How's that sound? I know neither one of us wants to cook."

"That sounds terrific." And it did. Anything to break up the monotony of her day and get her mind off Kristor.

Carly smiled. "It will be great catching up. Did you know the bank is planning an Alaskan trip? We're giving a discount if they can get twenty people to go."

"Are you going?"

Carly shook her head. "No way. So far, most of the people who have signed up are elderly. I think as soon as you have Katie trained, we can finally take that cruise we've been wanting to go on, though."

"A cruise sounds really good right now." But running away wouldn't solve Ria's problems. Not thinking about them tonight would at least help. "So what are we doing?" she asked.

Carly shrugged. "We haven't gotten to talk girl stuff in a long time. I had that godawful cold, then you sort of hooked up with your alien. . . ."

Ria hugged her friend's arm. "You're right. Let's watch *Beaches* or *Steel Magnolias*. How's that sound?" And please don't mention my alien again, she silently begged.

Carly grinned. "And cry until we run out of tissues."

They both laughed. Ria realized just how much she valued Carly's friendship. They'd been through nearly everything together. This was exactly what they both needed. It would be great to forget about the fact she was part alien, and a shapeshifter at that.

She studied Carly for a moment. What would her friend say if Ria told her that she had shifted into a frog? She grimaced. Carly would probably cry through a box of tissues and tell Ria not to worry that they would find help for her. Probably even mention the doctors in Dallas.

No, she couldn't tell her without proof, and Ria had already decided never to shift again. Tonight, they would relax, and Ria wouldn't worry about a blasted thing—including being part alien. And she especially wouldn't think about Kristor.

But she couldn't stop the niggle of frustration that Kristor wouldn't be around. Not around to hold her, to caress her, to make passionate love to her.

How's that for taking a trip—a guilt trip. Carly was her friend and they hadn't done a girls' night in a really long time and all Ria could think about was Kristor. They would make up for it tonight.

They went shopping, then met back at Ria's. The pizza was in the oven, and they each had a glass of wine when a motorcycle roared in Ria's driveway. Carly looked at Ria, her eyes accusing.

"I swear, I didn't know he was coming over." Ria still couldn't stop the flutter in her chest as she got up from the sofa and went to the door. She pushed the screen open. "Kristor, hi."

He strode inside, his presence filling the room. Carly came to her feet. Ria looked between the two.

"We were having a girls' night," she told him. It was only fair that she keep her promise to Carly.

Kristor looked between the two women. "I have interrupted." He caressed her face with the back of his hand. "I'll see you tomorrow."

"No," Carly spoke up, a smile pasted on her face. "Stay with us. Unless you're afraid to be in the room with two women who plan to watch a really sappy movie."

He squared his shoulders. "I am a warrior. I fear nothing."

Ria chuckled, but sobered when she looked at Carly. "Are you sure?"

Carly nodded. "More than sure."

Ria felt as if she had the best of both worlds. It was strange, but she wanted Carly to like Kristor. Maybe it was a good thing he'd dropped by the house. It would give Carly a chance to get to know him better.

"The pizza should be ready," Ria said, and made her way to the kitchen.

"How do you like Texas?" Carly asked as she followed.

"It's very different from my home," Kristor said.

Carly reached into the cabinet and brought down the paper plates. "I hope you don't mind paper plates. Ria and I always eat off them when we have a movie night so we don't have to do dishes, but I'll get out the real thing if you'd prefer."

"A paper plate is good."

Carly acted as if Kristor was a guest who wouldn't be around much longer. At least, that's how it seemed to Ria. It was almost as though Carly were marking her territory.

Ria shook her head. She was reading too much into the situation. Carly was doing no such thing. She was only being polite.

They carried their pizza back into the living room. Kristor had chosen an orange soda rather than wine. The guy was getting a serious addiction to orange flavored drinks.

"Where exactly are you from again?" Carly asked.

"New Symtaria. It's very far away."

Ria cast a warning look in Carly's direction, but Carly refused to meet her gaze.

"And what exactly do you do in New Symtaria?"

"I am a warrior, a prince. My father and mother rule the land."

Ria groaned.

Carly's mouth dropped open, then snapped closed. "You're a prince?"

"Yes."

"Then what the hell are you doing in Miller Bend?"

"I've come to take Ria home. She is part Symtarian. A princess in her own right."

Carly was looking at Kristor, but when his words sank in, her head whipped around to Ria. "You knew all this, but you haven't said a word to me? When were you going to say something? When you were boarding the plane?"

Ria cast a look at Kristor that should have had him cringing, but he only looked confused. It seemed as if he wanted to explain he hadn't told Carly that Ria was part alien, or that he was an alien and Symtaria was another planet, but from the look of deep disappointment on Carly's face, he might as well have told her everything.

"I'm not leaving with him," Ria tried to explain.

"Not yet, you mean. I can see the way you look at him. He'll convince you to leave. And I wouldn't blame you." She set her drink on the coffee table and rose. "He's a prince, and you're a princess. It's a fairy tale, and what's a fairy tale without a fairy-tale ending?"

"Being a princess means nothing to me."

Carly gave her a weepy smile. "That's what makes you so special. You've never cared about anything except the excitement of being alive. Not everyone can be like you, though."

Ria stood, taking a step toward Carly, but Carly held up her hand. "No, you really need to go with him. You're a princess." She laughed, but it came out sounding more strangled than anything. "You were meant to be a princess."

"I would've told you, but I was afraid you'd think I was crazy."

"I never did in the past when people would say something about you talking to the voice in your head. I always sided with you." She grabbed her purse. "I'm feeling kind of tired. I think I'll just call it a night."

"Carly?"

"No, it's okay. We'll talk tomorrow."

"Are you sure?"

Her eyes shone with the unmistakable glitter of unshed tears. "I'll be fine."

Ria watched from the door as Carly made her way to her car and got in. Then Ria watched her drive off.

"I like your friend," Kristor said. "And pizza."

Ria turned. She was going to absolutely kill him.

"What?" he asked.

"What? How can you sit there and ask what? It will take me spending all day on the phone with Carly to make sure she understands I'm not leaving with you. Why did you tell her all that?"

"You said you were her friend. I thought you would have explained some things to her."

"I haven't told her anything. And now she's hurt because I didn't." She marched over to her wineglass and downed half the contents.

"Why?"

"Why what?" she asked.

"Why did you not explain anything to her? At least to tell her our relationship is more than what one would think."

"I couldn't."

"Yet, you say she is your best friend."

"I don't just say it, I know it." He was about to drive her to tossing the rest of her drink in his face!

"But you can't tell her this."

"She wouldn't understand."

"Carly is a friend. A friend would understand." He came to his feet and walked over to her. "You must prepare her for when you do leave."

She shook her head. "But I'm not leaving."

He took her glass, setting it on the coffee table. "Are you sure?" He lowered his lips to hers.

Suddenly Ria wasn't so certain. When the kiss ended, she was out of breath. "If you tell anyone else you're here to take me back to New Symtaria, or that I'm an alien, I swear to God I'll castrate you when you're sleeping.

"Castrate?"

"Cut off your balls."

"You would do that?" His expression said he wasn't convinced.

"Just try me."

Carly brushed the tears from her face. Donald had been right. Ria was going to leave with Kristor. He was a freakin' prince, and Ria was a princess. Why the hell wouldn't she leave with him?

Her footsteps were heavy as she trudged up the stairs to her second-floor apartment. She unlocked the door, went inside, dropping her keys on the little table. There was a mirror above it. She stared at her reflection.

Plain Jane, that's what she was. Plain Carly. There was nothing exciting about her. Dull, dishwater-blond hair, dull blue eyes. That was her in a nutshell. Dull. And she had a zit coming up on her chin. For Christ's sake, she was almost thirty. She wasn't supposed to have zits!

She stomped to her bathroom, grabbed the toothpaste and dabbed some on the zit. "Not fair. Not fair at all."

After washing her hands, she went to her refrigerator, brought out her bottle of wine, and took it to the counter. Then she poured the merlot nearly to the rim of her glass.

"This might not be fit for a prince, but it suits me just fine. Dammit, Ria, you were supposed to marry someone from here." Carly took a healthy drink, then topped it off again. This was going to be one of those nights, but right now, she didn't care.

She armed herself with a carton of double-chocolate, fudge ice cream from the freezer, not bothering with a bowl, only a spoon. With her arms loaded, she went to the sofa.

"Life is so unfair," she said as she curled up on the sofa. Ria was cute and sexy. Carly loved her friend. And Ria deserved to be a princess.

On the other hand, Carly was tall, five-eight and a half.

And she still got zits. And now she was going to have a pity party, because she wanted to, and no one could stop her. Not that there was anyone around who would.

She dipped the spoon into the ice cream, and shoved it into her mouth, then squinched her eyes closed when she got cold throat. As soon as it was almost gone, she took a big gulp of the wine. Of course, she'd get cold throat. It was the story of her life.

Ria would leave. She'd be crazy not to. My God, look at Kristor. The guy was a walking, talking, in-the-flesh fantasy.

What did it feel like to be a princess? To have the fairy tale? Carly closed her eyes and tried to imagine a knight in shining armor rescuing her from her dull life. The vision didn't come.

Ria hadn't looked any different. At least, not like Carly imagined a princess would look like. She certainly hadn't put on airs. Not that she ever would. No, Ria would always be Ria.

Carly frowned. Where the hell was New Symtaria? She didn't know of it, and she was a travel agent. It was her job to know all the countries—big and small.

The spoon stopped halfway to her mouth. Her heart pounded like a big bass drum inside her chest.

She'd never heard of New Symtaria, in fact. That was strange. If anyone should know about the country, it would be her. Right? Apparently they had kings and queens there, too.

Unless it was all a scam?

But why scam Ria? Money? No, she didn't have a whole lot. Not that Kristor would know that.

But Ria did have her own business. A thriving business.

Carly had read about men who took advantage of women, stole all their money, then left them practically suicidal, and wondering what they had done wrong.

She came to her feet and marched into the kitchen. She jammed the ice cream back into her apartment-size freezer, and dropped the spoon into the sink. If Kristor was scamming Ria, Carly planned to out him. No one messed with her friend. She went back to the living room, grabbed her wine, and headed for the bedroom where her computer was set up.

New Symtaria. If anyone could find out about this place, it was her. She wasn't a travel agent for nothing!

Chapter 16

R ia opened the door to her parents' house and called out, "Mom, it's me."

She hadn't seen her mom since the night of her parents' party. Sheesh, she was neglecting everyone lately. But her mom had sounded cheerful when Ria phoned earlier. Still, she decided to drop by and visit.

"In the kitchen." Her mother's words traveled to the front of the house.

Her mother was always in the kitchen. Maggie Lancaster had once told Ria that it was her sanctuary. She could think better with flour on her hands.

Ria walked in, then stopped and closed her eyes as she inhaled the aroma of . . . she sniffed . . . homemade rolls. Her mother made them from a starter mix that had been passed down from her mother.

The starter was the most godawful smelling stuff. Once, Ria had been about to throw it out when she was cleaning the refrigerator and her mom walked in. Her mother almost had a heart attack. Ria had been about fourteen at the time, and even now she couldn't understand how something that smelled so bad could make the most mouthwatering rolls.

"Want one?" Maggie asked as she pulled the pan from the oven.

Ria grinned. "Do you even have to ask?"

"Get the butter then."

She opened the refrigerator and grabbed the tub, then a knife from the drawer.

"I've always imagined that when I die and go to heaven, it will smell like your bread, Mom."

"Kris ate six of them last time so I thought I'd make another batch. That's the way to thank a cook, eat what she puts on the table. And he's such a nice, single young man."

Her mother was so subtle—not! "I don't think you've ever had a problem with people not eating what you set out, Mom." Ria decided to ignore the innuendo.

Maggie was thoughtful for a moment. "True. I've always thought everyone had something special they can do in life. For me, it has always been cooking. With you, it's your grooming. You've always had a way with animals."

"Except Sukie."

"That's because Mrs. Miller spoils the mutt as if Sukie was her own child. The dog is cute, but rotten."

Ria spread butter on her roll, watching as it slowly melted. She had to tell her mom sometime. This wasn't something she could keep to herself. And she didn't want to, if the truth be known.

She and her mother had a close relationship. Ria had always told her everything . . . most of the time. And maybe she needed her mom to give her a reason to stay. Kristor was giving her too many reasons to leave.

"Have you ever wondered why I'm good with animals?" She didn't meet her mother's gaze.

Her mother took a bite of her roll, a look of rapture on her face. "The best batch ever."

"You always say that." Ria smiled.

"Because I'm always right."

Maybe today wasn't the day to mention she was part alien. Maybe no day would ever be good. Did she really want her mother to think she was crazy?

"You've always had a special way with animals," her mother said, picking up the conversation. "Remember that little parakeet we bought right after we brought you home? You were only three so you might not remember Fred."

"Fred?" Ria sat straighter. "Yes, I do remember."

"You used to point at him and say *bird talk*. Sometimes I wondered if the bird actually did communicate with you. It was strange." She chuckled, shaking her head. "Nonsense, of course."

But Fred *had* talked to her. There had been silent communication between them, but she had heard the bird's thoughts.

"When that bird died, you cried for hours and hours. It nearly broke my heart."

"It did talk to me, Mom."

Her mother's eyes widened with surprise, then she visibly relaxed. "I'm sure you thought so. Little kids love to play make-believe."

Ria knew there was no turning back. She had to say it. "I'm part alien."

Her mother drew in a sharp breath, then slapped a floured hand to her chest, creating a little puff of flour. "I . . . oh, my . . ."

She suddenly grabbed a dishtowel and wiped at the flour on the front of her shirt.

"Ria, you know better than to say something like that. For a moment, I thought you were serious. I mean, really, what am I to think when you blurt out something like that? I'm sure—"

"Mom," Ria interrupted. "It's true. I'm an alien. At least, part alien."

"It's okay. There are doctors in Dallas. I knew we should've taken you there sooner, but I just didn't want to admit there was something wrong with you." She sniffed, then wiped her eyes with the hem of her apron.

"No, Mom, I'm not crazy. I really am part alien."

Her mom looked around as if hoping it would all go away. Then she said, "I don't think I feel very well."

Ria hurried around the counter. "It will be okay, Mom. I'll explain everything. And don't worry. I'm not crazy." Now that Ria thought about it, crazy might be better.

She took her mother by the hand and led her to the sofa in the living room, then made her sit. Ria continued to hold her hand while she explained everything.

"Kristor is from New Symtaria, a planet of shapeshifting aliens. He's a prince, and I'm a princess, but we're not related. The voice in my head . . ."

Her mother drew in a sharp breath. "I thought you said you didn't hear it anymore?"

"I do. Shintara is my animal guide."

"Shintara?" She sniffed. "You've named it?"

Ria pulled some tissues from the box on the end table and handed them to her mother, who dabbed at her eyes before blowing her nose.

"You said you stopped hearing the voices years ago." Her mother's voice quivered.

"Just one voice, Mom. Shintara is my animal guide. A hawk. That's why I could communicate with the parakeet. And it did talk to me, in its own way."

"My poor baby, we'll get you help, I swear."

"I don't need help, Mom. I really am part alien. I shifted into a frog. Which wasn't the best experience in the world, but I did shift."

"I thought it was a hawk?"

"No, I'm still afraid of flying."

Her mother waved her arms. "Of course, you can't shift into a hawk because you're afraid of flying. It makes perfect sense to me." Her words caught on a half sob. "Why is your father never around at times like this?"

The front door opened and Kristor walked in. Thank God. Now maybe her mother would believe her. She had hoped to break the news to her a little more gently, but had totally screwed everything up.

But Kristor would make it right. "Tell Mom I'm an alien, part alien, that is," she told him.

His face paled and he reached toward his lower regions. "There are no such things as aliens," he said.

Oh, Lord, she'd forgotten about her warning. "No, I promise I won't cut off your"—she glanced at her mom— "any part of your body, but you need to tell Mom the truth. I've explained everything to her. I just need you to confirm it." God, she felt as though the hole was getting deeper and deeper.

"Confirm that you're part alien?"

She breathed a sigh of relief. "Exactly."

He stood taller. "Rianna is part alien."

Her mother sobbed into her hands. "You don't have to lie for her, Kris. I know we have to get her help. Her father and I had hoped she would outgrow the voices and everything. But my poor baby hasn't."

"No, Mom, I'm not lying. See watch, I'll shift."

Ria had sworn she wouldn't shift again, but she had to if she was ever going to convince her mother she wasn't living in a fantasy world.

She closed her eyes. What could she shift into so as not to cause her mother to have a heart attack? A puppy. Yes, that would work. A cute little puppy.

But a puppy would probably piddle on the carpet and it was brand new. That would really upset her mother.

"What are you, dear?" her mother asked.

Ria opened her eyes. "Huh?"

"What have you transformed into?"

"Nothing." She frowned.

Oh, hell, now her mother was placating her. She quickly closed her eyes. She had to think of something.

"What's going on?" Ria's father asked as he came into the living room.

Ria jumped.

"Shh, dear. Ria is . . . is trying . . . to change into a . . ." She sobbed into her tissues. "A hawk! Oh, Ron, she's completely lost her mind. She thinks she's an alien, or a hawk, or something. I don't want men in white coats to lock her away in a cold, sterile institution. What are we going to do?" She jumped from the sofa and ran to him, throwing her arms around his neck.

"There are doctors in Dallas." Her father patted his wife on the back.

"I'm not crazy!" Ria jumped to her feet and began to pace the room. She looked to Kristor for assistance, but he only shrugged. A lot of help he was.

Her mother got her sobs under control, except for a few sniffles and hiccups. She stepped out of her husband's arms and squared her shoulders. "I love you as if I had carried you for nine months. I will never stop loving you." She blew her nose into a tissue. "And we will get you the help you need."

"She's telling you the truth." Kristor walked to Ria and took her hand in his.

"Now listen, young man, we think the world and all of you, but you're only hurting our daughter by encouraging these fantasies and I won't allow it." Her father wore the dark scowl he had used when a boy came to the door to take Ria on a date when she was in high school. It didn't seem to have any effect on Kristor. Not like it had on other dates.

"I'll prove it." Right before Ria closed her eyes, her gaze landed on a pretty figurine of a horse. Without stopping to think about it, she concentrated as hard as she could on a horse.

Whatever she shifted into had to be something her parents couldn't deny. A horse was as good as anything. When the burning sensation started, she had to wonder if she really was doing the right thing. No, she had to do something.

Think horse. Think horse. Think horse.

She collapsed to the sofa, then rolled off, hugging her middle. From a long way off, Ria heard voices.

"What's going on?" her mother asked. "Ron, I'm scared."

"I can't see a damn thing in all this fog," her father said.

"It's going to be all right. Rianna is shifting," Kristor told them.

The burning sensation was strong inside her. She couldn't catch her breath. It was as though she'd been running for a long time.

She stretched her legs out, then her arms. Why the hell had she thought this was the only way she could prove to her parents that she was part alien? Surely there would've been a better way to go about showing them. She could've had Kristor shift. Hell, he did it all the time.

"Ron!"

"There's a horse in our living room," her father said. "What have you done with our daughter?"

Ria blinked several times. Again, she felt as though she looked through someone else's eyes and, in fact, she did. She raised her head and whinnied.

"He's a magician," her mother said, then laughed, but it came out weak at best. "You're a very good one, Kris, but I have to ask you not to bring animals into my house."

"This is Ria," he said. "We are a race of shapeshifting aliens."

"This is not my daughter!" Ron exploded.

Ria walked over to her parents, then nuzzled her mother's arm.

Her mother leaned closer, staring into the eyes of the horse. "Ria? Is that you in there?"

"Helloooo . . ." The front door opened and her mother's best friend, Vickie Jo, walked inside carrying a plate of cookies. "I had the urge to bake and thought you would help me eat a few—" She stumbled to a stop, the plate tilting, and a couple of the cookies toppled to the floor. "You have a horse in your living room. Why is there a horse in your living room, Maggie?" She took a step back.

"No, it is only Ria," Kristor told her. "She has shifted into a horse."

"Ria?" Vickie Jo looked around the room. The plate crashed to the floor right before she ran out the door and across the yard, her arms flapping as if she would take off in flight at any second.

Oh, hell, Ria thought. Vickie Jo might be her mother's best friend but she was also Tilly the dispatcher's friend, too. There was no telling what would be all over town by this afternoon.

You could've been a hawk, Shintara's thoughts filled her. *It would've been easy saying it had flown in through the back door. But no, you had to be a horse.*

Shut up! I certainly don't need your help right now.

I was only stating facts.

Ria closed her eyes and thought about being herself again. The burning began to churn inside her. She went to the floor as hooves became legs and arms. The fog rolled in. She couldn't see. Voices became distant.

The throw on the sofa was gently placed around her and someone picked her up. She blinked, then looked up. Kristor, of course.

"Ria?" her mother tentatively spoke.

"I'm okay, Mom. Just a little woozy."

"Your clothes are on the floor."

And a little bit naked. Thank goodness Kristor had grabbed the throw. She glanced at her father. He looked more dazed than anything.

"I'm sorry, but it was the only way to convince you. As soon as I get dressed, I'll explain everything, I promise." She looked at Kristor. "I can walk." But when he set her on her feet, she wasn't quite as steady as she had thought. It wasn't easy going from human to horse, then back again to human.

Ria managed to scoop up her clothes and head for the bathroom, dressing as quickly as she could. She shuddered to think what Kristor was telling her parents. And why the hell would he tell Mom's friend that she was part alien? His timing was really off the mark.

As soon as she was dressed and had run a brush through her mane—hair—she joined everyone in the living room.

"I don't know how I'm going to explain this to Vickie Jo," her mom said.

"We'll think of something, Mom."

Her mother sucked in a gulp of air and ran to Ria, throwing her arms around her, and pulling her close. "Oh, my poor baby. You're not losing your mind after all."

"No, Mom, I'm just part alien, but I'm not sure which is worse."

Kristor frowned.

Great, now she'd trampled on his feelings.

"I think you'd better start from the beginning." Her father cast a look in Kristor's direction that was more than a little wary.

"Let's all have a seat first," her mother said. "Would you like something to drink or eat? I suppose Vickie Jo's cookies are out of the question now since they're scattered over the carpet."

"Mother, come sit down." Ron patted the cushion next to him on the love seat.

"Yes, I suppose that would be best." Her hands fluttered about her face. Then she smoothed her collar, before placing her hands neatly on her lap.

Ria hated that her parents had to go through this, but they needed to know their daughter was an alien. It wasn't fair to keep it from them.

Kristor sat on the sofa opposite the love seat. Ria sat on it as well, but kept a bit of distance between them. Just being near him made her knees weak.

"We just thought you were a nice young man," her mother said. "We didn't know you were an...an..." She cast pleading eyes upon Ria.

"Alien," Ria spoke softly.

"I didn't even know they existed," she said. "Of course, everyone has heard of Area Fifty-one, and seen sightings of spacecraft, but I always thought it was nonsense. I guess I was wrong." She looked at her husband as if silently asking for his help in understanding.

"Maybe you should start from the beginning," her father said, looking at his daughter.

"I was out running when a hawk landed in front of me on the trail. Then a fog rolled in, and the hawk shifted into Kristor."

"Then what you told Heath was true?" he asked.

She nodded.

Her father turned to Kristor. "Why now? What is your purpose with my daughter?"

"I'm here to take her back to New Symtaria with me," Kristor told him.

Ron's frown deepened, his face turning dark red. "I won't allow it. My daughter's not going anywhere with you, especially to outer space. It's much too far away."

"Dad, it's okay, I'm not planning on leaving. You know how scared I am at the thought of flying."

"True." He relaxed.

"Her life is in danger," Kristor said.

She glared at Kristor. Pulling his danger card out was not *even* fair.

"What!" Her father sat forward.

"Danger?" Her mother's hands began to flutter again.

"Do you have to tell them everything?" Ria hissed.

The corners of Kristor's mouth turned down. "You tell me to say I'm alien, then not to say I'm alien. Then when your mother's friend comes over, you don't like it when I'm honest. Then when I try to explain to your parents, you get angry again. Women are very confusing on Earth."

"At least we agree on one thing," her father said drawing frowns from both the women in his life. He cleared his throat. "Maybe you'd better explain more about the danger Ria is in. I don't like the thought that harm might come to my daughter."

Kristor quickly told her father and mother everything he knew about the rogue Symtarians trying to get rid of the impures. When he finished, her father stood, then went to the window. When he turned back around, his eyes looked sad.

"I always knew you would fall in love and get married. Probably move away. I just never thought it would be to another planet. If it will keep you safe, then you have to go with him."

Chapter 17

Kristor breathed a deep sigh of relief. Good, her father understood the danger Rianna was in and agreed she needed to leave Earth. But when he looked at Rianna, she didn't appear to feel the same way. What was it that she didn't understand? He'd made it all perfectly clear. His patience would not last much longer.

"I'm not going anywhere," Rianna said, crossing her arms in front of her and casting a stubborn look in his direction.

"It doesn't look as if you have a choice," her father told her.

"I can take care of myself," she said.

"Ria, maybe your father and Kristor are right. I certainly don't want any harm coming to you." Maggie dabbed at her eyes with more tissue. "I'll miss my baby. It's not as though you'll be across town. Or a phone call away."

Ria went to her mother and knelt in front of her. "I won't leave you, Mom."

"Are there nice people on New Symtaria?" Ria's mother asked.

Kristor shifted in his seat. Emotion ran high between the two women. He noticed the father didn't look any more comfortable than Kristor felt.

"Rianna is of royal blood. She is a princess."

The mother smiled through her tears. "You always loved

pretending you were a princess when you were . . . were . . . little. You loved fairy tales. Now you have your own."

"Maybe we should leave them alone for a while," Ron said, looking uncomfortable. "This is a lot for Maggie to take in."

Kristor breathed a sigh of relief. "That sounds good." He had a feeling Ron Lancaster didn't know what to do either when women became emotional. He was discovering it was a sickness that affected all men.

Ron went to the refrigerator and opened the door. "I can use something to drink. How about you?"

"Orange soda?"

Ron chuckled. "I think I'll have a beer. I'm in need of something with a little more kick." He handed Kristor an orange soda, grabbed a beer for himself, then shut the door. "Let's continue our discussion in the backyard."

They walked outside to a table and found seats. Kristor popped the tab on his drink and took a long swallow, then waited for the questions that he knew would come. Ron only needed a little more time to digest everything.

"I remember when we first brought Ria home from the orphanage. Maggie and I couldn't have children of our own, but the minute we saw Ria, she stole our hearts. When she toddled over to where we were standing, we knew Ria had chosen us."

Ron took a drink from his beer, then set the bottle on the table. Kristor knew he had more to say, so he waited.

"I went out and bought that silly little parakeet. I named the bird Fred." He laughed. "It was the damnedest thing the way she seemed to communicate with it. I guess now I understand why." He sighed, running his finger through the condensation that had formed on the side of the can. "How much danger is our little girl in?"

"The rogues have killed before. They murdered Ria's biological father. Her mother left her at the orphanage. I think to keep her safe. She later died in a vehicular accident."

"Ah, jeez. That's too bad."

Kristor looked Ron straight in the eye. "The rogues won't be afraid to kill again. Impures don't have the strength or abilities that a pure Symtarian has. Ria would not be safe on her own."

"She's afraid of flying, you know. We thought she would enjoy the air show since she liked birds so much, but there was an accident. The pilot parachuted to safety, but the plane crashed. She had nightmares for a long time. Ria has been afraid of flying ever since. We had to drive whenever we went on vacation."

"She has to have the courage to connect with her animal guide, the hawk. If she doesn't, part of who she is will die."

"Animal guide?"

"When we shift, our animal guide is released. We coexist. If Ria doesn't connect soon, her guide will cease to exist."

"Ria would never intentionally hurt anything. It would destroy her if she did."

"I know." And so, they understood each other.

"Will you help her?"

"Yes."

Ron studied Kristor. Kristor didn't look away, but having Rianna's father study him was uncomfortable. He'd never really met any of the fathers of the women he had mated with in the past. He didn't like the feeling.

"Do you love her?"

"I think we are destined to be together. A Symtarian mates for life."

"Have you convinced Ria of that fact?"

He frowned. "No. She is very willful."

"That she is. Just like her mother. Has a mind of her own. It took me many a month to convince Maggie to marry me." He smiled.

"Are they all this emotional?" Kristor had stayed in the outlying areas on New Symtaria so hadn't been around women or any real length of time. He was finding they were quite confusing.

"This isn't anything, boy. You should be around them when their hormones are raging." He shook his head. "Scary. You want to stay away from them as much as you can. They can heat a pot of water with one scorching look, believe you me."

Kristor glanced toward the house. Not one of his brothers had mentioned this. He would have a long talk with them when he returned. He only hoped it wouldn't be long before he could convince Rianna to leave. He didn't want to resort to force.

Ria handed her mother fresh tissues.

"I'll be okay," her mother said. "I must be almost out of tears." She sniffed again.

"Mom, it will be all right once you have time to think about it."

"I always knew you were special." She suddenly hugged Ria. "My little alien princess. I didn't even know aliens existed, and here I've raised one. I wonder if we'll ever see you again after you leave."

"Mom, I'm not going anywhere."

"But you have to, dear. Kristor said you were in danger. I would rather you go to another planet than to be in danger. Damned rogues! If they touch one hair on your head, I'll give them what for."

Ria laughed. She couldn't help it. Her mother had such a fierce look in her eyes. "I don't have to leave. Not with you and Dad in my corner."

Just as quickly her mother deflated. "But we can't save you from these rogue aliens. We're just not strong enough." She drew in a deep, shuddering breath, then her face paled. "Oh, no, Vickie Jo." She looked at the plate of cookies scattered on the carpet. "She'll tell everyone in town. Then they'll find you and Kristor. I can't let that happen." She grabbed the phone and dialed her friend.

Ria went to the cookies and started cleaning up the mess, but listened as her mother tried to explain that Kristor was actually a magician, a very famous one, and he was trying to keep a low profile.

Ria hoped her mother's lies worked. She carried the plate to the kitchen, dumping the cookies into the trash. She set the plate on the counter and hurried back.

They were still talking. It was another five minutes before her mother hung up. Maggie slumped against the back of the sofa.

"I've never lied in my life. Well, at least, not intentionally."

"Do you think she bought your story?"

"The only alternative is to believe in aliens and that would make her as crazy as—" A guilty flush stole over her cheeks.

"As crazy as me."

"You know I didn't mean it like that. But you have to admit some of the things that have happened over the years have made you seem a little . . . different from others."

"It's okay, Mom. There for a while I thought I was crazy, too."

"It must have been terrible living with that burden. I'm sorry I couldn't help you more."

"You've always been there for me, Mom, and that's all I've ever wanted."

"Does it hurt?"

"Hurt?"

"Shifting into a horse."

"It's strange. Very uncomfortable. It burns, and it's hard to breathe."

"I always wanted to be a horse," her mother said with a dreamy expression.

Ria couldn't help it, she laughed. "You would make a great shapeshifting alien, Mom."

"Do you think we would ever get to visit your planet?

Your father and I had planned on taking a trip next year. Of course, we had been thinking more along the lines of a cruise or a trip to an exotic island."

Ria should've known it would make no difference to her parents that she was part alien. Their love had always been unwavering. She only hoped Carly would feel the same way when she finally told her.

Ria had a feeling it wouldn't be quite so easy with her friend. Maybe if she took things just a little slower, Carly would be more accepting.

Cutting short their movie night hadn't been good. Carly might not be ready to listen to anything Ria said that might remotely have to do with Kristor. But Ria had to try. She didn't have a choice.

Carly had been searching for a place called New Symtaria until her eyes were starting to cross. She had even called in sick today so she could keep looking. But so far, she'd gotten nowhere.

Her legs trembled when she pushed away from the computer. She stumbled into the kitchen to put on a pot of coffee, and heat a danish in the microwave.

She had to face facts: There was no New Symtaria. Kristor was an alien all right. An illegal alien.

She grabbed the counter for support when she realized exactly what was happening. Kristor needed a green card so he could stay in the country. That had to be it. That's why he was seducing Ria.

Not that Ria wasn't a catch. Her friend was hot.

But Kristor was using Ria's vulnerability. Really, Ria would believe anything. She was too gullible, too trusting. Hadn't she told everyone that Kristor was an alien from another planet?

Aliens did not exist. Scams existed. Carly was constantly reading about them on the Internet. How many times a day did she get e-mails to enlarge her penis? Uh, yeah, whatever.

Or the ones where she had won a lottery. Like that was ever going to happen. No, Kristor was scamming her friend and Carly was about to put a stop to it.

But how? She wasn't a detective. She didn't even read mysteries. Nor had she ever played the game of Clue.

She looked at the phone. She hesitated, then went over to it and picked it up. Her stomach churned. God, she really hated doing this, but there was one person who would know what to do. She wanted to puke.

She looked up the number, then called Donald.

"Hello," he said after the third ring.

"Donald, this is Carly. I have a problem." If Ria ever found out, she would kill her.

"So? I'm not a therapist. Call your parents or someone who cares."

"It's not about me."

"Then who is it about? Not that it will make much difference."

"Ria. It's about Ria and Kristor."

Silence.

Then, "What kind of problem?" he asked, a hard edge creeping into his voice.

"There is no New Symtaria. That's where Kristor said he was from. I was up all night long searching on the Internet. I even contacted others in the travel business. They've never heard of it, either. It doesn't exist."

"It still has nothing to do with me, and maybe it'll teach her a valuable lesson. Good-bye."

"No, don't hang up!"

"Damn, did you have to yell in my ear?"

"Kristor said he was from New Symtaria. Don't you see? He's lying. He's only after her money or a green card or something. She doesn't deserve this and you know it, dammit!"

The silence was different this time. Carly waited.

"You're sure he said he was from this New Symtaria place?" he finally asked.

"Positive. And there's more." She bit her bottom lip, wondering how much she should tell Donald.

"How much more?" His words came across hard, steely.

She said a quick silent prayer for forgiveness. "They're sleeping together. I think he's scamming Ria." She could almost feel Donald's grip getting tighter and tighter on the phone.

"They're sleeping together?"

Carly knew Donald had dated Ria for a few months and had to settle for kisses. Now here was Kristor, and they had only known each other for a short time, yet they were already sleeping together.

Not good.

"Maybe I shouldn't have drawn you into this."

"No, you did the right thing. I'm as worried about her as you."

"What should I do? I don't think she'll listen to me." And that really hurt, but she was pretty sure Ria was falling head over heels in love with a scam artist.

"Call immigration. Tell them what you told me."

She walked to the sofa and plopped down. "Isn't that a little drastic?" Kristor had seemed nice. What if she was wrong? Ria would never forgive her.

"Do you want to take the chance that he could destroy her emotionally? If he is here legally, then no harm. But what if he is out to scam her? What if he takes everything away that she's worked so hard to get? Then how will you feel?"

He was right, of course. "Okay, I'll do it."

"Try to be around Ria as much as possible, too."

"Are you sure? What if I accidentally say something that alerts Kristor to the fact I'm on to him?"

"You're not stupid, Carly. Just be careful what you do and say. But if you really want to protect Ria, then be there for her. Find out as much information as you can. For Ria."

"For Ria." Yes, she would do anything for her friend.

They hung up, with Carly agreeing to give Donald updates

on the situation. If she was wrong, Ria would hate her for the rest of Carly's life.

She called information, then waited for the number of immigration.

"Please let me be doing the right thing," she prayed.

Chapter 18

Ria opened the door to the travel agency and walked inside. Empty. Carly must be in the back.

She was walking down the short hallway when Carly stepped from the supply closet holding a handful of pens. Her friend looked up, screamed, and threw the pens in the air.

"I'm sorry. I didn't mean to scare you. I figured you heard the bell jingle." Ria stooped and started picking up the pens. When Carly continued to stand frozen to the spot, Ria looked up. "Are you okay?"

Carly jumped into action, scrambling to scoop up the pens. "Yes, fine. Why wouldn't I be? It's like you said, you startled me."

No, something wasn't right. Carly dropped about half the pens she'd picked up because her hands were shaking so badly. She grabbed a couple more, then stood, hurrying to her desk. Ria followed, wondering what exactly was going on with her friend.

After Carly shoved the pens into a cup, she smoothed her hands over the front of her slacks. "So, why are you here? I mean, nothing is wrong is it?"

Oh, yeah, she was acting really weird. "No, nothing is wrong with me." Ria had serious doubts about Carly, though.

"Good." She sat down, leaning her hands on the desk, then quickly moving them to her lap.

"I thought maybe you'd want to come over tonight. We never did get to finish our girls' night out."

"Has Kristor left town?"

"No. Why?"

"Oh, no reason. I only wondered when he would be leaving town. You two seemed pretty hot and heavy." She pursed her lips.

Could Carly be jealous? Ria knew Carly didn't have a lot of friends. Her family was so boisterous that she often became invisible. So much so that she rarely went anywhere by herself. Carly had always been there for Ria, though, and she wouldn't do anything to hurt her best friend's feelings.

Ria chose her words carefully. "I like him."

Carly took a pencil out of the cup and pressed her thumb against the eraser. "I'm sure he's nice enough. I don't want you to get hurt when he does leave."

"But you're still my best friend, and always will be." Did Carly blush?

"We don't have to do the girls' night out or anything." Her shoulders sagged. "Besides, I planned to work late tonight. I need to catch up on some things."

"I want to do something. My assistant is running the shop by herself tomorrow with Jeanie. Instead of staying in and watching a movie, let's go into the city and shop. We haven't been in a long time."

"Really?"

Ria grinned. "Yes, really."

"I'd like that."

"I'll pick you up around ten in the morning?"

"That sounds good."

Ria left the travel agency and walked back to her shop. She had a puppy pedicure in about thirty minutes. But as she walked back, she couldn't help but wonder what in the world was going on with Carly.

Maybe she was still upset their girls' night out had been interrupted. Carly had always been a little clingy, and then along comes Kristor. Then Ria had neglected their friendship. Another guilt trip. They were getting tiresome.

But all that was about to change. She had a plan: Neil, the sheriff's deputy. He liked Carly. Ria was about to turn up the burner beneath their feet.

She was doing it for Carly's own good. Not that she had a choice. What if the rogues came after her? Ria twined her fingers together. It could get dangerous for Carly to even be around her. No way would Ria ever intentionally put Carly in harm's way.

When had life gotten so complicated?

She opened the door to her shop. Kristor was talking to Jeanie, half sitting on the corner of her desk. Jeanie laughed at something Kristor said. They both looked up when she opened the door and walked into the shop.

That's when Ria realized she knew exactly when her life had gotten so complicated. But she supposed, in a way, it was a good complication. At least, now she knew who she was. Or better, *what* she was. She wasn't crazy. Only part alien. One who was apparently in danger from rogue aliens.

"I missed you," Kristor said as he slowly came to his feet.

Jeanie looked between the two of them, then cleared her throat. "Uh, I'm taking off now to look at more houses, but if it gets busy, I'll have my cell. You sure it's okay?"

"I told you this morning it would be fine."

"I'll be back in about an hour."

As soon as she was gone, Ria downed her head and hurried to the back. "I have a puppy pedicure in about ten minutes. I need to get ready for it." Yeah, like get out the clippers. That should take her a good thirty seconds.

She heard his heavier footsteps behind her and realized they would be all alone in the back. Bad move! But it didn't stop her body from tingling to awareness. They would probably have time for a quickie.

Christ, she was pathetic. Ten minutes would not be nearly long enough to satisfy her. Besides, she certainly didn't want to give people something more to talk about. They had enough gossip to fuel them the rest of the year.

At least her mom's friend hadn't told everyone Kristor was an alien. But it was all over town he was some kind of famous magician traveling incognito.

She turned around and faced Kristor, ready to tell him that she had a business to run, but she forgot what she was going to say when he took her into his arms and kissed her. The heat of his lips scorched downward, making her toes curl. It was the kind of heat that burned in all the right places, and the only scars it would leave would be the ones on her heart.

She knew he wanted her to leave with him, but she shuddered with fear every time she even thought about shifting into something that could fly. Visions of when she was a child and the airplane exploding at the air show sent shivers down her spine. She'd had nightmares for months, and could still smell the strong odor of the fuel, and the burning plane.

And even Kristor's kisses couldn't block out the memory.

He ended the kiss but wouldn't let her pull out of his arms. "Leave with me. Let me show you my world."

"I can't."

"I won't let any harm come to you."

"This is my home."

He looked her in the eyes. "I'll give you a week, then I will have to leave."

Tears filled her eyes. "I don't want you to go." She caressed his face.

"I have to. It's not a choice. My time here is almost up."

"I'll miss you."

His eyebrows drew together. "I won't leave without you. I cannot protect you if I'm not here. I was only letting you know *when* we would leave."

She pushed away from him. "I beg your pardon. I've told

you I'm not leaving. You can't make me." She crossed her arms and raised her chin.

He pulled her back into his arms, nuzzling her neck with his lips. "You think not?"

Her body turned to mush as he started an aching need inside her, but just as quickly, she caught on to his game. "Oh, no, seducing me won't work. When you get on that spacecraft, or whatever brought you here, you'll be the only one on it." She put distance between them.

He planted his hands on his hips and glared at her. "You will leave with me, even if I have to throw you over my shoulder and force you."

"You don't scare me!"

"I have your parents' approval."

She opened her mouth, then snapped it closed. They had said it would be safer if she left with Kristor. It didn't matter. "They're confused."

"No, they're not. They were reasonable. Unlike some people I know."

"I'm not leaving."

"You better start learning to face your fears. In a week, you won't have a choice."

The bell over the door tinkled. "I won't change my mind," she said as she hurried past him.

"I don't care if you do or not. Just be prepared to leave. One week."

When she parted the curtains and stepped out, her next customer was waiting. When she took Sir Otis to the back, Kristor was gone. Good. She was furious that he thought he could force her to leave. What was he—a freakin' caveman? He'd better think again if he thought she wouldn't raise hell at being forced to do anything. If he wanted a fight, she'd give it to him!

Her gaze fell on the back door. It was slightly ajar. She marched over and locked it. Not that it would keep him out if he really wanted to come in. It made her feel better, though. She began working on the black lab, and tried not to think about zooming through space. The mere thought made her queasy.

No, Kristor could think all he wanted about her leaving, but it was not going to happen. She had a business to run and she wasn't about to give it up. Her parents were here. Her friends. What would the Women's League do without her? Okay, maybe they would continue on, and probably not even notice she wasn't there. Hell, they'd probably volunteer her for a bunch of stuff, and then wonder why the hell she didn't show up.

It didn't matter. She didn't want to go anywhere. Kristor would just have to leave without her.

Ria paused when it hit her that Kristor was leaving. What the hell would she do when he left?

Tears filled her eyes. How could she have started to like him so much in such a short time? It was the sex. Good Lord, she'd never had orgasms like the ones she'd had with him. It was like riding a roller coaster at breakneck speed to that last big downhill dip that took her breath away.

"I can't leave with him just because the sex is good, Sir Otis."

Sir Otis licked her face as she clipped a nail. Bleh! It was a big, sloppy, wet-tongue lick.

"Thanks, but I can do without your kisses." She grabbed a towel and wiped his slobber off her face.

Really, what did she know about Kristor? He liked anything with an orange taste, and couldn't stand coffee. He was good with Sukie, and he'd helped get Fluffy out of the tree. He played a hell of a game of flag football. Her parents liked him. He could move objects with his mind. . . .

And he made her feel like she was the only woman in the room, even when bombshell Mary Ann came on to him. And he had a nice laugh.

"What the hell am I doing? I can't leave with him."

And why not? Shintara asked. *Everything you've mentioned is a good enough reason to go. What is really keeping you here?*

"Have you forgotten I have a business, a home, friends, parents who love me? Or did you only hear the things you wanted to hear?"

You'll never be satisfied with anyone else. Kristor is your soul mate.

"Pffft, you don't know what you're talking about. We barely know each other. How the hell can we be soul mates?"

You only have to listen to your heart.

She finished clipping the last nail. Was it that simple? Just listen to her heart. It sounded easy, but . . . Wait a minute. "I read that in *Cosmo* last month. They did an article on soul mates. You're plagiarizing them."

Does it matter? You thought everything in the article made sense. Now you've found your soul mate and you'll let him slip away. Never see him again.

"That's not what you're worried about. You only want me to shift into a hawk."

It's true, but do you blame me? Shintara coughed. *I grow weaker every day. Soon, I won't be around. It will be as if . . . as if I never existed.*

Was she getting weaker? What would it be like to never hear her animal guide's voice? To have a dead hawk soul living inside her?

Eww.

She mentally shook her head. Could she live with the guilt? Could she . . . Suspicion filled her. "You're lying. You are not getting weaker."

How would you know? You never seem to miss me when I don't voice my thoughts. You don't care about me.

"That's not true. I do care about you," she admitted.

Then shift.

"I can't."

It won't be as bad as you think. Sort of like riding a bicycle.

"I always fell off my bike."

But at least you never gave up. You always got back on. And remember what it felt like to have the wind on your face? It's like when you run now.

She brushed Sir Otis, running the bristles through the dog's thick coat. He would need a trim soon.

You're not concentrating.

"I'm trying not to," she mumbled. Ria felt bad that she didn't have the courage to shift. "I'll try," she finally said, then wondered why she'd said she would.

When?

"I don't know."

The bell jingled.

A reprieve, although Ria had a feeling it would only be temporary. Shintara had once kept her up all night because she'd wanted to talk about something that bothered her. She only hoped she didn't decide to do that again.

Ria laid the brush down and escorted Sir Otis out. She didn't bother with a kerchief. Sir Otis ate everything. He was only a couple of years old and still playful, mischievous, and into everything. She did give him a dog cookie, which he practically swallowed whole. The dog and his owner left a few minutes later.

She was alone again, and with enough time until her next appointment to wonder what in the world she was going to do. It was one thing to be part alien, and another thing to go live on an alien planet.

Chapter 19

Ria was glad she had made Carly go shopping. They both needed today. Carly needed it so she would know that they were still best friends, and Ria so that she could get her head screwed on straight.

Sure, Ria could probably start her own business on New Symtaria. What better place to have an animal grooming shop than on a planet where everyone shifted into animals? She could make a fortune.

Her only problem would be getting a loan. Their small town bank was progressive, but she was pretty sure her loan officer would consider it high risk. What would happen if she defaulted? They certainly couldn't foreclose.

And even though Kristor had told Ria she was a princess, she was almost certain it would turn out to be an empty title. It wasn't likely that she had a castle and a trunkful of gold. No, she was much better off right where she was.

"You're miles away," Carly said.

Startled, Ria looked around. She remembered she was waiting for Carly to try on an outfit that Ria had to practically force on her.

Ria smiled. "More like a zillion miles." When Carly looked confused, Ria laughed. Then she got a good look at her friend.

"Wow!" The snug black jeans rode low on Carly's hips

and the white top hugged her curves, veeing low in front to show the swell of her breasts and short enough that her belly button winked.

Carly blushed. "Wow? Really?"

"Oh, yeah. Really wow."

Carly turned and faced the mirror, then blinked. "Good Lord," she breathed. "Ria, I look . . . so different. This isn't me. I feel as though I'm looking at someone I've never met."

Ria walked up behind her. "You look sexy as hell. This is the woman you should've met a long time ago. I've been trying to get you to dress like this for years, but all you ever wear are dull brown clothes. You remind me of a little mouse."

"But my brothers would kill me if they saw me dressed like this."

"Because they have some mistaken idea that you should be forever pure. Look at the women they date, for pity's sake. They wear a lot less than what you're wearing right now."

"You're right, they do. And my brothers all act like idiots when they come around. Maybe I should stop caring about what they think."

"That's the attitude! Finally!"

Carly turned to the side and ran her hands over the top, tugging at the hem. "I look so tall, though. Someone like me shouldn't wear heels."

"Neil is tall."

She frowned. "What does that have to do with anything?"

"You like him, but you don't feel confident around him. When he sees you dressed like this, believe me, his eyes will pop."

Carly's shoulders slumped. "You're just saying that because you're my friend." She turned to the other side. "I don't know, I'm just not sure about this new look."

Was she blind? Apparently. Ria looked around, and spotted a couple of hotties in business suits walking down the sidewalk. She dragged Carly over to the window.

"What are you doing?"

"A test." She knocked on the window. The men stopped and looked at her. Ria pulled Carly from behind, waving her hand in front of her.

One guy grinned. The other rushed toward the door.

"Ria, what have you done?"

Oops. She hadn't expected quite this kind of reaction. The guy opened the door and rushed over, sliding to a stop on the tiled floor.

"Can I have your phone number? I mean, was that some new way to ask a guy out? It worked." He grinned.

Carly stepped closer and whispered, "Do something, Ria."

"Actually, uh, my friend wanted a man's opinion to see if her husband might like what she has on."

His face fell. "Oh, you're married." He brightened. "Ever wanted to have an affair?"

"No," Carly said over Ria's shoulder.

"Opinion?" Ria asked again.

He grinned and Ria wondered if she shouldn't at least get the guy's number for Carly, but then thought about the wishful look she'd seen in Neil's eyes. No, that wouldn't be right, and she wouldn't do that to him.

"Hot. If she models that in front of her husband, expect to be in bed in under ten." He turned his attention to Ria.

"We're both married," she quickly told him.

"Just my luck." He smiled once more, winked, then joined his friend on the sidewalk.

"I can't believe you just did that," Carly said.

"I was tired of you not believing me. Now, will you buy the outfit?"

Carly walked back over to the mirror and looked at herself from all angles. "I always thought I was too tall."

"I'd kill for legs like yours."

"And Neil will like this look?"

"Oh, yeah."

Carly took a deep breath. "Then I'll buy it."

When Carly went into the cubicle to change back to her street clothes, Ria came to a decision and made a call. This was not distancing herself from Kristor, but she needed his help. They talked for a few minutes. She was just saying good-bye when Carly stepped back out.

"Mom." Ria smiled and waved the cell before dropping it back into her purse. A small lie, but it was for a worthy cause.

They shopped some more, then chose a tea room for lunch. The frilly atmosphere was the perfect place. There were white Christmas lights draped through a grapevine edging the ceiling, rather than molding, and around fake trees. The tables were covered with red cloths with little bouquets of dried roses, and the room smelled like sweet potpourri.

The waitress showed them to a corner table beneath an alcove, then gave them a couple of menus. After she left, Ria inhaled. "Ginger spice. Isn't it wonderful?"

"We haven't been here in a long time," Carly said. "It's very relaxing."

"Mom and I came a few weeks ago. I can't get enough of their flavored teas."

They decided on what they wanted, then placed their order. Ria completely and totally relaxed as she drank in the Victorian surroundings.

"So, what is going on with you and Kristor?"

Sucker-punched. "Going on?"

Carly raised her eyebrows. "Don't play coy."

"I don't know," she answered truthfully.

"But you like him."

"Yes, I do. If the circumstances were right, he'd be the ideal man."

"And they're not?"

Ria shook her head. "He wants me to leave with him. Go back to his . . . home. He's leaving next week."

Carly drew in a sharp breath. "You're not, though."

Ria didn't say anything.

"You haven't known him long. Please say you won't go

without letting me know. He could be here illegally or something."

Here illegally? That was pretty much a gimme.

"I promise you'll be the first to know if I decide to leave." She really hated that she might have ruined their outing, but she wanted to prepare Carly for anything. Or was she preparing herself?

"She's in the bathroom so I can't talk long," Carly told Donald. "Kristor is leaving next week, and Ria might go with him. We can't let her. Not until we know more about this guy."

"You called immigration, right?"

"Yes. I already told you that. They acted like they were bored and underpaid." She frowned. They probably were. "Maybe I shouldn't have hinted rather broadly that Kristor was an alien from another planet."

"Why the hell would you do that?"

"I was desperate for a response from them and I thought they might pay more attention."

His sigh came across the phone. "I'll see if I can't be a little more persuasive. Stay close to her, and find out everything you can about this guy."

"I've gotta go, here comes Ria." She snapped her cell closed and dropped it back in her purse. "Moms." She chuckled, knowing it came out sounding strained.

"Let's pay the bill, then run get a manicure and pedicure," Ria said. "I feel the need for more pampering."

"I'm all for that."

Carly needed something to relax her jangled nerves. She was not about to let her friend leave town with a man from God-knows-where, to an imaginary country just so he could murder her or something. Even if it meant that what she was doing would end their friendship, she was willing to take that chance. Ria meant too much to her.

There was a place in the mall that took walk-ins. They

were lucky and got right in. Maybe it would settle her nerves. What if Ria never spoke to her again? Her stomach did flip-flops just thinking about it. She glanced at Ria. What was she thinking? Did Ria suspect that her best friend had notified the authorities that Kristor might be here illegally? She didn't look as though she did.

Ria eyed Carly out of the corner of her eye. She was starting to act a little funny again. Kind of nervous. Ria wondered what was going on with her.

But then, maybe she was just anxious about wearing her new clothes in public. The girl had looked seriously hot, though.

"What would you ladies like done today?" the receptionist asked.

Ria turned her attention away from Carly and glanced at the woman's nametag: DEBBIE. "We'd like the works, Debbie. Manicure, pedicure, and eyebrow waxing."

"I'm not sure about the eyebrow waxing, Ria." Carly looked skeptical.

"It doesn't hurt." Okay, another small white lie. But Carly was looking bushy. Probably because she'd never had them plucked or waxed.

"You'll barely feel a thing," Debbie agreed. "Your eyebrows really need a trim."

"Well, okay."

Ria breathed a silent sigh of relief. "Let's do the wax first." Might as well get it out of the way. By the time Carly finished with her manicure and pedicure, maybe she would have forgotten about the waxing.

They followed Debbie to a chair in the back and Carly made herself comfortable. Debbie spread the sticky solution around the eyebrows and in between.

"That's warm," Carly said. "Kind of nice."

When Carly closed her eyes, Debbie and Ria exchanged looks. Co-conspirators. Debbie smoothed on the little pink pads, pressing them down nice and firm.

"Ready?" Debbie asked.

Before Carly could ask ready for what, Debbie pulled the first pad off. Carly's mouth dropped open and she sucked in air, but before she could say anything, Debbie jerked on the other pad.

Carly glared at Ria. "You said it wouldn't hurt!"

"It doesn't, if you're not a bushman."

"I just need to do a little plucking," Debbie said, holding up a pair of tweezers.

"It will be so worth it. I promise."

"Pluck you," Carly growled, but laid back and closed her eyes, wincing as Debbie shaped her eyebrows.

But the transformation was unbelievable. Ria had tried to talk Carly into doing this years ago, but she always refused, wanting to keep her look natural. It was another lie one of her dumbass brothers had told her: That natural was the best look.

Maybe the thought that Neil liked her had changed her mind, and that's why Carly wasn't protesting overly much.

Ria parked in front of her house, put the car in park, and turned the key off.

"You mean you're not tired of my company yet?" Carly asked.

"Never. I have plans."

"What kind of plans?" Carly's smile slipped.

"Good plans. Trust me."

"The last time I trusted you . . ."

"Carly!"

"Okay, okay." She laughed.

"And bring in the bag with your new clothes."

Carly groaned. Ria only hoped she would thank her in the morning.

They went inside, taking the packages to the bedroom. Ria glanced at the clock. They had an hour. "Go ahead and change into the black jeans and that little white top."

"And what will you be doing?"

"I'm changing, too."

"Oh, we're going out together?"

"Yes."

Carly relaxed and smiled. "A whole day together. We haven't done that in a long time."

Ria pushed her toward the bathroom, then hurried to the kitchen and poured two glasses of courage—merlot, to be exact. She wanted her friend nice and relaxed for their evening out. Yeah, she knew Carly thought they would be alone, and her friend might want to kill her when she learned the truth, but it was worth taking the chance to see Carly finally happy with a guy.

When she returned to her bedroom, Carly was just coming out of the bathroom.

"You really look hot," Ria said and handed her one of the glasses.

Carly faced the full-length mirror. "Wow, I do look pretty good. Who would've thought waxing your eyebrows could make that big of a transformation?"

"How many years have I been trying to tell you that?"

"Okay, okay, you were right and I was wrong. Correction—my brothers were wrong."

"Now sit." She motioned toward a chair.

"Why?"

"Have I killed you yet?"

"No, but there was the time you convinced me we could rappel off the side of that mountain."

Ria frowned. "It wasn't a mountain, only a little hill. And I really thought I had the rope anchored pretty good."

"You didn't."

"Duh. I realized that when you made it to the bottom in about two seconds."

"I sprained both my ankles."

"Bruised, not sprained. Big difference. I said I was sorry,

and I waited on you for a month. And I know your ankles were a lot better after the first week."

"It was nice having a servant, though."

"Sit," Ria ordered.

"Okay, okay." Carly walked over and sat in the chair. "No hot wax."

"Not even a little bit. I promise. You'll like what I'm going to do. Now, drink your wine and relax."

She went to the bathroom and gathered everything she would need, then piled it all on the dresser. Carly took another drink of wine, then Ria took the glass from her and set it down, but within reach.

"Close your eyes."

Carly hesitated, then closed them.

Ria began rubbing moisturizer on Carly's face.

"That feels good. It smells nice, too."

"You need to moisturize your face every morning and night."

"I don't have wrinkles."

"You don't want to get any either, do you?"

"This will stop wrinkles?"

"It will help." She handed her the glass of wine. "Drink."

Carly took a drink, then handed her back the glass.

Foundation, drink, blush, drink, then powder. Ria studied her handiwork. Not bad. Carly's complexion was evened out now.

Ria still couldn't believe she was letting her do all this. Never once had Carly wanted to do girly things like makeup. Maybe she was mellowing. Must be from all the times they watched *Beaches* and *Steel Magnolias*.

"Can I look?"

"Not yet."

Smoky eye shadow, dark brown eyeliner, and then mascara. And the final stroke from the artist's brush, deep red lipstick. Ria stepped back. "Open your eyes."

Carly did as she asked.

Ria's eyes widened. She wasn't sure what she'd expected but holy cat shit, it wasn't quite this.

"What?" Carly asked. She turned in her chair until she faced the mirror again. She stared at her reflection in the mirror above the dresser. "Is that me? Really me?"

"Oh, yeah." Ria nibbled her bottom lip. "Do you like it?"

"Like it? Do you need to even ask? Crap, why didn't I let you do this years ago?"

"Because you grew up surrounded by brothers who tried to make you think being a girl was silly, and that women who look like you do now couldn't possibly have a brain."

"You're absolutely right. I just never realized how wrong they were."

Ria handed her the glass of wine.

"Isn't this yours?"

"Drink it. I'm going to the bathroom to change and then we'll be ready. I can't drink and drive."

"Oh, yeah. I feel like I'm doing all the taking. What are you getting out of all this?"

Ria chuckled. "Don't you know? Friends enjoy giving. Besides, you're always doing things for me. I'm not keeping score."

"Then get changed. I'm ready to party."

Ria grabbed the bag with her new clothes and hurried to the bathroom to change. She only hoped Carly was ready for what Ria had planned.

Chapter 20

"I feel very mellow," Carly said. "I shouldn't have drunk so much wine." She snorted, then quickly covered her mouth. "Get it? I might get drunk if I drunk too much wine." She frowned. "No, that isn't right. Odd, it was funnier when it was still in my head."

Oh, great, she'd gotten Carly loopy. Deep breath. All was not lost. The first drink or so always made Carly tipsy, but it never lasted for some strange reason. She said it was because her grandfather had been a bootlegger, and a little alcohol ran through her veins.

Ria took the glass of wine away from her. "Just remember, you look hot." Carly didn't say anything. Was she losing her confidence? "Say it."

"What?"

"That you look hot."

Carly eyed her. "You look hot."

Ria shook her head. "Not me. You. Say, 'I look hot.'"

"I look hot."

"With more conviction."

Carly stood tall, squared her shoulders, and raised her chin. "I look hot!"

"That's better."

A car door slammed.

"Our ride's here," Ria said.

"Ride?"

"Don't hate me."

"Ria! What did you do?" Carly looked around the room as if she would turn and run, but Ria grabbed her arm.

"Neil is your date. You can do this. You look hot. We're just going out to dinner. No biggie. I'll be there with you." She squeezed her hand for reassurance.

"Ria," she whimpered.

"Repeat it: I am hot," Ria frantically whispered.

"I am hot, I am hot, I am hot."

"Okay, now paste a smile on your face and I'll open the door and let them in."

"I can't do this," she whispered.

"Look me in the eyes." When she did, Ria took Carly by the shoulders. "You can do this."

She nodded, took a deep breath, and repeated, "I can do this."

Ria breathed a sigh of relief and hurried to open the door. "Kristor, Neil, please, come in."

Ria held her breath, looking from Carly, then back to Neil.

"Carly?" Neil asked.

Carly's shoulders slumped. "You got roped into the blind date, too, I see. Hey, it's okay if you want to bail."

He shook his head. "Nope, I knew exactly who I was going out with tonight. You just look different. I've always thought you were beautiful, but now you're like—wow."

Ria grinned. She had a feeling that was the most Neil had ever said to Carly, or any girl for that matter, but it was exactly what Carly needed to hear.

She glanced Kristor's way. He studied her. "Are we ready to leave?" she asked with false cheerfulness.

They took Neil's car to the restaurant so that left Ria and Kristor in the back. Her and Kristor's first real date, and Ria realized she was a little nervous. The last time she'd been with Kristor, he'd given her an ultimatum—and her answer was still no, she wouldn't leave with him.

Then why did you want to make sure Carly would be taken care of if you weren't planning on leaving? Shintara asked.

That is so not the reason. Neil likes Carly and she likes him. Since it would've taken them forever to get together, I nudged the relationship a little.

Yeah, right.

Shush!

The only reason she had gotten them together was because they liked each other, and that was the only reason. Shintara was only trying to get her to shift into a hawk. Ria wasn't ready.

Don't forget your promise, Shintara said.

I only promised I would try to overcome my fear. Her hands began to sweat at the thought of shifting again.

Kristor reached across the seat and squeezed her hand. "Tonight we won't think about anything except enjoying each other's company."

Had he read her mind? Heard her conversation with Shintara? No, of course, he hadn't.

He lightly rubbed his thumb over the palm of her hand. Her body tingled and she found herself wanting more. The way he looked at her, she kind of thought he might, too. It would be difficult for her when he left. No man had ever made her feel the way Kristor did.

They arrived at the restaurant, and after they went inside, and the waitress seated them, Neil talked the girls into trying an Italian margarita. Kristor chose his usual orange soda, even when the waiter gave him a funny look. Neil had iced sweet tea since he was driving.

"The restaurant is beautiful. I love the Tuscan look," Carly shyly spoke up.

"Have you ever been to Italy?" Neil asked.

She shook her head. "I've never left Texas."

"You're a travel agent. I figured you'd traveled all over the place before I moved back."

"She'd love to, but we've never had the time to go," Ria said. "At least, not at the same time. I've been busy starting my business. Then when I could go, she's had something to do."

"But it never stopped us from dreaming," Carly said.

"Maybe we can manage a trip sometime," Neil suggested. "My hours are a little more flexible, and I would love the chance to travel. I bet you know a lot of places that would be great to visit."

"Oh, uh, I . . ." Carly blushed as she looked around the table at everyone.

"Sorry," Neil quickly spoke up. "I guess I'm moving a little too fast."

Carly shook her head. "No, it's just that . . ." Her posture relaxed and she smiled. "I think I might like that."

She let out a breath as if it had taken a lot for her to admit that much. This was working out a lot better than Ria could have hoped.

They ate dinner, then saw a new show that was out. A romance with a happily-ever-after kind of ending that was the cherry on top of their evening, and left Ria feeling warm. Neil dropped Kristor off at her parents' home, then drove Ria to her house.

"I'll get my things tomorrow," Carly told Ria.

Ria kept a straight face. She knew Carly didn't want to end her evening with Neil quite so soon. She nodded and shut the car door. They waited until she had her front door open before driving off.

Ria tossed her keys on the table by the door, then stepped back outside to enjoy the lazy summer breeze that whispered through the pines. She felt good that the evening had gone so well. This was what Carly had needed.

As she leaned against the porch post a hawk landed on the railing. She didn't move, didn't breathe, then realized who the hawk was.

"Hello," she said softly.

Before she could do much more than that, a fog rolled in, wrapping around her. She heard his groan. Before the fog could even clear, Kristor picked her up in his arms and carried her inside.

"I've wanted to pull you close to me all evening, but I understand why you needed to take care of your friend, so she would not be so alone when you leave her."

When she wiggled, he set her on her feet. "That is not why I was doing it. I did it because Neil likes her. She likes him, too, and they were taking forever, and feeling miserable because of it."

He stood tall, and very naked. Her gaze couldn't help but drop lower. Her mouth went dry as she remembered how it felt when he sank inside her moist heat.

"Even now you want me."

Her gaze jerked up. "Just because I want you doesn't mean I want to travel to your planet."

Her eyes drifted downward again. She shook her head in an attempt to clear it of her naughty thoughts, and what she'd like to be doing right now.

"Wait here," she said and hurried to the bathroom. She grabbed the largest towel she had and marched back into the living room, shoving it toward him. "Put this around you."

"You do not like my naked form?" he asked, but took the towel and knotted it at his waist.

"It's hard—"

"You make me that way." He took a step closer.

Ria quickly backed up. "That's not what I was talking about. It's hard . . . I mean, difficult to talk to a naked man."

Especially when she already wanted to jump his bones. He

certainly didn't make her life easy, but then, she didn't think that was his intention.

"Then what did you want to speak about?" he asked.

"I won't be going back with you, and you can't take me back by force."

"Yes, I can. My strength is superior. Remember, I am a warrior. You don't even have any muscles. Your puny strength is no match for me."

"I have plenty of muscles, thank you very much!"

"Not as many as I do."

That was easy to see when she was looking at such a broad chest and all those sexy muscles. She quickly cleared her mind and squared her shoulders. Not that she really thought he would be intimidated, but she wanted him to see she wasn't backing down. Not one little inch.

"I won't be leaving with you, and I know you won't force me. It's just not in you." She crossed her arms in front of her and smiled smugly.

His forehead wrinkled when his eyebrows drew together. "I am a warrior."

"So you've pointed out more than once. But you would never force a woman to do something against her will."

His lips clamped together, but just as quickly, he relaxed and sauntered toward her. For a moment, she couldn't think as her nipples strained against her bra.

She quickly took a step back, holding up her hand in front of her. "No, I won't let you seduce me into leaving with you, either."

"You're very obstinate." He strode to the front porch.

Ria waited, but when he didn't return, she walked to the door and looked out. The fog was back. She waited for it to clear. When it did, her towel was on the front porch. She went outside and picked it up.

Her body ached to feel his touch, to feel him buried deep

inside her. But she knew the other side of her bed would be cold tonight.

And so would she.

You're the obstinate one, Labrinon told Kristor. *Throw the woman over your shoulder and force her to go with you. Be done with this once and for all. I grow weary of Earth and stubborn Earth women.*

You know I can't. I swore an oath to my mother.

She will forgive you.

Have you forgotten the spell she cast on me when I refused to dance with the Princess Quara? It made me impotent for many days . . . and nights.

A mere inconvenience.

Easy for you to say, Kristor grumbled.

You'll have to continue seducing her. It may take longer than I had thought. You're losing your touch. A few years ago, you could have had her panting to do your bidding.

I am not old. Ria is only very stubborn. I like that about her.

That's where you are similar—unfortunately.

I will convince her to leave with me.

Some men lose their minds when separated from their life-mates. What will you do if she continues to refuse?

Kristor didn't voice his thoughts. He'd already begun to think about an alternative plan.

You can't remain on Earth and give up everything that you care about. You are a warrior! A warrior without a war. That will destroy you just as fast.

Then it would seem I am doomed either way.

"What are you thinking?" Neil asked.

Carly still couldn't believe that Neil had wanted to go out with her. Maybe it was because she'd had a secret crush on him for so long.

"I'm glad Ria set this up," she admitted.

"Me, too."

She nibbled her bottom lip. "I'm worried about her. She told me Kristor wants her to leave with him. She knows nothing about the man. I think their relationship is moving way too fast."

"Heath is checking him out. I'm sure there's nothing to worry about. Ria's a big girl, and the guy seems nice enough."

That bothered her, too. Being around Kristor had changed things. She found him likable, and his size wasn't quite as intimidating as it had been in the beginning.

He also seemed to care a lot about Ria. Maybe she had been too quick to jump to conclusions. Not that what she'd done mattered. It wasn't like anyone was swooping down on him with arrest warrants.

"You're right," she told him.

"I'll walk you to your door." He opened his car door and walked around to her side.

Carly's stomach twisted in knots. What if he wanted to come inside? Or more? She had never had much luck in the sex department, mostly because she was so scared and embarrassed.

She looked up at the stairs, and suddenly there was a hangman's noose at the top. Each step she took brought her closer to the death of this relationship.

Then she was standing outside her door. She swallowed past the lump in her throat. "I had a good time tonight." When Neil smiled, her heart thudded inside her chest.

"I did too, sexy lady."

He scraped the back of his hand over her cheek, then leaned in close. His mouth covered hers in a gentle, non-threatening kiss. When he moved back, she sighed.

"I'd like to take you out again. Just me and you," he said.

"I'd like that."

"Friday?"

She nodded.

He grinned. "Friday, then." He turned and went down the stairs.

She touched her lips, feeling the warmth that still lingered. She was smiling when she went inside and closed the door. Butterflies tickled her stomach. Tomorrow she would send Ria a box of chocolate. Life was sweet.

Chapter 21

Ria flung the cover away and swung her legs off the bed. Her body didn't follow. With supreme effort, she forced herself to a sitting position. But when she tried to open her eyes, they wouldn't cooperate. She was tempted to lie back down and pull the cover over her head, but she knew from past experience that she wouldn't be able to go back to sleep.

She'd had a horrible night, filled with nightmares of Kristor flinging her over his shoulder, and forcing her to return to New Symtaria with him. Her mother and father had been smiling, and waving her off as if she were only taking a short vacation.

That nightmare had ended only to go into another one where Kristor *didn't* fling her over his shoulder and force her to return with him. She'd been left all alone and wishing for something more.

She was so confused. What was she going to do? It would seem she was damned if she did, and damned if she didn't.

She closed her eyes for a moment and slowed her breathing. Flying might not be so bad. She'd been a little girl and the explosion had scared the crap out of her. She really should get over it. Other people overcame their phobias. Why not her?

What would it feel like to have the wind currents lift her higher and higher?

Something banged in the kitchen.

Her eyes opened wide.

Ruffles? Nope, the cat's tail swished out from under the bed to tickle Ria's heel.

Burglar?

It's nothing, Shintara screamed inside Ria's head. *Go back to concentrating. Think hawk. You can do it.*

"Shh."

Ria's heart banged against her chest wall. She grabbed her cell phone off the nightstand and punched in 9-1-1.

"Nine-one-one, what's your emergency," Tilly's voice came over the line.

Ria grimaced. "This is Ria Lancaster. I think there's an intruder in my kitchen," she whispered.

"Are you sure it's not a naked alien?" She snorted.

"Do you want to start looking for another job when they replay this call after they discover my lifeless body?"

"I'll send Heath over," she said, but Ria thought she still sounded snarky.

"Tell him to hurry."

Ria closed her phone, looking around. Her heavy flashlight was in the other room. She stood and tip-toed to the bathroom, picking up her hairbrush. Yeah, right, that would scare the hell out of the intruder. Hairspray? It might work like mace. She supposed it was better than nothing.

Holding the can close to her chest, she crept into the hallway wanting to get to the living room, and then outside where it would be safe. She could hide around the corner until Heath got there.

"Ria, you're awake. Good," Kristor spoke from behind her.

She jumped, whirled around, and without thinking, sprayed toward his face.

He coughed. "Ugh! That's awful tasting. Worse than the stuff you sprayed in my eyes."

"Oh, Kristor, I'm sorry. I thought you were a burglar. How

the hell did you get in here, anyway? I know I locked my doors and windows last night."

"Mind over matter."

"Oh. I forgot. Where did I spray you?" Dammit, she needed more sleep. And coffee.

"My mouth and my cheek. What is that stuff?"

"Hairspray." She grabbed his arm and pulled him along with her as she hurried to the kitchen. "You need to rinse your mouth. I'm so sorry."

She grabbed a glass out of the cabinet and filled it with water before handing it to him.

He took a big gulp, then spat water into the sink and rinsed again.

"Why are you here? You weren't that happy when you took off last night. I didn't think you would show up until later in the day."

"Coffee." He rinsed some more.

She brought the orange juice out of the refrigerator and poured a glass. "You don't like coffee." She handed him the juice. He drank half in one gulp.

"I was going to surprise you."

"You did."

"I guess the burglar is gone?" Heath said as he stepped into the kitchen, gun drawn.

Ria screamed and aimed the hairspray, but Kristor jerked her arm down and away as she sprayed so the spray didn't land on anything except the floor.

"You called me, remember," Heath said as he holstered his gun. "You're not supposed to attack the good guy."

Kristor took the hairspray away from her and set it on top of the fridge. God, she'd probably aged ten years this morning. "I'm sorry, Heath."

"I take it this is your burglar?"

She nodded. "Kristor was going to surprise me with coffee this morning."

"Not the first time that I've almost plugged a boyfriend

who wanted to surprise his girlfriend." He pushed the button on his radio. "Tilly, no problem at Ria's."

Static, then, "I didn't think you'd be discovering her lifeless body."

Funny.

"Would you like some coffee?" she asked Heath.

Heath eyed the pot. The coffee was so thin you could read a newspaper through it.

"I think I'll pass." He tugged on the brim of his hat. "Try to stay out of trouble today." He headed for the door.

She followed him out to the porch. The neighbor was watering her plants. Ria smiled and waved, then realized she was still in her pajamas. Great. At least she'd worn a T-shirt and shorts to bed.

Well, except the T-shirt was really big so it looked as though that was all she had on. More gossip. Not that Tilly would stay quiet. No, she'd be eager to tell everyone the latest news at her canasta club.

Ria turned and went inside to the kitchen and poured herself a cup of coffee. She added sugar, but skipped the cream. Kristor went to the refrigerator and refilled his glass with more orange juice. Lord, they acted like they were married or something.

"I thought you were angry with me because I said I wouldn't leave with you," she said.

"I'm no longer angry."

"Then you're fine with my decision?"

"No."

"Oh." He confused her. But then he turned that devastatingly sexy grin on her and she melted.

"Do you work today?"

She shook her head, more to clear it of the visions she was starting to have. "We're closed today."

"Then change. I want to take you somewhere."

"Where?"

"Go change."

She might as well. The coffee tasted like crap, but she didn't want to hurt his feelings by telling him. She would only hope there was a Starbucks nearby.

She took a quick shower and changed into shorts and a tank top. When Ria joined him in the living room, Ruffles was curled in Kristor's lap, purring like she was in kitty cat paradise. She gave Ria a snotty look, then jumped down and padded back to the bedroom.

"Are you going to tell me where we're going?"

"You'll see."

When Kristor went outside, she followed. He got on his motorcycle and handed her a helmet. She climbed on the back and fastened the helmet in place. Did it really matter where they were going? As long as she was snuggled up against him, nothing really mattered. She sighed. It would take more than a week to say good-bye.

She closed her eyes, resting her cheek against his back. She could hear the beat of his heart, feel the warmth of his skin through his shirt.

She opened her eyes when he slowed. The zoo. Why had he brought her here? It wasn't even open.

Kristor stopped the bike and turned the key. She removed her helmet and climbed off. He followed suit.

"Come on." He pulled on her hand.

"Where? It isn't open. They're not going to let us in."

"Yes, they will."

"You cannot act the warrior and barge your way in. They'll arrest us."

"I asked them if we could go inside before the zoo opens."

Nope, she didn't believe him.

"I gave them money."

"And where did you get money?"

"Database."

Of course. She should've known. That was a good way to stay under the radar—flash lots of money around.

They stopped at the ticket booth. The young woman on

the inside had her back to Kristor. He tapped on the window. She jumped.

"Oh, it's you, Kris," she said, then smiled.

What? Did he know everyone? Sheesh. Ria would admit it wasn't that difficult. The town was small. The zoo was small. More of a mom-and-pop operation, which was why he had been successful bribing his way inside before they opened.

The girl came around and opened the gate. "Hi, I'm Frannie." She turned back to Kristor. "Remember the rules I mentioned. And don't get up against the cages. The animals are wild."

"Of course."

"You'll have about an hour before the gates officially open."

"Thank you," Kristor said as she pushed a button that would let them in.

"Now where are we going?" Ria asked when they were away from Frannie. "And why? I don't understand." She needed coffee—strong coffee.

"You don't have to know, only to trust me." He stopped, leaned down, and kissed her.

Her breath caught in her throat and she automatically moved closer. How could one touch steal her thoughts? Did he have some kind of magic power that made her forget everything except him?

He stepped away, but it took a few moments for her head to clear.

"Labrinon flew over the enclosure. We took a closer look, and after talking to your father, I knew I had to bring you here."

"Labrinon?"

"My animal guide."

"Oh, of course. And why did you want to bring me here?" She didn't even want to know what her father had to do with any of this.

"Have you ever been to this zoo?"

"When I was a kid, but not in years."

"Then come with me. I'll show you a bit of New Symtaria."

She pulled her hand free. "I told you, I'm not going to fly off to your planet. It's not going to happen." What, had he left his spacecraft hidden somewhere inside the zoo?

"New Symtaria is here. On your Earth."

The guy had lost his freakin' mind. Maybe Symtarians weren't supposed to breathe too much of Earth's polluted air. What if it affected their brains or something? She'd humor him. Kristor was fun to be with and, for a warrior, he could be quite sentimental. She had a hard time picturing him slicing and dicing people.

They passed a sign that pointed to the bird sanctuary. She should've known that's where he would take her. He was trying to convince her she should leave with him.

They went inside a small house with cages on either side. "It's kind of sad that all the birds are caged." You could put a quarter in what looked like a gumball machine and seed would go into a tray so the birds could eat. She supposed it cut down on expenses.

"Wait." Kristor led her to the back. He stopped at a door that said NO ADMITTANCE, then placed his hand on the doorknob and closed his eyes. After a moment, he turned the knob, and opened the door.

She only stared, then shook her head. "It's amazing how you do stuff like that."

"Come."

"We're going to get into trouble."

"Probably, but I will give them more money."

"Of course. Just give them more money." He had learned fast how things worked in America.

They went down a dark hall with a light at the end. Great: Walk toward the light. She felt as if this was her death march. Since she wasn't quite sure where he was taking her, it could very well be the end.

But when they stepped into the open, Ria felt as though she had entered heaven. There were trees and dark green grass and birds singing everywhere. They were in a large enclosure, but it didn't feel like a cage.

"Watch." He stuck his arms out to his sides and whistled softly.

Ria looked around as everything stilled. Then there was a flapping of small wings. Dozens of birds landed on his outstretched arms.

"Good Lord, I feel as if I've stepped into a scene from *Cinderella*." Except Kristor had suddenly become Prince Charming. This was so not good.

She needed to change her way of thinking. Birdman of Alcatraz? No, she didn't like that visual, either. Maybe a . . . a . . .

She stopped thinking when a little yellow parakeet landed on her shoulder. Slowly, she turned her head and they stared at each other. The bird opened its beak and a pretty melody cascaded over her. It reminded her of Fred. Tears filled her eyes. She rapidly blinked them away.

"You're so pretty," Ria whispered.

Thank you. The bird's thoughts filled her mind.

"The bird talked to me," she said.

"You only have to listen to hear them," Kristor told her. "I think you stopped listening to the birds. When your father told me about your pet bird as a child, I knew I should bring you here, so you could reconnect."

Ria had a feeling she was in deep trouble. No, Kristor wouldn't force her to leave. But he was tempting her. Oh, dirty pool!

Chapter 22

Ria had five little birds on her shoulders, and she was hearing their thoughts all at once. They were like chattering children, much like Fred had been. She laughed. Another bird landed, then another. Ria looked at Kristor.

"This isn't fair," she said.

"Yes, I know. Sometimes when you wage a war, you concentrate on winning the smaller battles before you conquer all." He looked around, then his gaze came to rest on her. "Did I win this battle?"

"The battle, but not the war."

His slow grin told her that he hadn't stopped fighting, either. A flutter of excitement rushed through her. Maybe she was glad he hadn't.

"So, you said you would show me what New Symtaria was like." It might be prudent if she changed the subject. Besides, she wanted to know where her ancestors had lived, even if she would never go there.

"There are lots of birds where I live, and they will stop and communicate much like this."

"And you have your own home?"

"I have a castle."

"You really are a prince?"

"Yes. Does that bother you?"

"I don't know." But then, he'd said she was a princess. No, she couldn't wrap her brain around that. She didn't feel like a princess. Especially when she had to clean house or wash dishes. "Do you have servants?"

"Yes."

Okay, it might just be worth going to live there if she never had to wash dishes again.

The door opened and Frannie stuck her head inside. "You're not supposed to be in here," she frantically whispered. "My father's going around checking things before the gates open. You'll have to leave." She stopped talking and looked around. "What did you do? Hypnotize the birds?"

"They are only friendly," Kristor said.

"Aren't you Ria Lancaster?" Frannie asked.

"Yes." Ria didn't think she'd ever met the girl. She looked as if she was still in high school.

Frannie slowly nodded. "I've heard about you." She looked around at the birds. "Now it makes sense. But you both still have to scram."

What made sense? Ria didn't think she liked her insinuation.

Kristor gently waved his arms and the birds flew away. Ria's birds followed. She was disappointed they were gone. She'd make a point to come back for a visit, but she didn't think it would be the same without Kristor. It wouldn't be as easy to get inside the cage since she couldn't do the mind-over-matter trick that he could.

They left, going back to his motorcycle. Rather than go in the direction of her house, he went to the city. She didn't know what he had planned, but she wasn't too concerned because in the city they had Starbucks. She still needed a big cup of java, or a latte would be nice.

He parked at the mall. Did he want to shop for souvenirs? Maybe he just wanted to look around. He was leaving soon. Ria didn't care what they did as long as it was together.

"Do you have malls on New Symtaria?" she asked.

"We have tradesmen, and we can get products from our database."

"And does everyone have a database?"

"Only the royals."

"That doesn't sound fair."

"If everyone had a database, then no one would have need of anything."

"And that would be bad because . . . ?"

He looked at her. "If you can have anything you want with the touch of a button, then you would have no need to do anything. Think about it. We have to keep the day-to-day operations running smoothly. Having everything you want would be frivolous."

"Like your motorcycle?"

"That was needed for transportation."

She nodded. "As opposed to say, an older model car with rust spots."

"I'm still a royal and have a certain image to maintain. If I had things that were in disrepair, I would be deemed unworthy to have the title of prince."

She knew he just liked the cycle, but she had a feeling it wouldn't do any good to argue with him. They strolled hand in hand inside. The air-conditioned mall was a great escape from the heat.

"Coffee." She aimed toward the little shop, inhaling the rich coffee bean aroma. Except Kristor pulled her hand and pointed her in a different direction. "I really need coffee," she told him.

"I want to show you something. It's better if your stomach is empty."

That didn't sound good.

They went to the end of the mall and turned the corner.

"All that's down here is the game room. Video games, pinball . . . things like that."

"I know." He held her hand as they went inside. "This is

what I wanted to show you." He pulled her over to a machine that looked sort of like a plane, but on a much smaller scale.

She cocked an eyebrow. "Simulated flying."

He stood taller. "It will cure you of your fear."

She laughed. "I doubt that, but it was a nice thought. Come on, I need coffee, then food."

But he held her hand, not letting her escape. "You're afraid?"

"I am not." She glared at him. Teens and kids looked their way. "I am not scared of a video game," she said a little quieter.

"Then why do you run away?"

"I wasn't running away. I just don't see how a video game could cure anyone of anything. And believe me, I've ridden my share of roller coasters at Six Flags. I am so not scared of a video game." He only stood there looking like a very determined warrior. "Okay, fine, I'll try it." No video game would get the best of her.

Ria climbed inside the one-person cockpit. What was there to be scared about? It looked like a plane, but it wasn't like the thing was going to get off the ground. When the ride was over, she would still be in the game room. At least maybe then they could get some coffee. And food. Her stomach had started rumbling.

The fake plane sucked up the five-dollar bill Kristor put in the slot while she adjusted her seat, checking out the pedals, and the steering wheel.

"Headphones," he said, pointing to the ones on the hook near the steering mechanism.

Of course, couldn't forget those. She placed them over her ears.

"Ready?" he asked.

She nodded.

Kristor pulled the black curtain over the top. The fake plane wasn't quite as cool anymore. In fact, it was a little too convincing. But she wasn't a coward and no matter how spooky real it was, it still wasn't going anywhere.

A screen in front of her came on. Cute, she was on a runway. She hoped the kid that had been playing the pinball machine in front of her moved out of the way. She snorted. There was no way a toy was ever going to cure her of her fear of flying.

The sound of jet engines starting up filled her ears. Then she was moving. Not really, it just felt like she was. The plane tilted back and suddenly she was taking off, surrounded by blue sky.

"Just a simulation, just a simulation," she muttered. Kristor was standing right outside probably thinking he was pretty smart to think this up.

The plane climbed higher and higher. Blood rushed through her veins, pounding inside her head. It was getting harder and harder to breathe. Just when she thought she couldn't stand any more, the plane began to level out. Clouds drifted past.

This was better. Maybe. It was sort of like watching a 3-D movie.

She took a deep breath and slowly exhaled. Not as bad as she'd thought. Had she been afraid for nothing all these years?

"Flight commander, we have a situation."

She grinned. That was probably her. She was a flight commander. Carly would not believe any of this. Ria wondered what kind of situation they had. They would probably have to land early. Five dollars' worth of fuel would only go so far nowadays. Hopefully, Kristor wouldn't put in another five bucks.

"The tower has enemy planes on the radar."

Ria sat a little straighter. What enemy planes? Wasn't this a commercial flight? She had figured they were out of peanuts or something. Kristor hadn't said anything about this being a war plane.

"There they are, sir!"

A black ugly plane appeared in front of her. She swerved to the right as it fired.

"Good move, Commander, but you have two bogies on your tail. Watch out, sir."

Bogies? What the hell was a bogie? She looked at the screen and could see two more black planes coming up on her tail. She stepped on the gas and swerved to the right, then the left. She couldn't shake them. They fired. Her wing caught on fire.

"Commander, Commander, you're going down!"

She was going down? No, she was too young to die! But the screen showed her plane aiming toward the ground and there was a strong smell of smoke and fire.

She screamed.

The curtain over her head was flung back. Ria jerked the headphones off, and scrambled out, falling into Kristor's arms and sobbing.

Kristor looked at the screen. "You said she would get over her fear of flying in the simulation." He glared at the young teenager.

He took a step back. "Well, yeah, but she crashed. That probably didn't help. Most ten-year-olds don't crash the plane."

"It crashed. Just like when I was a kid." Her stomach rumbled as she wobbled to an upright position. "I think I'm going to be sick."

"We have bags inside the cockpit for that."

She curled her lip. The boy couldn't be more than sixteen, smacking gum, wearing shorts that showed his underwear, and a T-shirt that claimed he was too smart for his shirt. The shirt lied. She should barf all over him.

"You'll feel better soon," Kristor told her as he led her away from the game room. "Do you want some coffee? You said before you wanted coffee and food."

He had to be joking. He didn't look as if he was joking. "I

need the ladies' room so I can wash my face." Maybe the cool water would help.

"Over there."

He walked her over. She stopped him at the door. "I can make it from here by myself."

She went inside. There were several ladies waiting in line, but they moved farther to the side when they got a good look at her. Hell, as soon as she saw her reflection, she understood why. People could actually turn green. More of a pale green, but green just the same. Maybe she had a Martian in her ancestral tree.

She splashed water on her face. Much better. Never ever would she get on a plane. She hadn't been able to stomach the damned simulator. No way would she spend as much time as needed to get to another planet.

"I'm sorry," Kristor spoke from the other side of the door.

The women turned to look at her. Maybe if she ignored him, he would go away.

"I didn't know it would make you this sick. Are you okay?"

He wasn't going away. "I'm okay."

"Your first?" a little gray-haired woman asked.

"Yes. And my last." She was not going near anything remotely related to flying. She grabbed a rough paper towel from the dispenser and patted her face.

"But when you hold that baby in your arms, you'll feel differently."

"Baby?" Sudden realization hit her. The woman thought . . . "I'm pregnant?" This was priceless.

A stall opened and Tilly the dispatcher stepped out. "I thought I heard your voice, Ria Lancaster."

Crap! "Listen, I'm not pregnant. It was a misunderstanding."

"Crackers will help calm the stomach," the old woman said.

Tilly turned and looked at her. "Seven-Up is good, too."

"Oh, yes, I've heard that, too."

"Great," Ria mumbled and left as the two women continued their conversation about babies. She supposed this would be all over town before she even made it back home.

"Now we will eat," Kristor said as she emerged from the ladies' room.

"I think I'll just have crackers and maybe a soda." She might not like more rumors being spread, but she would take their advice about settling her still-churning stomach.

"I thought it would help," Kristor said.

"It didn't."

"I could see that."

She sighed. "It's the thought that counts." But no, she was doubly sure she couldn't get on his spacecraft, and it hurt knowing he would be leaving without her.

She held tight to him as they made their way back to her house. At least she had this moment. And she had a few more days. And she had tonight.

Kristor dropped Ria off at her home. She hesitated before going inside. He knew she wanted him to join her. Driving away was probably the hardest thing he'd ever had to do. He needed to get away and think, and he couldn't do it at her house, nor her parents'.

So he just drove—down paved roads, down dirt roads. He drove where there were no roads. Nothing seemed to help so he finally went to where he'd hidden his spacecraft. Unless someone walked into it, they would never know it was there, because he'd used the invisible shield to hide it.

He stopped the motorcycle beside a tree and turned the key. When he pushed a button on his remote, the door on his spacecraft opened. Once inside, he relaxed in one of two seats.

The craft was small, with a large window. He imagined Rianna would be terrified to travel anywhere in it.

"Have you completed your mission?" A soft feminine voice came through the speakers.

"No."

"Are you ready to leave Earth?"

"No."

"You seem tense. Is there a problem?"

Yes, she was starting to get on his nerves. His brother had made sure he would have all he needed for the journey, including having his craft programmed with a female monitor so he would not get lonely on his mission. Right now, he was tired of all females.

That was a lie. He wasn't tired of Rianna. Even now, she filled his thoughts. He wasn't sure what to do about her. This mission was nothing like any battle he'd ever fought, and he didn't know how to win. She used everything in her powers to conquer him. Rianna fought with sad eyes, angry eyes, and a smile that made him want to lay his sword at her feet and vow his undying love. When her eyes filled with tears, she could take him to his knees. How did someone fight against that?

"Prince Kristor?"

He ran a weary hand over his eyes. "I'm fine. I only need to think."

"Of course. I will leave you to your thinking."

Good.

Annoying, that's what the monitor was. He had a feeling Rogar had the female voice installed for just that purpose. Kristor had made a wrong turn around Mars and the monitor had acted as if it was the end of the world.

He shook his head. The voice was computer programmed. A mere chip, not as big as his smallest fingernail, yet here he was, acting as if she had form and substance.

Earth had made him crazy. Correction: Rianna had made him crazy. Even now he could close his eyes and imagine her naked body pressed against his. Did she feel the same way? Did she need him as much as he needed her?

He suddenly sat straight up in his chair. That was it. She did need him. He knew it with every fiber of his being. She would miss him after he left. He would give her a taste of what it would be like without him around.

I don't think that's a good idea, Labrinon said. *If you're not around, she will forget about you.*

I don't think so, Kristor said.

Are you willing to take that chance?

Yes, I am. I have no other choice.

And if it doesn't work?

I'll throw her over my shoulder and force her to leave with me.

She won't like that. What will you do then?

I will seduce her all over again. He grinned, liking his plan. It definitely had merit.

If you would have listened to me, you could have already done that and be home. I suspect if you go along with that plan it will hurt more than help. She is your lifemate.

He sobered. *Yes, I know. For that very reason, I can't leave without her.*

But could he win her back if he used force? His bed might be cold for many passings of the moon before he could convince her that he hadn't had a choice.

Chapter 23

Where was he? Ria's mother said Kristor hadn't been staying in her old room. They hadn't seen him at all. Ria walked to her shop's large plate-glass window that looked out onto the street.

The usual traffic drove down the two-lane road. There were the same people that she saw every day strolling down the sidewalk, as they went about their daily routine. Some just walked for the exercise, mostly older people. The park wasn't far.

Then there were the ones who didn't care as much about exercising anymore and sat on one of the benches. They watched the day slowly pass, or met up with others to talk about days gone by.

But as Ria scanned the area, she didn't even catch a glimpse of Kristor. Two days had passed, and nothing. Had he decided she was a lost cause, and gone back to New Symtaria?

A shiver of fear ran down her spine. What if the rogue Symtarians found her? What if they came after her? She had no way of protecting herself.

The bell above her door jangled and Carly came inside.

"I waved, but it was as if you didn't even see me. You must have been really lost in thought."

"Unfamiliar territory?" She smiled at her attempt at humor, but knew it was weak at best.

"What's the matter?" Worry creased Carly's brow.

Ria glanced toward Jeanie, who was filing papers at her desk, and gave an imperceptible shake of her head. Carly glanced at her watch.

"It's lunchtime. I dropped by to see if you wanted to get something to eat. Do you have any appointments?"

She shook her head. "And Katie is coming in to take care of the afternoon ones."

"Then get your purse."

"I don't want to leave Katie alone again."

"Is she any good?"

"She's great."

"Are you the boss?"

"Okay, okay. Let's go." She grabbed her purse out of her office and they walked to the Dairy Queen. Ria couldn't deal with Donald today, so they passed by his restaurant.

After placing their order, they found a booth in the back, away from the crowded front.

"Now, tell me what's going on? You look as if you've gotten some really bad news. Whatever it is, we can work through it."

"It's Kristor."

"Did you two have a fight? Whatever it was about, you can work it out."

Ria's eyes widened. "I didn't think you liked him. I would've thought it would make you happy if he left and never came back."

"Don't get me wrong. I don't want you leaving with him, and I'm still not sure I trust him completely, but the other night when we went out, I saw how much you both care about each other." She shrugged. "And he certainly didn't act like a criminal."

The waitress brought their drinks and burgers and set the

tray down between them. They waited until she'd left before resuming their conversation.

"And there's something else, too," Carly said.

"What?"

"Well, Neil likes him, and he's a good judge of character. I trust his opinion."

"Really?"

Carly picked the pickles off her burger, eating them one by one as she'd done for as long as Ria had known her.

"We're going out again." She sighed, a dreamy expression on her face. "He's exactly what I've needed. He makes me feel so alive." She blushed. "He thinks I'm beautiful."

"You've always been beautiful."

Carly shook her head. "Not before you took me shopping." Her eyes narrowed. "Do you know my brothers thought it was just terrible that I'd changed the way I look?"

Ria didn't doubt that for a second. "So what did you tell them?"

"That they were full of bull, and that when I see them dating frumpy women, I might go back to dressing like I used to. That shut them up quick enough."

Ria chuckled. "Then the waxing was worth it?"

"Yeah, it was."

They ate in silence for a while. Ria could tell there was something else on her friend's mind. She clearly wanted to ask something, but it didn't look like she would without a little prodding.

"Okay, what else do you want to know?"

Carly took a deep breath, setting her burger on the paper wrap. She opened her mouth, but then snapped it closed. "It's nothing, really. Stupid, in fact."

"What? Now you have to tell me."

"Okay, but don't get upset."

"I promise. Now what?"

"Are you pregnant? Is that why Kristor left? It's okay if

you don't want to tell me, but I want you to know that if you are, I'm here for you. Anything you need, just name it."

Silence.

Then Ria burst out laughing. She tried to smother it when people turned to stare. "Where in the world did you hear that?"

"My mother heard it from Wanda, who heard it from Becky. She heard it from Sandy, and I think she got it from Tilly, who said you admitted it in the ladies' room at the mall when you were having morning sickness."

"I'm not pregnant."

Carly released a deep breath. "Good. Especially since Kristor skipped out—" Her face took on a rosy hue. "I mean, since he, uh. I'm sorry, Ria. I hoped to make you feel better, but I think I did the opposite."

"You did make me feel better. You always do." But she couldn't help wondering about Kristor and where he was. What if his animal guide had been shot while soaring through the sky? No, she would not even go there. But where was he?

It doesn't appear as if she's too distraught that you're not around, Labrinon said as he perched high on a building and watched Rianna and her friend, Carly, leave the eating establishment. *Rianna smiles and laughs as if you were never in her life.*

Kristor had to admit that Labrinon was right. He'd only thought Rianna cared about him. She would not suffer emotionally if he left. She would easily move on with her life.

He watched through the eyes of the hawk as she hugged her friend good-bye, then got in her car and drove toward her house without a care, without a worry.

Leave. Now. I don't wish to watch her any longer, Kristor said.

What will you do?

Just go back to the craft.

Kristor closed his eyes as Labrinon caught the air currents that would take them back. But closing his eyes didn't stop the anger from building inside him. How could Rianna not care about what they had shared? It was as though she had tossed their whole relationship away.

Did she not realize he would probably go crazy without his lifemate? Did she not care that she would destroy him?

Labrinon glided into the craft, landing on one of the chairs. The change began. Kristor welcomed the burning sensation, the pain that accompanied shifting. And when he was back to himself, he dressed, his movements stiff as he tried to contain his anger. Then he climbed on his motorcycle and went to Rianna's house. He would confront her.

Her car was parked in the driveway. He pulled in beside it and turned the key off. She didn't even come to the door in greeting. Had she already dismissed him? How could she so easily wipe him from her mind when all he could do was think about her? Every waking moment he'd been consumed with thoughts of her. And when he'd slept, his dreams had been filled with visions of Rianna.

As Kristor climbed the steps and walked across her porch, he understood why some men were driven crazy without their lifemate. He thought he might already be halfway there.

He opened the door and went inside. Rianna still didn't rush to greet him. His frown darkened as he strode to the kitchen. Empty. He listened. Heard water running. It stopped.

He turned on his heel and marched to the bedroom. He was halfway across the room when the bathroom door opened. Rianna looked up, slapping her hand to her chest. It was all Kristor could do to take a breath. She stood there with a towel on her head and one wrapped around her body.

"Kristor?" Tears filled her eyes.

Oh, no, he hadn't meant to make her cry. He'd expected anything except tears.

She launched herself at him, throwing her arms around his neck. "Where have you been? I've been so afraid something happened to you. That you were hurt or dead. That you might have left without saying good-bye. I've missed you so much."

His anger evaporated. All that mattered was that she did care. He had a feeling she'd only let him win a few skirmishes. Rianna had won the battle. But if he took her back by force, would he lose everything?

"Kiss me," she said against his neck, the warmth of her breath igniting the flames inside him.

He lowered his lips to hers, tasted her once more. By the gods, he'd missed holding her close, loving her. He caressed her tongue with his, gently stroking, when all he wanted to do was throw her onto the bed and plunge inside her heat. He held back, though it took a supreme effort on his part.

He ended the kiss, buried his head in her neck, and breathed in the fruity aroma of her hair. His hands slid down her back, tugging at the towel until it came loose. He stepped back and gazed upon her beauty.

Full breasts, a tiny waist, gently curving hips, and a flat stomach, but the thatch of dark curls covered what he most wanted. He wanted to feel her legs wrap around him and pull him in deeper before much more time passed.

"I want you," he said.

"I want you, too."

He jerked his T-shirt over his head and tossed it to the floor. He shoved the button through his jeans, then jerked the zipper down, before shoving them and his briefs to the floor.

"I don't know how much longer I can wait," he warned, then almost lost it when he saw she was looking at his erection, not his face.

"Me either," she said, then dragged her eyes upward as he kicked his clothes away. "You shouldn't have stayed away. Why did you?"

"Because I'm a man, and a warrior, and we often do stupid things when we're around women."

He picked her up, then laid her on the bed, joining her. She parted her legs, but he would do nothing to hurt her. He slipped two fingers inside her and discovered she was already damp with need. The pressure inside him built. He moved between her legs, slipped inside and, for a moment, didn't move. He wanted to savor everything about her. The way her body automatically tightened around him, enclosing him in the liquid fire that was her body. He almost lost it when she wrapped her legs around his waist, sucking him deeper inside her heat.

"More," she whispered.

He growled, rose above her, then plunged deeper.

"Yes, harder."

He watched her face in the throes of her passion. The way she bit her bottom lip, strained toward that first quiver that would overtake her body.

She rose to meet each thrust, her breath coming out in little pants. Straining, drawing nearer.

"More," she cried out.

He plunged deeper, faster, harder.

Her body tightened. She gasped. A tear slid from the corner of her eye.

The fire built inside him. He drew almost all the way out of her body, then sank back inside. Fire licked at his erection as her heat stroked down his length, then back up.

And then he came. Explosions of light went off around him as intense pleasure filled his mind and body. He sank into her softness with a moan of deep satisfaction before rolling to his side, taking her with him, pulling her against him.

"Don't ever leave me again," she murmured.

He barely heard her words. Didn't answer. He wasn't sure it was a promise he could keep. At least, not without causing her pain.

They clung to each other, as though they knew their future was uncertain at best. Would they even have one together?

She sighed, her breathing even. He kissed the top of her

head and closed his eyes as the familiar burning pain gripped him. He used to welcome the shift after sex so he wouldn't have to answer a lot of questions. But now he only wanted to feel Ria's body pressed against his, grasping every moment as if it might be their last.

Chapter 24

Ria woke to the sound of her shower running. She grumbled as she rolled over in the bed. Then it hit her. Kristor was back, and all was right in her world. Butterflies fluttered inside her stomach.

She stretched and yawned. There was a thump under the bed. She leaned over the side and raised the dust ruffle. "Hello," she told her cat.

"Meow."

Ria smiled. Ruffles looked pretty satisfied. The cat closed its eyes and visions of chasing a mouse filled Ria's head.

She stilled.

Why would she imagine that? She looked at the cat again. Ruffles had gone back to snoozing.

Okay, no more concentrating. She didn't even want to see Ruffles catching the stupid mouse or what she would do with it when she did.

Ria rolled out of bed, grabbing her fluffy white robe, and slipping her arms inside. She was tying the belt when Kristor stepped out of the bathroom wearing only a towel knotted at the waist.

Good Lord, did he realize what he did to her? She wanted to pounce. Who wouldn't? All that tanned exposed skin, sinewy muscles, broad chest, rock-hard abs . . .

"If you keep looking at me like that, I don't think we'll leave the house today."

And that would be bad because . . . ?

Her stomach rumbled. She had only picked at her lunch today and suddenly she was starved. She glanced at the clock. It was already four. Too early for dinner, but she had plenty of munchies. Cheese, crackers, fruit, and wine . . . then more sex. Oh, baby, that sounded good to her.

"I'll shower and then see what I can hunt up for us to eat."

"Hunt? I am a warrior. I will do the hunting."

She chuckled. "Well, everything is in the pantry in the kitchen. Go for it."

She watched as understanding dawned.

His smile was a little sheepish. "I thought you meant you would kill our food."

"I know. Sorry, I couldn't resist teasing you."

"Teasing me?" He nodded. "I have a sister like that."

It was difficult for her to wrap her mind around the fact he had a family on another planet far away. And that he would be joining them soon.

She cleared her mind of those thoughts. Not today. They would spend the day together and not worry about the future.

"I won't be long." She started past him, but he pulled her into his arms and kissed her. Her arms entwined around his neck as she pressed her body closer.

They were both panting when he ended the kiss. For a moment, they held each other. She knew if she didn't take her shower, it might be a while before she got that chance, and besides being hungry, she wanted to know everything about Kristor.

"I'll join you in a few minutes." She hurried inside the bathroom, closing the door behind her. He mumbled something about needing a cold shower. She grinned.

When she joined him in the kitchen, he was bending over

looking at something on one of the lower shelves in the pantry. She stopped, staring at his nicely formed ass that was only covered by a bit of towel.

Now who needed the cold shower?

"Find anything?" she asked.

He jumped, bumping his head on the shelf above the one he was looking at. When he turned, she saw the smear of chocolate at the corner of his mouth.

"Ah, I see you found my stash of chocolate bars."

He held up a half empty bag. It had been full! So maybe their relationship wouldn't work. He'd eaten most of her chocolate, and you just didn't mess with a lady's chocolate. She cocked an eyebrow and planted her hands on her hips.

He held up the bag. "I'll share."

Okay, maybe it would work out. She sauntered over and grabbed the bag from him. "Of course, you will. It's my chocolate."

He leaned forward until their lips touched. The kiss was light. He tasted of chocolate. Chocolate and Kristor—a heady combination.

"I have ice cream in the freezer," she said as she put a little distance between them.

"I don't know this food."

"Oh, it's a major food group. Milk. Eggs." When he still looked confused, she continued. "Trust me." She tossed the chocolate on the table and grabbed the gallon of strawberry-shortcake ice cream out of the freezer. Rather than getting bowls, she just got two spoons. It would save on dishes.

"And orange drink?" he asked.

It was a good thing she'd bought more. The guy had a serious addiction. Hmm, apparently they didn't have any of this on New Symtaria. Maybe she could get him hooked on junk food and he'd stay. It was an idea.

"Did you see the moon pies?" she casually asked. A good addictive food. She was so evil.

He stopped in the process of removing the lid from the ice cream and stared at her. "You have pies from the moon?"

"No, they're just called that." Her forehead puckered. "Do you?"

"Of course not. It's a barren wasteland filled with craters. No one lives there."

"We sent men to the moon." She went to the pantry and grabbed the moon pies.

"Were they being punished?"

"No, they were explorers."

"Then you should have sent them someplace better." He dipped one of the spoons into the ice cream and brought it to his mouth. He closed his eyes and moaned, a look of pure rapture on his face. "This is good."

"Better than what you have on your planet?"

"No, but it will do for now."

So much for getting him hooked on junk food. Apparently, they had their own on New Symtaria.

She set the moon pies on the table and poured them each a glass of orange soda. It wasn't the sophisticated meal she had imagined, but this would probably be a lot more fun.

She joined him at the table and, after setting the drinks down, grabbed a spoon. The ice cream was good.

He took a drink, then reached for a chocolate bar. She had a sudden light-bulb moment of inspiration. "Do you know what else you can do with chocolate?"

He paused in tearing off the wrapper. "What?"

"Don't eat it yet." She stood and went back to the pantry. She glanced over her shoulder when she heard just the slightest sound of ripping paper. "Don't eat it," she warned, then grabbed a bag of marshmallows and a box of graham crackers.

"You have a lot of good food," he said, eyeing the new treats.

"Too much. This is why I have to run every day." She

ripped open the bag of marshmallows and brought out two. Then one cracker each, and broke them both in half. "Okay, give me the Hershey bar."

He looked at the bar, then back at her.

"Trust me, you'll love this."

He reluctantly handed her the bar of chocolate. She broke it in half and placed one half on the cracker, topped it with a big white marshmallow, and smashed a cracker on top of it. Then she repeated everything.

He reached for one.

"Not yet. We have to put them in the microwave first."

He flinched.

"What?" she asked.

"Rogar said microwaves are dangerous."

"Well, they're not."

"He said they make pretty lights on the inside, then begin to smoke and burn."

And she wondered what exactly he'd put in the microwave. "But then, I know what I'm doing."

He didn't look assured.

"What? Do you think women aren't capable of doing anything?" She hoped he didn't come from a planet of cavemen. If he did, she was more than ready to set him straight!

"Women are equals. They have been rulers, and contribute as much as men." He grimaced. "Their powers are much greater than men's, which can cause discord at times."

"Greater powers, huh?"

He nodded, not looking very happy.

She put the s'mores on a saucer and carried them to the microwave. He followed. "Why does it bother you so much that women can be superior? I mean, why can't women have greater powers?"

"Because they are more emotional than men. They sometimes act before they think."

She had a feeling he'd caught the brunt of more than one

woman's anger. She didn't care too much for the thought of his being with other women.

"Any woman in particular on New Symtaria?"

"A witch."

"Witch?"

"It does not matter."

And she had a feeling it didn't. At least, not to him. She was glad he didn't have someone waiting for his return. Not that she could do anything about it if he did. Now she really needed chocolate.

She turned the microwave on and watched through the glass as the conglomeration began to melt. After a few seconds, she took them out, and carried them back to the table. Rather than follow, he opened the door of the microwave, waved his hand inside, then shut the door.

"I think you're right. It does not look dangerous."

"Try this. Be careful, though. They're probably still hot."

He tentatively took a bite, then closed his eyes in rapt delight. He didn't say anything until he finished eating all of it. "More."

She waved her arm over the table. "They're almost as much fun to make. Go ahead."

"I don't cook."

She arched an eyebrow. "If you want another one you will."

"You're stubborn."

"I know."

He reached for a cracker, then unwrapped another chocolate bar and placed half on top. Next came the marshmallow, but when he put the cracker on top and smashed it down, the cracker broke into small pieces.

"It didn't work," he said.

"It'll still taste just as good."

He carried it over to the microwave and did exactly as she

had done, then carried it back to the table and sat down. He seemed quite proud of himself.

"You conquered the microwave," she said.

"Of course, I'm a warrior." He grinned. He took a bite and chewed. "How did you learn to make these?"

"My mom. We used to go camping a lot. Dad loves to fish. At least twice a year we would go to the mountains and pitch a tent. At night, Daddy would build a fire and we'd roast hot dogs, and then after supper, marshmallows."

"You love your family very much."

"Don't you love yours?"

"Yes. There are many, but we are very close. We have celebrations throughout the year."

"What do you celebrate?"

He shrugged. "Our ancestors, the gods. We give thanks that we found a new home. Sometimes you don't realize how precious something is until you've lost it."

Was he talking about the two of them? Warning her that when he left, she'd never see him again?

"You have chocolate right here." He stood, came around to her chair, and slipped his hands beneath her arms, raising her to her feet. Then lowered his mouth.

He kissed her as if it was the last time he would ever kiss her. Tears filled her eyes, and slipped down her cheeks. He held her close, not letting her go when they broke apart.

"Shh, don't cry," he whispered.

"But what are we going to do? I can't see myself flying through the air. Do you know how long it took me to get up the courage to swing? I was twelve! I'm pathetic, but I can't help it."

She looked up at him with pleading eyes. "Why can't you stay? You like the town and the people all seem to like you. We could make a life here—together."

"And what would I do?"

"I don't know. Get into security or something. We could

work something out. Or we could run my grooming shop together. You're really good with animals, especially Sukie."

"I can't. I have responsibilities."

Sadness filled her. "So do I."

"It would seem there is no solution to our problem."

"It would seem like it."

Her cell rang. She moved away from him and went to answer it.

"Hello."

"Ria, this is Jeanie."

She immediately went on alert. "What is it?"

"Katie isn't feeling well. I think she's getting the crud that's
going around. She told me not to bother you, but she looks
like death warmed over."

"I'll be right in." She closed her phone. When she turned,
Kristor was right behind her. "I need to go to the shop. Katie
isn't feeling well."

"Of course."

"I shouldn't be too long. I could grab a pizza on the way
home."

"I like pizza."

"I know." She smiled. He pretty much liked everything ed-
ible. And he consumed a lot. "Don't eat too many sweets or
you'll ruin your supper."

"You think so?"

"Probably not."

"I'll wait for you here."

She let her gaze roam over him. "Wearing just a towel?"
Talk about a fantasy come true!

"Is that how you want me to wait for you?" His gaze
moved over her in a slow, seductive move that left her breath-
less.

"Oh, yeah, just like that."

"Then this is how you will find me when you return."

She was still smiling as she went to the bedroom to dress.
Maybe she would close up early. Tempting thought.

She pulled up to the shop fifteen minutes later. One thing about being in her line of work, she didn't have to wear makeup unless she wanted to.

She went inside, reprimanded Katie for not calling and letting her know she was ill, then sent her home with orders not to come back to work until she felt better.

And as she took over the grooming, she watched the clock and counted the minutes until she could leave, until she could lie in Kristor's arms.

Ria had just sent the last dog off with its owner, and was breathing a sigh of relief that she could turn the open sign around to closed, when the phone rang.

"Closed," Ria mouthed. They could bring their animal in tomorrow.

But Jeanie didn't tell them the shop was closed. Instead, she nibbled her bottom lip and cast a worried glance in Ria's direction. "I think you'd better take this," Jeanie said, handing the phone to Ria as she stepped closer.

Fear snaked its way through her, curling inside her stomach. "Hello."

"Ria, it's Mom."

"Is Dad okay?"

"He's fine, sweetie. It's Kristor."

Her heart crashed to her feet. "What?" she whispered, grabbing the edge of the desk for support.

"There were some people here from immigration looking for him. They say he might be in the United States illegally. Ria, I'm scared."

"Oh, God, Mom," Ria said. "I thought you were going to say Kristor was . . . dead or something." Her heart rate slowed to less than a hundred-and-twenty beats per minute.

"I'm sorry," her mother apologized. "But this is serious. He's an illegal alien, but what if they find out just how alien he is?"

She could feel the color drain from her face. "Ohmygod,

Mom. That can't happen. It could open a can of worms that we might not be able to close."

Silence.

"Mom?"

"What if they find out *you're* part alien?"

Her pulse sped up again. "If they did that they might—" What? Dissect her? Lock her away in some kind of institution? An eight-by-eight cell with a two-way mirror so they could observe her? She barely swallowed past the lump in her throat.

And what about her parents? They would definitely be at risk for harboring an alien all these years. Ria had to do something, and she had to do it fast.

"Mom, I'll call you back. I need to get home." Kristor would know what to do. She handed the phone back to Jeanie, hands shaking.

"What's wrong?" Jeanie asked, biting her bottom lip.

"I can't talk about it right now." She grabbed her purse, then pulled the curtains closed and locked the door. "Can you lock up the back?"

"Yeah, sure."

"After you do, go out that way, too. And hurry. If anyone talks to you, tell them I'm out of town for a few days."

"If you need anything, call me," Jeanie said.

Ria stopped before stepping into the back. "Thanks, Jeanie." And she was so glad Jeanie didn't press for more answers.

She glanced both ways before stepping outside. All clear. She hurried to her car and unlocked it. After tossing her purse inside, she slid under the steering wheel and started her car.

Someone tapped on her window.

She jumped and screamed at the same time, her hand flying to her chest.

Chapter 25

Kristor looked up when someone knocked. Ria hadn't said she was expecting anyone. He glanced down at the towel still knotted at his waist. A promise was a promise and he tried never to break a promise. He sauntered to the door and opened it. Three men stood on the porch, all wearing the same kind of black suit, white shirt, and black tie. An uneasy feeling washed over him.

"Are you Kristor Valkyir?" the oldest of the men asked.

There was something about him that immediately put Kristor on his guard. He looked at the other two men, then quickly dismissed them as followers, rather than leaders.

"Yes, that is who I am."

"I'm Agent Adam Richards. May we come in for a moment?" Without waiting, he pushed his way inside. "We have reason to believe you might be in the United States illegally."

"Why would you think that?"

Agent Richards smiled, but he looked more pleased than anything. "An anonymous phone call alerted us to the possibility. Of course, if you can produce papers, then we'll be on our way."

Kristor glanced over the man's shoulder and saw the black van. If they were only here to check for papers, why have three agents and a van, when one agent and a car would have been enough?

Kristor smiled. "Of course. My papers are in the bedroom. I will get them." His database was on Ria's nightstand. He could produce a set of papers in only a moment or two.

He turned and walked toward the bedroom. In the mirror above the sofa, he saw Agent Richards motion to the other two men. Kristor grabbed a chair and flung it toward them, but they must have been expecting something because they dodged it and tackled him.

"Cuff him," Agent Richards said.

With the biggest of the agents sitting on top of Kristor, he could barely breathe let alone try to move. As soon as he was cuffed, they dragged him to his feet. The towel slipped to the floor in the process.

Agent Richards wore a look of disgust. "Get him some pants on."

The two agents led him toward the bedroom.

"Wait!" Richards said and walked closer. "That's an unusual birthmark on your ass."

It was the mark all Symtarians wore: A small rose. But it was not just any rose. No man could ever duplicate the mark.

"Not so unusual," Kristor said.

"Oh, you think not?" His words rang with superiority.

His gut clenched. There was something about the man. A knowing smirk. Kristor wondered how he knew he was an alien. And he did know. Kristor was almost positive.

"Get him dressed. I want him out of here pronto."

While they helped him pull on a pair of jeans, Kristor wondered if he would ever see Ria again.

Chapter 26

Ria looked out her window. Donald. "No time," she mouthed.

"Immigration," he mouthed back.

Oh, God. Oh, God. Had they been all over town asking questions? Oh, no. How long would it take them to get to her house? Maybe she could hide Kristor at Carly's. Yes, that was it. That's what she would do.

Donald wasn't leaving. She pushed the button on her window and the glass silently slid downward. "I'm in a bit of a hurry. Would you please move." Or risk losing your toes or something else he might want to keep attached to his body.

"People have been asking about your friend," he said with a snarky smirk plastered on his face.

"So I've been told. I really do have to leave."

"Too late. I heard they were already on their way to your house. You might want to keep a safe distance. I'd hate for you to get into trouble with the law. Of course, we both knew this Kristor was bad news from the start."

He looked a little too smug. "Donald, move the hell out of my way or lose a body part." She slammed the car into reverse and stepped on the gas. Donald barely jumped out of the way before getting hit. Still, he tripped over the concrete parking slab and landed on his butt. She wished she had time to see the expression on his face. She was pretty sure he wasn't quite so smug anymore.

It served him right. Ria had a feeling he had something to do with immigration agents being in town in the first place. It was the whoopee cushion incident all over again, except this time the stakes were a lot higher.

As she hurtled toward her house, she speed-dialed Carly. Ria breathed a sigh of relief when her friend answered on the first ring. She really needed Carly right now.

"We'll take you to places you've only dreamed about at Wilson's Travel Agency—"

"Carly," Ria interrupted.

"Ria, what's wrong?"

"Immigration might be on the way to my house. Can you meet me there? I know I'm asking a lot, but can Kristor stay with you? Just for a little while. Until it's safe. I'll explain more later."

"Yes, of course. Oh, God, Ria. I'm so sorry. I—"

"I'll talk to you when you get here. Hurry."

"I'm on my way."

She snapped the phone closed and dropped it inside her purse. Please don't let them already be there, she prayed. If they weren't, she would get him into her car, and they would get away as fast as she could drive.

Then what? Shintara asked.

"I don't have time for this," she told her guide. "And where the hell have you been?"

I was busy.

Busy? Doing what?

Ria didn't ask as she slid around a corner practically on two wheels.

I'm too young to die! Shintara screeched.

"You're not going to die."

Crap, that was it. Kristor could shift into his animal guide and fly away. If only she had a phone in her house she could call and warn him, but all she had was her cell. She didn't think calling her nosy neighbor would work. What would she say? Could you run over and tell the alien who's staying with me that he needs to shapeshift into a hawk and fly away before immigration arrives and carts him away? Nope, that wouldn't cut it.

She pulled up to her house and slammed on her brakes, skidding to a stop just before she plowed into the unmarked, black government van. It had exempt license plates. What the hell else could it be?

Her heart plummeted.

There was nothing she could do. She could only sit and watch as they led him out of her house in handcuffs, wearing only a pair of jeans.

Everything moved in slow motion. She vaguely knew when she opened her car door and got out. A man in a suit hurried over to her.

"Are you Rianna Lancaster?"

Dazed, she could only look at him.

"Ma'am, I'm Agent Jack Stafford and I'll ask you one more time. Are you Rianna Lancaster?"

"Yes," she finally answered. "What are you doing?" She started to go to Kristor, but suit-man put out a hand to stop her.

"It's best you keep your distance for now. We have reason to believe the man who has been staying with you is an illegal alien. He can't produce any papers. Do you realize it's against the law to harbor someone who is in the United States illegally?" He glared at her.

She realized just how official he looked. There were three of them. All wearing the same style dark suit, black shoes, white shirt, and black tie. And they all wore the same deadpan expressions, except the one glaring at her right now.

"He's not from another country," she told him. Not exactly a lie, but she hoped it would keep Kristor out of jail. Not that she really thought it would work.

"What do you mean?" he asked.

"I just don't think he would lie about something like that."

The man's eyes narrowed. "Has he done anything strange or out of the ordinary?"

Her heart skipped a beat. "What do you mean?"

"We looked through our records and a woman called about a possible alien from another planet, but the person taking the report laughed it off, except there was a blip on the radar about that same time. So, I'm asking you again, is there something strange about this Kristor guy that you're not telling us?"

She swallowed hard, then cocked an eyebrow. "Are you going to stand there and tell me you believe in aliens?"

He let out a deep breath and relaxed just a little. "No, I don't, but there was enough evidence to at least check him out." His expression changed to one of pity. "I'm sorry, ma'am. You need to be careful who you take in. I know you have your own business. Women like you are ripe for the picking. He's probably a scam artist."

"No, he's not."

"We'll know soon enough."

"But I love him." And she did. With all her heart. Why hadn't she just left with him in his spacecraft? She could've taken enough drugs to knock herself out. She wouldn't have even known when they left the ground. Maybe.

She looked around. But could she leave everything behind? Her business, her family? She met Kristor's gaze across the expanse of her front yard. He looked furious, but quickly masked his feelings, and smiled at her. Even now, he was trying to protect her. What had she gotten him into?

"I'll get you out of jail," she called to him. She turned to the agent. "How much is his bail?"

"I'm afraid there isn't any. If he's here legally, we'll let him go. If not, we'll deport him."

"Deport him?" She'd like to see them try. "Where are you taking him?"

Before he could answer, Carly pulled up, her face as white as a sheet. Ria ran to her as she got out of the car.

"They're taking him away," Ria sobbed, falling into her friend's arms.

"Let's get you into the house."

"They won't let me."

"They're leaving."

Ria whipped around. "No, they can't." She ran toward the black van, but it sped off in a small cloud of dust.

"I have to go after them."

Carly pulled her toward the house. "It won't do you any good. If he's not here legally, then they'll deport him. But I'm sure he'll try to contact you. Besides, they'll probably lock him up here. Heath and Neil will make sure they don't harm Kristor." Once inside, Carly shut the door from prying neighbors.

Ria paced the living room. "You don't understand. There's more to it than that."

"More what, Ria?" Carly watched Ria with troubled eyes. "What haven't you told me?"

Ria stopped, and looked at her friend. It was time to tell her everything. She took a deep breath. "He's an alien."

"I figured that one out," Carly said. "But all they'll do is deport him. I'll get you a discount ticket and you can go to wherever he's from."

She shook her head. "Only if you can get a ticket to another planet."

Carly opened her mouth, then snapped it closed. Her forehead puckered in thought, then her eyes widened. "He scammed you into believing he's an alien from another planet? You have got to be kidding me."

"He wasn't scamming me. He's a shapeshifting alien from the planet New Symtaria, and I'm part alien. My father was part alien; my mother was from Earth."

"You haven't been smoking anything, have you?" She scanned the room. "We didn't do drugs in school. Why would you start now?"

"I'm not on drugs."

A car pulled up out front, and doors slammed a few seconds later. She ran to the door and opened it.

"Mom! Dad!"

They rushed inside.

Ria fell into their outstretched arms. "Men in black suits came and took Kristor away. What am I going to do? What if they discover he's an alien?"

"I'll call Heath. Maybe we can break him out of jail," her father said.

"I could bake a pie and hide a file inside," her mother suggested.

"Whoa!" Carly looked at each of them. "Have y'all lost your minds? He's not an alien from another planet and you can't break him out of jail! That's illegal. Do you want to spend the rest of your lives behind bars?"

Her mother and father looked at each other. "You haven't told her?" her mother asked.

"It just never seemed like the right time."

Carly threw her arms into the air. "Oh, puleeze! This is so not happening."

"I have to see him. Make sure he's okay." Ria looked at her father. He would know what to do. He always knew what to do.

"I'll call Heath. He'll be able to tell us what Kristor's rights are. I'll hire him a lawyer. Whatever it takes."

But before her father could make the call, Heath and Neil pulled up in the patrol car and jumped out. Running toward the porch, they took the steps two at a time, which didn't take long to reach the top since there were only four steps.

Her father flung the screen door open. "We have a mess on our hands, fellas."

"You can say that again," Heath said.

Neil went to Carly's side. "You okay?"

She shook her head. "They've all lost their minds." She hiccupped back a sob.

"What are they doing to Kristor?" Ria asked.

"I don't know," Heath said with a worried frown.

Ria froze. "What do you mean, you don't know? Isn't he locked in your jail?"

He shook his head. "They took him back to their office. One of them said they'd gotten some information Kristor was more than an illegal alien. That he might be from another planet." He shook his head. "I know, it sounds crazy. That's the government for you, though."

"That's what the agent told me, too. That they got an anonymous phone call." Ria sat down on the sofa with a hard thud. "Who would tell them such a thing?"

"Me," Carly squeaked. "Oh, God, don't hate me. I was desperate, and scared for you."

"Why?" Ria asked, tears welling in her eyes. "I thought we were friends. You could've just come to me, not strangers."

"I was protecting you. I'm so sorry. When I couldn't find New Symtaria on any map, I called Donald for advice and he encouraged me to call immigration."

Ria's lip curled. "Yeah, I just bet he did." It was a good thing Donald wasn't here or she'd flatten him. She came to her feet, ready to put a stop to all of this. "Where are they taking him?" she asked Heath.

He shook his head. "They told me they were taking him to an undisclosed location. I'm sure he'll be okay, though. The worst they'll do is deport him."

"No, that isn't the worst thing. I have to know where he's going. What direction did they leave in?"

"East. But you'll never catch them now," Neil said. "All you can do is wait."

I can find them, Shintara said. *After all, I have the eyes of a hawk.*

Fear filled Ria at the thought of shifting into her animal guide. Could she do it if it meant saving the man she loved?

No, she couldn't.

The thought of flying terrified her. She didn't want to crash in a blazing ball of fire: She hadn't married or had children or anything.

Of course, the man she loved was being carted away to God knows where, to possibly be dissected by mad scientists. If they did that, she would probably live a lonely miserable life, then die an old maid.

You can do it, Shintara's words whispered through Ria.

I'm scared.

Face your fears. You can do it. I'll be there with you every step of the way.

Ria had a feeling she was going to regret what she was about to do, but she couldn't see any way around it. She took a deep breath.

"I can find him," she said. "If I shapeshift into my animal guide."

Chapter 27

Kristor shifted on the hard bench. They had forced him into the back of the hot stuffy van. An agent was in the back with him, the one called Jack. The guy looked nervous. Why, Kristor didn't know.

Maybe because he was young and oozed inexperience. The older agent seemed to enjoy Jack's discomfiture when he'd told Jack that he would be riding in the back with the prisoner.

Kristor glanced around, weighing his options. He could mentally unlock the restraints, but they had his hands bound behind his back. He had to be able to look at them to unlock them.

"So, where you from?" the young agent asked, trying for the voice of authority.

It came out more of a squeak. He might intimidate women and children, but not Kristor. He had a feeling the young agent knew that, too.

Was it a trick question? Was the young man only acting nervous? He studied him for a moment. Jack's expression only showed curiosity.

"Not from here," Kristor finally said.

"Yeah, I can't really blame you for not talking." He nodded his head toward the front of the van. The only thing separating them from the two men up front was a glass panel. "Adam can be an ass."

"Adam?"

"He's the lead agent. Been one for about twenty-five years. Gung-ho and all that. Agent Adam Richards." He snickered. "He thinks you're an alien from another planet. Can you believe the guy? I think he might be doing drugs on the side."

"He told you he thinks I'm an alien?"

"Not in so many words, but on the way down here, he told us that was what our mission was about. To make sure you weren't an alien. Crazy, I know."

"Yeah, crazy."

"So, what do you lift?"

Why did everyone wonder what he could lift? "Anything I want." It seemed to satisfy the guys he'd played flag football with that day.

"Yeah, I kind of figured that. I'm not much for weights, but I'm a fast runner."

And for the next hour, Agent Jack talked about running, working out, and what it meant to be an agent, and how proud his family was of him. Kristor had a feeling he could talk long enough that a prisoner would be willing to give away all his country's secrets just so Jack would shut up.

Kristor's eyes narrowed on the man sitting in the front seat as Jack droned on. The lead agent. Adam Richards knew Kristor was an alien. Kristor had seen it in the man's eyes when he saw Kristor's birthmark.

The other two thought their leader was a little crazy to think aliens might exist. He'd seen that in their body language, and the way they'd cast knowing looks at each other. But that knowledge would do Kristor no good. They obeyed their leader, and would follow his command. He respected them for that, but it didn't help his situation.

With his wrists bound by metal shackles, it was too late for him to shift. His only hope was Rianna. But could she set him free before they found out the truth? She'd been more distraught than determined when they shoved him into the back of the van, and pulled away from her house.

There was always her father. He had come across as an intelligent man. She might be able to enlist her father's help. He would know what to do. As they left town, Kristor knew it would be impossible if they didn't know where he was being taken.

The glass that separated him from the front slid open and Adam shifted in his seat. His grin was mocking. "You two nice and cozy?"

"It's hotter than Hades back here," Jack said.

"Where are you taking me?" Kristor asked, before the other man could say anything to Jack.

Adam looked at him. "Somewhere we can question you properly. We don't want any of those country yokels interfering with our interrogation."

"You don't have to scare him, Adam," Jack said.

Adam glared at the other man. "Yeah, well we don't know exactly what he is, now do we? I've been in this business a lot longer than you, boy, and I've seen things that would make you think twice about whether aliens exist or not."

The man stiffened. "My name is Jack, not 'boy,' if you don't mind."

"Whatever." Adam slid the glass closed and turned around in his seat, facing front again.

"Might as well make yourself comfortable. It's going to be a long ride," Jack said.

Kristor didn't like the sound of that. There was no way Rianna would ever find him, even if she could help. His mission was in jeopardy of completely failing and his identity becoming known.

Or it could be worse. He'd heard of the secret testing they did. It was whispered throughout the galaxy that aliens from other planets had been captured and no one ever saw them again. He had thought the rumors false, a way to scare children into completing their daily tasks.

His mother had told him more than once that people from Earth would come get him if he didn't clean his room. When he was young, he'd believed her but, of course, as he'd gotten older, he realized Earth wasn't nearly as advanced as New Symtaria.

But now he began to wonder. Maybe Adam was the monster from his childhood after all.

Chapter 28

"Oh, Ria!" Carly ran to her friend and threw her arms around her neck and sobbed.

Heath cleared his throat. "Maggie, Ron, you know they have some pretty decent doctors in Dallas who can help your girl. John Ratcliff took his son over there, you know. The one that's a little touched and would throw things all the time. He's a lot calmer now. They said the doctors were a blessing. I bet they could help Ria."

Maggie squared her shoulders. "I beg your pardon, Heath, but our daughter is not touched. She's only part alien. It's not even close to being the same thing."

"Mom, we can't blame them for not believing." Ria untangled herself from Carly, who then threw herself into Neil's arms. A much better fit, Ria thought. "I don't have time to go into a lengthy explanation. I need to follow them to see where they're taking Kristor."

"Are you sure, baby girl?" her father asked.

She nodded. "I've never been so sure about anything in my life." Then she silently prayed she could follow through with her bold statement.

Woo-hoo! We're going to shift! Finally!

Ria ignored Shintara for now. If she hurried, and didn't think about what she was about to do, then she might not get scared and back out at the last second.

She took a deep breath and stepped away from everyone. "Okay, you'll see a thick fog. Don't worry about it. Then, if everything works out right, I'll shift into a hawk."

"Oh, Ria." Carly raised her head from Neil's shoulder and sniffed loudly.

Neil pulled a hankie out of his back pocket and handed it to Carly. She wiped her eyes, then delicately blew her nose.

"Quiet. I need to concentrate." Ria looked at each one of them, registering their expressions. Heath looked as though he was ready to call for the men in white coats. Neil looked confused. Her mother looked worried, her father full of pride that she was facing her fears, and Carly was just plain old scared. When Ria saw her reflection in the mirror over the sofa, she saw determination.

Yeah, well, she might be determined, but she was also scared silly.

You can do this. We can save Kristor. Ria, we're his only hope.

I know. Just don't fly into a tree or anything.

Pffft, as if that would ever happen. Just watch and see what I can do!

That was exactly why Ria was afraid. But Shintara was right. Ria was Kristor's only hope, and she wouldn't fail him now.

Ria closed her eyes tight. *Think animal guide.*

She swallowed past the sick feeling at the back of her throat.

Think hawk.

Something was starting to happen. She grit her teeth.

"What is that?" Carly asked.

"Just the fog, dear," Ria's mother explained. "Remember, she told everyone there would be a fog."

Ria heard their words as if from a distance as the burning pain grabbed hold. She groaned, slipping to the floor.

"Think hawk," she murmured.

"Ria, where are you?" Heath's voice bounced off the walls.

"I don't think she can hear you. She's too busy shifting into a hawk," Ria's mother told him. "I've always told everyone that our daughter was special. And she is. Certainly better than Vickie Jo's daughter who is just a pharmacist. Ria's a shapeshifting alien. Just watch and see."

The voices faded. Ria stretched her arms and feet out. They drew back as the shift began. Beak, talons, and feathers replaced her human form.

I can feel it, Shintara's thoughts came to her. *Ohmygod, this is what it feels like to be me. I think I might cry.*

Did hawks cry? Ria didn't care as she was engulfed in the transformation. Her breathing became ragged. She heard the cry of a hawk. Fog swirled around her.

The burning eased.

Ria blinked, and looked through the eyes of a hawk, then quickly closed them tight.

I'm alive! Shintara spread her wings.

I'm frightened.

Don't be scared, Ria. Open your eyes and see through mine. Now we are truly connected.

Ria tentatively opened her eyes as the fog began to lift. For the first time Ria felt the strength of Shintara's emotions as they flooded her entire being. She finally realized the pain Shintara had felt being unable to shift into her true form.

"Ria?" Carly asked.

"Hello, Shintara." Ria's mother knelt in front of them.

The hawk screeched a hello.

"Shintara?" Neil asked.

"Her animal guide. They coexist," her father explained.

"The voice she talks to," Heath said. "All these years it was real." He nudged his cowboy hat higher on his forehead. "I'll be damned. And the naked man in the woods that day was Kristor. Everything she said was the truth. Aliens do exist."

Carly moved closer. "You're part alien."

We need to leave, Ria.

Ria's stomach churned. *Then let's do it.*

Shintara flapped over to the screen door. Her father opened it. Once out on the porch, Ria had second thoughts.

No turning back. Shintara stretched her wings. The span was impressive, to say the least, and she took off. It was more like a dodge-and-wobble takeoff, though.

I thought you said you could fly!

All hawks can fly, but you have to remember this is my first flight. It will take a little getting used to.

Getting used to! Shintara hadn't said anything about having to get used to flying. Oh, God, Ria was going to be sick. She looked up as a large object appeared in front of them.

Tree!

I see it. Calm down.

Branches!

I see those, too

Could hawks vomit? Why the hell hadn't she read up on them? Anyone with half a brain would have googled hawks if that was their animal guide. But noooo, she'd never thought she would have to shift into one.

She could feel the wind on her face. That wasn't bad. Kind of like when she went running. She glanced down as they flew over the town. Oh, God, she was going to die!

Drama queen. You're not going to die. And if looking down bothers you, then don't freaking look down.

You've really copped an attitude lately, you know.

And you've let something that happened when you were a child consume you with fear. All your life, it's held you prisoner. Now we're both free.

She was right.

Of course, I'm right.

You heard my thoughts?

You didn't block them.

I can do that?

Sometimes, Shintara reluctantly admitted.

Ria would file that away for future reference. She didn't want Shintara knowing everything she was thinking.

There's the van, Shintara said. She swooped down closer, flying near the window on the driver's side.

Truck! Ria's mind screamed.

Shintara swooped up and out of the way with barely a feather being ruffled. *I saw it. Remember, my eyesight is superb.*

I'd just as soon not play chicken with oncoming traffic if you don't mind.

I'm a hawk, not a chicken.

Whatever. But she was glad Shintara had found Kristor. Now she would be able to free the man she loved. Well, as soon as she figured out how she would go about doing it.

Kristor thought about Rianna, wondering if he would ever see her again. She was special. His family would like her— that is, if she decided to make the journey to New Symtaria. A deep throbbing pain ripped through him. He couldn't imagine life without her.

Adam turned slightly in his seat, glancing back at Kristor. Kristor returned his gaze with stoic indifference. Adam's eyes narrowed before he faced front again.

The man was taunting him. It was a maneuver meant to intimidate the opponent. Kristor had used it. By the time they arrived at their destination, he was supposed to be ready to tell them whatever they wanted to know. Adam's ploy wouldn't work. Not this time.

According to the clock on the dash, they'd been in the van two-and-a-half hours. Kristor shifted on the bench, but no position helped ease his discomfort. Jack looked even less comfortable and had already loosened the tie around his neck and removed his jacket.

They passed a sign that said Dallas was twenty-five miles away. He'd been there when he searched for Rianna. It was big. Much bigger than any town on New Symtaria. Would Rianna or her father be able to find him among so populated a place?

But they turned off the main road a few minutes later. Jack sat straighter.

"This isn't the way to the office."

A tingle of worry crept up Kristor's spine.

Jack tapped on the glass. Adam turned, sliding the partition open.

"Did you make a wrong turn?"

"We're not going to the office. Like I said, I've been in this business a long time, and I've seen a lot more than you have."

"So where are we going?" Jack asked.

"You'll see."

Kristor knew he would have a better chance of escaping from a place with fewer people. They'd just made it easier for him. But ten minutes later, he wasn't quite as sure as they drove up to a small building with glass windows surrounded by a twelve-foot fence.

A guard stepped from the building as they approached. The driver of the van slowed, then stopped, his window sliding silently down.

Adam leaned forward. "Agent Adam Richards," he said, then handed his identification to the guard.

His words were muffled on the other side of the glass partition, but Kristor could understand what was being said.

"One moment, sir," the guard told him.

He went inside the building. Kristor watched as the man raised a phone to his ear and spoke. He put down the phone and returned to the van, handing Adam his identification.

"Once inside, turn to the right. The buildings are lettered. You'll be going to C Building. Someone will meet you there." He went back inside. The metal arm rose in front of them to let them through.

Kristor looked at the buildings as they drove past: cold, stark-gray buildings. They pulled in front of Building C and parked. Maybe he could make a run for it. Woods surrounded the perimeter. If he could get loose of the metal bindings, he could shift, then escape.

But when the back doors of the van opened, Kristor saw that two guards stood on either side of the doors. Jack grabbed Kristor's arm, and one of the guards grabbed the other. They didn't let go after he jumped to the ground. As they walked inside, Jack moved away and the other guard took his place. They didn't say a word.

"There's a cafeteria down at the end of the hall," Adam said as they went inside.

"Where are you taking him?" Jack asked, nervously looking at Kristor.

"It's classified," Adam said with a smile that didn't reach his eyes. "Someday you'll get to play with the big boys."

"Ass," Jack mumbled, but Kristor thought he was probably the only one who heard. He agreed with Jack.

Adam, Kristor, and the two guards turned and walked down the corridor opposite to where the other men were going.

"What do you think you'll find out about me? I'm nothing special," Kristor said.

"I don't *think* I'll find something, I know I will. Oh, yeah, I know exactly who and what you are."

They put him in a small room with a tiny window in the door. Chains were bolted into the back wall.

"Chain him," Adam said.

"You would treat me like an animal?" Kristor jerked away from the guards.

"But isn't that what you are—Symtarian?" Adam cast a fierce glance toward the guards. "I said chain him!"

Kristor fought against the men, but he was handcuffed and they were two to his one. Still, he managed to kick one on the shin. He would have felt a lot better if it had been Adam instead of the guard, who was only following orders.

His efforts were futile as two more guards came running at Adam's command. They managed to chain each wrist and both ankles to the wall. But they didn't do so without taking some bumps and bruises. At least they didn't look quite so stiff and stoic, and they were panting.

As soon as Kristor was secure, Adam waved the guards from the room and stepped in front of him.

"You might as well have just let us chain you, alien. What did you get for your effort? Pain?"

"I am a warrior." He stood tall. "That was not so much pain as it was gratification."

"I'm glad the thought of pain doesn't seem to bother you. Over the next few weeks, you'll have a chance to experience much more than what the guards gave you."

Kristor would not let Adam see that his words bothered him. He would find a way to escape. They could not hold him.

"Aren't you even curious to know how I guessed you're Symtarian?"

People like Adam enjoyed bragging about how much they knew. Kristor understood his kind well. They liked to push weaker men around, or men in chains. But when it came to real fighting, they were the first to run away.

Still, he wanted to know if there were more Symtarians caged. So he asked the question. "How did you know?"

Adam fairly glowed with anticipation. "I knew as soon as I met you that you were alien. The mark on your ass when the towel came loose proved it. You're Symtarian. All Sym-

tarians have the same rose symbol, different from a tattoo."
He laughed. "It will give you away every time."

"And how many Symtarians have you found?"

His chest puffed out. "My fair share." He frowned. "Some
of them didn't know they were Symtarians. I thought that
was strange at first. But then I figured that out, too. Your
people dumped them here so they could breed with people
from Earth." His lip curled in distaste. "Is that why you're
here? To breed with that slut you were shacked up with?"

Kristor tightened his fists. He wanted to kill this man like
he had never wanted to kill another person. But he couldn't.
Not right now. He had to keep Ria safe.

"Get her with child? I think not. I am a prince. She is not
worthy to carry my seed. But she did give me some relief, no
matter how distasteful it was to relieve myself by using her
body."

"Why, you filthy alien!" Adam doubled his fists and
punched Kristor in the gut.

Kristor sucked air, but not enough to let Adam know he'd
caused him anything more than mild discomfort. "Don't hurt
yourself," he told him.

The door suddenly opened and a gray-haired man wearing
a white coat stepped inside. "Agent, you've been warned
about harming the specimens. The last one died too quickly.
I think you can leave now."

Adam smirked. "I want to see him squirm."

"He won't be squirming today, so you can leave."

Adam cast one last glare in Kristor's direction before leaving the cell.

"I'm Dr. Rigby," the gray-haired man said. He nodded toward the door. "Agent Richards is an imbecile, but we have
found him useful for our needs."

"What? Torturing people just because they aren't exactly
like you?"

"We don't torture. We perform tests. If your people should ever attack, we need to know what makes you tick so we can defend ourselves."

"That will never happen."

"Attacking us?"

"Being able to defend yourselves."

The man looked taken aback by his truthfulness. Kristor continued, "We're far more advanced than Earth people. We're able to travel between planets. But we've learned something that you haven't."

The man looked genuinely interested. "What would that be?"

"Destruction breeds destruction. You gain nothing through wars so fierce that they will destroy your planet."

He sighed. "I wish our time together could be more pleasant. I would like to sit down and talk about your home. Those are not my orders, though."

"If you harm me, they will find you."

The man looked surprised that someone who was chained would threaten him. Just as quickly, he recovered his composure. "But they won't know we have you."

"Yes, they will. I don't think I've properly introduced myself. I'm Prince Kristor Valkyir, of New Symtaria. My parents rule our planet. I have brothers and sisters. None of them will appreciate people from Earth experimenting on me. So heed my words carefully. They will discover what happened to me and there will be destruction like you have never seen before."

The man's eyes grew wide as he stumbled backwards, running into the door. He turned, fumbled with the knob, and rushed out.

Kristor might still be chained, but he was satisfied that he had taken away some of the man's superiority. He wouldn't be quite so condescending the next time they met. And they would meet, but next time he wouldn't be in chains. He looked at the metal that bound his wrist. Metal that he could focus on.

Kid's play.

It would be dark soon. People would leave for their homes. That's what people from Earth did. There would only be a few left in the building. And then he would escape.

Chapter 29

Watch the fence! Ria said.

I see it, Shintara told her.

Shintara glided gracefully over the fence. Maybe Ria was a worrywart, but it wasn't easy overcoming a lifetime of fear in just a few hours.

There's the van. Shintara landed on a branch in the wooded area at the edge of the compound.

Ria watched as they brought Kristor out of the back. If they hurt one hair on his head, she'd kill them.

Kristor! Ria called.

Do you really think he can hear your thoughts?

So maybe he couldn't. Which was probably a good thing, but it had felt wonderful to call his name.

But damn, it had hurt to see him in handcuffs. If it was the last thing she did, she would help him escape.

We'll wait until nightfall, Shintara said. *There will be fewer people around.*

Ria wasn't a patient person. She was ready to storm inside the building right now. But Shintara was right. Besides, she would have to figure out a way to find clothes. She really doubted anyone would be afraid of a woman streaking through their building.

So what are we going to do until then? Ria asked.

Fly, Shintara said with more than a little exuberance.

Ria had to ask. She closed her eyes as Shintara dipped between the trees and dodged branches. After a while, she realized she could block out everything around her and let Shintara take complete control. Much better. Now she didn't feel quite so woozy.

Wake up! Shintara screamed.

Ria jerked awake, looking around. *Where am I?*

For the last couple of hours you've been snoozing. You snore, by the way.

I do not.

Whatever.

What time is it?

Late. Around ten. The compound has pretty much shut down. By my estimations, there are only about twenty people inside C Building.

How did you figure that?

There are twenty cars in the parking lot.

Smart ass.

I don't suppose you found me some clothes.

I'm good, but I'm not that good. Now, are you ready to shift?

As ready as I'll ever be.

But nothing happened.

Hey, Ria, Shintara said in a serious voice.

What?

Thanks for shifting.

I think I would have anyway.

Yeah, I'd already guessed you would. She cleared her throat. *I've got your back if you need me.*

Warmth swelled inside her. *Let's do this.*

Shintara swooped down closer to the building, landing around the corner from the door. Ria began to concentrate on her human form. Nothing happened at first, and there was a moment of panic. She didn't want to remain a hawk.

Just concentrate, Shintara's thoughts came to her.

Concentrate. Yes, that's what she needed to do. She closed her eyes and thought about how it felt to have Kristor hold her close, to feel his hands caressing her.

The burning began in the pit of her stomach. She moaned as her body began to change. The hawk screeched. Their thoughts blended and for a moment, they were one, no separation between them. An incredible feeling of bonding flooded through her.

The burning eased, but not the feeling that the two of them had merged and somehow grown closer, stronger in spirit.

Did you feel it? Ria asked

Yes, I did. We are truly one.

Ria sat up and looked around. It was quiet, dark. She slowly came to her feet. Leaning the palm of one hand on the side of the building, she caught her breath, letting herself regain control of her body again.

We need to hurry, Shintara urged.

I'm ready. Ria peeked around the side of the building. No movement. She hurried to the door and tested the knob. Unlocked.

God, she was scared shitless. Clothes would be nice. It wasn't cold, but goose bumps had popped up all over her body.

She eased the door open and took a quick look inside. No one was in the hallway. There were doors on either side. Maybe she could find something to wear in one of the rooms.

She slipped inside. The first two doors were locked, as well as the next three. She was halfway down the hall when she heard voices coming down one of the halls that branched off.

Oh, hell! Now what was she going to do? Shift!

No time!

Crap! She tried the next two doors.

Locked.

The next one opened. She slipped inside the room just as two men turned the corner. She left the door open just a hair to see what they would do. They stopped at the first door and unlocked it, then went inside. She breathed a sigh of relief, then looked around.

She was inside a lab of sorts.

Bingo.

There was a white lab coat hanging from a coat rack. She quickly slipped it on. A little too big, but beggars couldn't be choosers. There was something in the pocket. She pulled it out: a name badge with a barcode. She looked at the picture. Crystal Webb was in desperate need of a makeover. She dropped the badge back inside the pocket and opened a few drawers until she found booties like medical staff would wear over their shoes during surgery. If she saw anyone, maybe they would think she was also wearing shoes and worked there.

She still felt really naked, but at least the coat fell below her knees and it buttoned up the front. Now to find Kristor.

The men she'd almost ran into had been carrying Styrofoam coffee cups. Cafeteria? She decided to go in the opposite direction. But when she rounded a corner, she came face to face with a set of double doors blocking her path. There was a sign that read RESTRICTED AREA.

Kristor had to be somewhere behind those doors. She pushed on them. They didn't budge. To the right was a scanner, much like the ones used to slide a credit card through. *Pffft*, she knew how to use one of them. She reached inside the pocket of the lab coat and brought out the badge. It was worth a try.

She slid it through the slot. The doors beeped. She tentatively pushed on them, breathing a sigh of relief when they opened.

The hall was empty and dimly lit. On either side were doors again, but these had small windows. The first three were empty. She peered into the next window. It also looked empty. She opened the door to make sure.

Something grabbed her arm and dragged her inside. She opened her mouth to scream but a hand clamped over it.

"Don't make a sound or I'll have to silence you."

She nodded.

He slowly moved his hand away.

"Kristor?"

"Rianna? What are you doing here?"

"Saving you."

"I don't need saving."

"You're in a cell. I'd say you do."

"I was just about to leave. The guards make their rounds every hour from what I can tell. They just made them."

"Then let's get the hell out of here."

She opened the door and glanced out. "All clear."

They kept close to the wall as they made their way to the double doors. Just as she was about to swipe the badge, the doors opened and a man stepped through with two guards.

"Agent Richards." Kristor nodded toward the older man as if they were old friends meeting on the street.

The agent sloshed his coffee over the side of his cup, burning his hand. He yelped and dropped the cup.

"Sir, I—" The guard didn't get the chance to say anything else. Kristor threw one punch and the guy slumped to the floor. The other guard had barely opened his mouth when he met with the same fate.

Agent Richards turned to run, but Kristor clamped a hand on his shoulder and pushed him toward the cell.

"Maybe I should take you back to my planet and let you see how we question aliens from Earth."

"Oh, God, please, no."

Kristor opened the door and shoved him inside. Ria wondered if they really captured people from other planets. Did they poke them with probes?

It had been rather nice when Kristor had probed her. She mentally shook her head. Now was not the time to let her thoughts wander.

Agent Adam Richards was the man who had wanted to dissect the man she loved. She shoved up the sleeves of her lab coat. "Let me at him," she said. She wasn't sure what she would do, but she wanted to do something. Maybe punch his lights out.

Kristor shoved the agent against the wall, then clamped the cuffs on his wrists and ankles.

"Please don't. I swear I'll retire, anything, just let me go."

Was he actually crying? The tough expression he'd worn when Kristor was taken to the van was gone. The guy was actually sniveling.

"If you don't stop torturing aliens I will return, and I'll bring others with me. Do you understand?"

"I'm not sure I have the authority—"

"Whatever it takes, you will get it done." Kristor took a menacing step closer.

"Yes, I will. I will. Just don't hurt me."

Kristor grabbed Ria's arm and they started out, but he glanced once more over his shoulder. "Don't make a sound. If you do, I'll kill you."

He shook his head. "No, of course not. Quiet as a mouse. Promise."

"Then shut up," Kristor growled.

Ria thought Kristor was quite fierce. She rather liked this warrior side of him. He made her feel protected. Except they had to get out of there fast.

"How did you find me?" he asked as they slipped past the double doors and down the hall.

She glanced his way as they hurried down the hall and out the door. Fresh air was like a welcome caress on her face. He grabbed her arm.

"Rianna?"

"I shifted. There, I hope you're happy."

He grinned, then pulled her into his arms. His lips brushed across hers in a gentle kiss. Then it deepened with emotion as they both realized how close they had been to losing each other.

"I love you," he whispered after the kiss ended. He continued to hold her close.

She sighed. "And I love you."

"Then you'll leave with me?"

"Can we come back to visit?"

"Of course."

"Then yes, I'll follow you anywhere. As long as I have a bottle of Valium."

"Valium?"

"Yes, and Dramamine."

"I will make sure you have plenty then."

"Good. Let's go home."

The fog began to roll in as they both thought about their animal guides. Ria felt the burning pain, but this time she welcomed it like an old friend.

Shintara stretched her wings as the fog dissipated. She looked over at the hawk who was doing the same. *Nice wingspan.*

You're not so bad yourself, Labrinon screeched.

Ria mentally shook her head. Having her animal guide free was going to take a little getting used to. But as long as she was with Kristor, she had a feeling she could get through just about anything.

Her life finally felt complete. As it should.

Pick up DAMAGE CONTROL,
Amy Fetzer's latest novel in the Dragon One series,
in stores now!

Dr. Walt Arnold took slow breaths to keep from freezing his lungs. At thirty below, he was accustomed to the staggering temperatures, but it was hard to regulate his breathing when he was lifting sixty pounds of pipe and ice. He wrapped the core sample in plastic, then, with his assistant, levered it onto the transport, its metal shell intact. The temperatures were in their favor to keep the core sample from relaxing, as well as maintaining the chemical isotopes in prime condition.

His team took care of transporting the sample to storage as he returned to the drilling. He adjusted the next length of pipe, clamped the coupling, then glanced at the generator chugging to drive the pipe farther into the ice. The half dozen random samples would help correlate the data from the deeper drills. He watched the meter feed change in slow increments. Nearly three hundred meters. It was the deepest he'd attempted on this patch, and he was eager for data. His report wasn't due for a year, but making the funding stretch took hunks of time he needed for the study.

When the core met the next mark, he twisted, the wind pushing the fur of his parka as he waved a wide arc. His assistants jogged across the ice and he warned them again about exerting themselves unnecessarily. They brought it up, the sample laid out in sections. Overstuffed with down and thermal protection, his colleagues rushed to contain it in the storage trenches dug into the ice to keep the sample from relaxing or their measurements for chemical isotopes would be screwed to hell.

The drill continued and out of the corner of his eye, Walt watched the computer screen's progress. The nonfreezing drill fluid flowed smoothly and he could kiss the scientist who'd perfected it. Pipes locked in the ice meant abandoning valuable equipment. The crew transported the next length into storage below one degree to maintain the specimen. The rest gathered around the equipment housed over the site with a windscreen that would protect them, yet not change the temperature of the core samples. Walt ached for hot coffee.

Suddenly the core shot another twenty-eight feet and he rushed to shut it down. *Shit shit shit.* Not good, he thought, his gaze jumping between monitors. A pipe had come loose, he thought, yet the readings were fine. There wasn't a damn thing wrong with the equipment. That meant there was a gap. An air pocket in the glacier. His brows knit, his heartbeat jumping a little. The core depths so far were a sample of the climate eight hundred years earlier, give or take a hundred.

"All stop, pull up the last sample."

It was useless anyway. The inconsistent drill would change the atmospheric readings of gas bubbles if the core relaxed and lost its deep ice compression. Holes under pressure were usually deformed. The technician went back to securing the steel pipes. Walt switched on the geothermal radar, lowering the amplifier, then waited for the recalibration. The picture of the ice throbbed back to the screen, loading slowly. He didn't see anything in the first half that shouldn't be there. The feed showed an eerie green of solid glacier ice. Then it darkened, a definite shape molding from the radar pulse. Bedrock already? Or perhaps a climate buoy. Thousands of those were getting trapped, yet never this far below the ice flow.

A graduate student moved alongside him, peering in. "There's something in there."

Walt didn't respond, waiting the last few seconds for the pixels to clarify. "Yes, Mister Ticcone. There definitely is."

Don't miss Mary Wine's BEDDING THE ENEMY,
in stores now!

He was staring at her.

Helena looked through her lowered eyelashes at him. He was a Scot and no mistake about it. Held in place around his waist was a great kilt. Folded into pleats that fell longer in the back, his plaid was made up in heather, tan and green. She knew little of the different clans and their tartans but she could see how proud he was. The nobles she passed among scoffed at him but she didn't think he would even cringe if he were to hear their mutters. She didn't think the gossip would make an impact. He looked impenetrable. Strength radiated from him. There was nothing pompous about him, only pure brawn.

Her attention was captivated by him. She had seen other Scots wearing their kilts but there was something more about him. A warm ripple moved across her skin. His doublet had sleeves that were closed, making him look formal, in truth more formal than the brocade-clad men standing near her brother. There wasn't a single gold or silver bead sewn to that doublet, but he looked ready to meet his king. It was the slant of his chin, the way he stood.

"You appear to have an admirer, Helena."

Edmund sounded conceited and his friends chuckled. Her brother's words surfaced in her mind and she shifted her gaze to the men standing near her brother. They were poised in perfect poses that showed off their new clothing. One even had a lace-edged handkerchief dangling from one hand.

She suddenly noticed how much of a fiction it was. Edmund didn't believe them to be his friends but he stood jesting with them. Each one of them would sell the other out for the right amount. It was so very sad—like a sickness you knew would claim their lives but could do nothing about.

"A Scot, no less."

Edmund eyed her. She stared back, unwilling to allow him to see into her thoughts. Annoyance flickered in his eyes when she remained calm. He waved his hands, dismissing her.

She turned quickly before he heard the soft sound of a gasp. She hadn't realized she was holding her breath. It was such a curious reaction. Peeking back across the hall, she found the man responsible for invading her thoughts completely. He had a rugged look to him, his cheekbones high and defined. No paint decorated his face. His skin was a healthy tone she hadn't realized she missed so much. He was clean-shaven, in contrast to the rumors she'd heard of Scotland's men. Of course, many Englishmen wore beards. But his hair was longer, touching his shoulders and full of curl. It was dark as midnight and she found it quite rakish.

He caught her staring at him. She froze, her heartbeat accelerating. His dark eyes seemed alive even from across the room. His lips twitched up, flashing her a glimpse of strong teeth. He reached up to tug lightly on the corner of his knitted bonnet. She felt connected to him, her body strangely aware of his—even from so great a distance. Sensations rippled down her spine and into her belly. She sank into a tiny curtsy without thought or consideration. It was a response, pure and simple.

Keep an eye out for THE DEADLIEST SIN
by Caroline Richards, coming next month!

The air was like a heavy linen sheet pressed against Julia's face, yet a cold sweat plastered her chemise and dress to her body. It was peculiar, this ability to retreat into herself, away from the pain numbing her leg and away from the threat that lay outside this suffocating room.

A few moments, an hour, or a day passed. She found herself sitting, her limbs trembling against the effort. Guilt choked her, a tide of nausea threatening to sweep away the tattered edges of her self-regard. Why had she ignored Meredith's warnings and accepted Wadsworth's invitation to photograph his country estate? Julia felt for the ground beneath her, flexing stiff fingers, a film of dust gathering under her nails. If she could push herself higher, lean against a wall, allow the blood to flow . . .

The pain in her leg was a strange solace. As were thoughts of Montfort, her refuge, the splendid seclusion where her life with her sister and her aunt had begun. She could remember nothing else, her early childhood an empty canvas, bleached of memories. Lady Meredith Woolcott had offered a universe onto itself. Protected, guarded, secure—for a reason.

Julia's mouth was dry. She longed for water to wash away her remorse. New images crowded her thoughts, taking over the darkness in bright bursts of light. Meredith and Rowena waving to her from the green expanse of lawn at Montfort.

The sun dancing on the tranquil pond in the east gardens. Meredith's eyes, clouded with worry, that last afternoon in the library. Wise counsel from her aunt that Julia had chosen, in her defiance, to ignore, warnings that were meant to be heeded. Secrets that were meant to be kept.

She ran a shaking hand through the shambles of her hair, her bonnet long discarded somewhere in the dark. She pieced together her shattered thoughts. When had she arrived? Last evening or days ago? A picture began to form. Her carriage had clattered up to a house, a daunting silhouette, all crenellations and peaks, chandeliers glittering coldly into the gathering dust. The entryway had been brightly lit, the air infused with the perfume of decadence, sultry and heavy. That much she could remember before her mind clamped shut.

The world tilted and she ground her nails into the stone beneath her palms for balance. She should be sobbing by now but her eyes were sandpaper dry. Voices echoed in the dark, or were they footsteps, corporeal and real? Her ears strained and she craned her neck upwards peering into the thick darkness. There was a sense of vibration more than sounds themselves, hearing as the deaf hear. Footsteps, actual or imagined, would do her no good. She felt the floor around her, imagining a prison of rotted wood and broken stone, even though logic told her there had to be an entranceway. Taking a deep breath, she twisted onto her left hip, arms flailing to find purchase, to heave herself into a standing position. Not for the first time in her life, she cursed the heavy skirts, entangled now in her legs, the painful fire burning higher.

No wall. Nothing to lean upon. If she could at least stand— She pushed herself up on her right elbow, wrestling aside her skirts with an impatient hand. The fabric tore, the sound muffled in the darkness. The white-hot pain no longer mattered, nor did the bile flooding her throat. Pulling her legs beneath her, she dragged herself up, swaying like a mad marionette without the security of strings.

The silence was complete because she'd stopped breathing. Arms outstretched, her hands clutched at air. Just one small step, one after the other, and she would encounter a wall, a door, something. She bit back a silent plea. Hadn't Meredith taught them long ago about the uselessness of prayer?

And then it happened. Her palms halted by the sensation of solid stone. Instinctively, she stilled, convinced that she was losing her mind. The sensation of breath, the barely perceptible rise and fall of a chest beneath her opened palms. Where there had been black there was now a shower of stars in front of her eyes, a humming in her head.

And then she saw him, without the benefit of light or the quick trace of her fingers, but behind her unseeing eyes.

She took a step back in the darkness, away from him. The man who wanted her dead.